Includes:

After the Flag Fell

A Choose Your Own Adventure-style bonus to *Heart of Brass*

Published by Odyssey Books in 2016

www.odysseybooks.com.au

A Cataloguing-in-Publication entry is available from the National Library of Australia

ISBN: 978-1-922200-58-7 (pbk)
ISBN: 978-1-922200-59-4 (ebook)

Cover design by Elijah Toten

Dedication

This book is dedicated to my family.

To the ones who made me (and put up with a lot)

To the one I chose (who also chose me)

And to the ones I made because I loved you before
you existed (and more every day).

Chapter One

Society doesn't allow young men to marry science experiments.

Tick, tick.

My heart beat loudly—too loudly. That's the trouble with brass.

Tick, tick.

Mrs Dawes would be calling shortly with her son, and I needed to stay calm or I'd give the game away. Everyone who was anyone wore metal, but I was the only person in London to wear it on the inside of my chest.

'You're ticking fit to burst, Emmeline!' said Arabella, putting my hairbrush down amongst my scent bottles, unguents, facial powders, and half a disassembled clockwork rat. 'They'll discover everything at this rate.'

'Hush. I already stopped the drawing room clock. The Daweses won't hear a tick out of place.'

She made a face at me in the mirror, scrunching up her eyes—the same blue eyes I'd also inherited from Mother—and I smiled back at her. I'd grown fond of having my baby sister set my hair instead of a maid.

One of Mother's pastoral watercolours hung in a wooden frame on the wall. The original gold frame had kept the servants paid for two months. It had been Arabella's idea to sell it. She possessed a natural flair for intrigue that worried me sometimes. Best to marry soon, and hope she followed suit before clever lies became too solid a habit for both of us. Or perhaps the lies would prove more useful than ever. I was hazy on the details of married life. The main thing was to get it done as quickly and profitably as possible.

'Soon it'll be you receiving the young men,' I said, pleased at the thought that if this afternoon went smoothly I'd be settled soon, and she could choose whomever she liked best.

Arabella stuck out her tongue.

'Or perhaps not,' I said.

She sniffed. 'Boys? I should think not.'

I stood, straightening my skirts so the discreet wheels keeping my petticoats aligned fell in a circle around my slippered feet. Arabella's opinions on boys would change soon enough.

She stepped back and examined me with a critical air. Despite her tender years she very nearly faced me eye to eye. 'Shall I tighten your corset a little more? Is the back vent lined up correctly?'

'There's not enough time to check.' I tipped my head to the side, listening to the rumble and clink of passing carriages on the hard macadam road outside. Iron wheels, wooden wheels, coster wagons, horse hooves, and the rain forever tinkling on rooftops and carriages. It was impossible to tell whether the Daweses had arrived or not, but they'd descend upon us any moment.

A quick knock sounded at the bedroom door, and Jem tumbled in without waiting for permission. 'All your fripperies done?' he asked.

'Don't be vulgar,' said Mother as she followed him inside. Her skirt floated exactly level with the floor thanks to her own set of precision-engineered crinoline wheels. It was one of the few creations of mine that she truly loved.

I stood by the window and pressed my eye to the viewer of my second-best brass periscope. The far end was welded into place in the bottom left corner of the glass. I'd considered using copper for the tubing, but the cleverer magic of brass was best for fine-tuning sensory detail. Copper only made things bigger or louder, while brass let me see through raindrops, and the aural attachment could filter out background noise.

At the touch of my hand, the street came into sharp focus.

Every time I used the periscope the magic responded faster, and with greater accuracy. The noise of the street clarified as suddenly as the view, and I jumped at the strident *oy-eh!* call of the dustmen.

Forgetting Mother wasn't meant to know about the reduced number of servants, Jem said, 'I hope Harry's quick to answer them, or he won't be in time to receive the Daw—'

Arabella conveyed a reminder of Mother's presence with a swift kick, aided by the Superior-Inferior Heels I'd made her, the points of which sprung out in a deadly manner.

Jem yelped and swore.

'Jeremy,' Mother reprimanded softly.

'Beef-head,' hissed Arabella, underestimating her volume by half.

Rather than choosing to hear Arabella's comment, Mother straightened the dangling satin ribbons of her cap.

'Dustmen!' Jem said with a flash of inspiration. 'I hope Harry's quick to receive the *dustmen.*'

'It has been awfully smelly downstairs,' Mother agreed, neatly changing the subject.

Arabella and I exchanged a glance. We both knew Father's laboratory—my laboratory now—was smelly because of rising damp, not because of any industrial by-products I might happen to produce between making tea and embroideries. The stench was an inevitable side effect of living in Britain's greatest city.

I turned back to the periscope and watched Harry haul our rubbish out to the waiting dustmen, who dumped it in their cart. Rain slicked down his grey hair. He jumped guiltily at something outside my view and hurried back inside to change clothes, dragging the empty boxes with him.

'They're close,' I said.

'Should we go to the drawing room now?' asked Arabella, trying and failing to keep the nerves from her voice.

'Wait a moment longer,' I said. 'I want to see Mrs Dawes.'

A monster-sized carriage drew up a moment later, drawn by

six horses—all satiny white except for the black mud on their legs. Four footmen jumped out and stood to attention. They were all exactly the same height and build. I was impressed.

Mrs Dawes's hand extended from the doorway and hovered in the air. Two of the men leapt to her side to help her down. I winced as my brass contraption amplified the creaking of her stays until the sound filled my room. Brass has a wayward sense of humour.

Mother coughed politely, trying and failing to mask the sound. I kept my eye pressed to the viewer.

Mrs Dawes bulged in every direction. Her arms bulged from her sleeves, and her eyes bulged from her bacony face. The footmen were discreet enough to avert their eyes as she alighted, but I had a feeling even her ankles bulged. When she shook off her men and advanced on the house I distinctly heard the tuneless screech of crinoline wheels in need of grease. My heart skipped a beat in sympathy. It didn't like being around shoddy maintenance, no matter how popular it might be this season.

Tick … tick.

Her son stepped down unassisted, swearing quietly at the vagaries of fashion as his steel waistcoat prevented him from bending low enough to easily clear the door. I sympathised, since no amount of leather lining made my steel corsets comfortable either.

The jawline I remembered fondly from last year's royal ball was as square as ever. I willed my heart not to overheat, steaming out of my safety valves and giving away my interest—not to mention my unique medical condition.

We'd spent every penny of our social currency covering up the initial installation of my heart years ago, and Father's subsequent execution by hanging. The slightest mistake on my part would expose the macabre truth and ruin us all. But if I didn't manage to catch Mr Dawes's interest, my remaining choices of suitor were limited at best. Father's last remaining business ventures had finally petered out and I needed to marry at once, before our thin veneer of prosperous respectability failed once and for all.

Mr Dawes moved with grace, as if we were still at the ball. When he glanced up I saw that his eyes behind their spectacles were outlined in girlishly long lashes, and bore a wistful expression. I remembered that from the ball, too.

'Should we go to the drawing room now?' asked Jem, tugging pointedly on my sleeve.

'One moment,' I said, unwilling to stop staring while my periscope gave me the advantage.

Mr Dawes followed his mother to the door.

She whirled and held up one hand to stop him. 'Remember, Ambrose, watch Miss Muchamore carefully. Rumour has it her father was secretly executed for murder!'

The revelation hit me like a physical blow, and I bit my lip to keep from crying out—whether in fear or rage I couldn't say. Fortunately the magical brass of my periscope only worked in one direction. It wouldn't do for them to hear my gasp and know I was using magic to spy on them from above as they approached my front door.

'How reliable is your source for that juicy morsel?' Mr Dawes smiled slightly, and my hopes rekindled. His natural scepticism might just save me. 'Was it Miss Smythe again?'

'They couldn't prove it, but it's God's own truth,' Mrs Dawes insisted. 'He cut out a young girl's heart.'

I touched the cool metal of the vent leading to the place where my flesh and blood heart used to reside. It always made me think of Father, and how much he loved me. My body was the canvas for his glorious art—mine, and no one else's. If only my genius could match his!

'Really?' Mr Dawes said. 'Whose heart did he take? And what did he do with her corpse?'

Mrs Dawes harrumphed loudly. 'I'm sure I don't know.'

'As I recall, he died of ill health—and you and I both attended the funeral. It was very tasteful. Your version of events is a trifle fantastic, don't you think? Like so many of your best rumours—more's the pity.'

'Then why the closed casket that day?'

'Apparently people don't look their best when ill. Especially after the illness proves fatal.' He sighed. 'Unless the family managed to arrange an entirely secret trial and an equally secret execution—with the help of some of the top doctors, lawyers and judges in the city—I think we'd best presume the late Mr Muchamore was innocent of slicing out the heart of a little girl.'

Studying Mr Dawes wasn't helping me calm down. The rate of my heart's ticking increased the longer I spent in his presence..

Mrs Dawes rallied her outrage for one last sally. 'The details of the case are irrelevent. Only remember, if you will, that this family has a reputation for peculiarity.'

'I do hope it's deserved.'

Mrs Dawes took several agitated breaths. 'Do be serious, Ambrose. I only mentioned the rumour so you could keep it in mind, just in case the Muchamores give some sign that proves it to be true after all. Try not to be distracted by Miss Muchamore's famous blue eyes. Blue eyes are not at all a suitable reason to marry.'

'I managed to remain calm when I saw them at the royal ball last year. Very distracted blue eyes—until I mentioned my admiration of Hungerford Bridge. Then they were sharp as steel.'

'Did you bore her with your engineering talk? You know you mustn't discuss all that rubbish in proper society.'

'I didn't have the chance. She danced on. I did, however, notice she possessed a very finely-engineered ankle.'

I wondered how he'd react when he finally saw my beautiful brass and silver heart for the first time—but of course that idea was sheer presumption. Until we were engaged, my secret had to remain hidden. There was too much at stake to trust anyone, even someone with such excellent taste in bridges.

'Well I never!' Mrs Dawes prevented further wickedness by motioning for Mr Dawes to ring our bell.

Chapter Two

I followed Mother in an uncommonly rapid stroll to the drawing room. All four of us stood in our most elegantly awkward poses. Jem tapped out a nervous rhythm on the left-hand section of his brass waistcoat until Arabella stamped on his foot, leaving a round imprint from her Superior-Inferior heel. She had a rare gift for communication.

While I had a moment, I slipped my portable hem-crank out of an inner pocket and adjusted my skirts so Mr Dawes would catch a tantalising glimpse of my wheels before I sat down. I remembered the way his brown eyes lit up when he spoke of Hungerford Bridge, and felt a flutter of anticipation. My heart responded to my nervous excitement by beating harder than ever.

Tick!

Mother quickly switched places with me so I was closer to the stopped clock. I opened the glass face and adjusted the hands to the correct time. Hopefully the Daweses wouldn't stay too long and notice something amiss.

I was secretly proud that brass was a part of me, no matter how appalled Society would be if they knew. Apart from anything else, my artificial heart gave me instincts far more accurate than women's intuition, and I had a good feeling about Mr Dawes.

Tick, tick.

Harry bowed at the door. 'Mrs Dawes and Mr Dawes,' he said, and I noticed he still had half a cast-off brass cog stuck to his trouser leg with grease. Perhaps no one else had seen it. I hoped not. Poor Harry was always trying and failing to tidy my laboratory. He still hadn't given up hope that it was all merely some childhood phase. I tried to resist the urge to share my latest wondrous discoveries with him on a daily basis. Sometimes I even succeeded for a day or two.

Mrs Dawes progressed into the room with all the pomp of a galleon under sail. She exhibited all the creaking and huffing of a galleon too, not to mention the discolouring spatter of raindrops across her chest.

Mr Dawes met my eye and smiled. His patented self-doffing hat wound itself upward on a long spring before leaning sideways and then flipping neatly into his crooked arm. It was elegantly done, and gave me time to admire the moulded shape of his steel waistcoat between the cravated V of his frock coat. Now that he was in the room, I struggled to maintain my focus. For a moment I wished we weren't chaperoned at all. Perhaps then I'd begin by telling him that his self-doffing hat had been invented in the basement of the very home in which he sat. I was struggling to conceal my excitement, and my heart wasn't helping one bit.

Tick!

We all sat and folded our hands politely. Mother excused the children. I knew they'd listen from the next room, probably assisted by another of my brass devices. It was only fair: Arabella had to learn flirtation somehow. I wished I'd had an older sister to observe at our most vital work. It seemed far too important to be made up as I went along.

A foolish fantasy popped into my mind about wanting a more important destiny than marrying well and looking pretty. I dismissed it at once. Harry was right: experimentation and invention was no occupation for a lady. Impressing the right young man was what really mattered.

'Tea?' said Mother.

'Delighted,' said Mrs Dawes, eyeing her carefully. Perhaps she suspected Mother might spontaneously sprout petunias from her nose. I could think of three different ways to make that happen, but failed to think of a practical use. Pity.

Mother tugged the bell-cord to let our upper housemaid know

her services were required. None of us were certain whether or not Mother had noticed the girl was now also our lower house-maid, and our cook. She gave no clear sign of having observed the change.

I rested my hands in my lap and left a space for Mrs Dawes to pick a topic of conversation that suited her. Instead she glared around the room without looking at me. She examined the porcelain figurines on the mantelpiece above the fire, then the genuine gold detail on the rose wallpaper, long since faded to brown. Her eyes rested above my head, and I knew she was examining the family portrait Mother had painted in oils the year before Father cut out and replaced my natural heart. I was Arabella's age, showing barely a sign of womanhood. Jem was a pouting child, and Arabella wasn't old enough to walk. Mother was slightly prettier than she should have been, and her blonde hair was a little smoother than real life would have it. She'd painted the entire portrait with all of us facing a mirror. As a result, it was very nearly truthful.

Mrs Dawes's eyes narrowed, searching for some new morsel of gossip to share with the world. I kept my breath and heart steady, grateful I hadn't sold the heavy gilt frame and replaced it with painted plaster—yet.

'The weather is very fine,' Mr Dawes attempted.

'Yes,' I said, trying very hard to think of something more inspiring. I failed, and blurted an honest comment instead. 'It was rainy all this week.'

He stifled a smile. 'Faithful British weather.'

I almost broke into a nervous laugh, but managed to keep my expression ladylike. 'Indeed.'

'Miss Muchamore, if I may be so bold?'

'Please,' I said, and saw his eyes brighten to reflect mine.

'Our families are on good terms, terms likely to improve.'

Tick!

A jet of steam scalded my back as it exited the main safety

valve between my shoulder blades, hissing loudly through the vent in my corset. Since I was seated close to the fireplace, the steam dissipated without causing comment. As long as I kept calm enough that no steam erupted from the secondary safety valve in my brass sternum, I'd be fine. Mrs Dawes was unlikely to appreciate the sight of her prospective daughter-in-law steaming violently from between the breasts.

'Yes, Mr Dawes?' I willed myself to keep my heart in check. 'Do go on.'

Tick, tick.

He blushed, and took off his spectacles to polish them. 'May we call one another by our first names?'

I didn't answer right away. To my surprise, even Mrs Dawes looked quietly pleased at the prospect of greater intimacy between us. The upside of having a notorious gossip guess one's family secrets was that she was unlikely to be believed. She didn't even believe herself.

Tick, tick.

My family would be safe, Jem and Arabella would grow up and choose their future in the same circles we'd enjoyed all our lives. The crucial task of my life was as good as done—other than bearing children, naturally. That had to be easier than this.

'Of course, Ambrose,' I said at last, hardly daring to look at him.

'Thank you, Emmeline.' He stared at his hands, hiding his expression, but my heart told me our meeting was going very well indeed.

Once again the image of my laboratory lying neglected gave me the illusion of dissatisfaction with my future. I shook it off: my happiness was virtually complete. Marriage would be far more interesting than the clammy hole where I spent so many of my leisure hours inventing unique contraptions and changing the world around me with modifications to everything from fashion to vermin. Harry would soon be proved correct: it was merely a girlish phase. I was about to grow up and leave that illusion of real joy behind me.

Mary knocked and entered with the tea-things. Ambrose and I dared an exchange of smiles as she set out the tray and left us.

Tick, tick.

Mother passed a fine bone china mug to Mrs Dawes—we'd sold all but four, and I was desperately relieved we'd kept the right number for this essential meeting. My heart hadn't betrayed me after all, and nor had our lack of funds. All our efforts at remaining part of society were about to pay off. My future was set in stone. Good British stone.

Tick, tick.

I was happy. Of course I was.

Clonk.

Oh. Oh no.

I took a careful breath and knew at once I was in dire need of help. That, and oxygen. I gasped for more air, knowing it was useless: the problem was inside me.

My mind sorted furiously through Father's medical and bio-metallic notes. Supernatural intuition from the clever brass of my heart told me one of my arterial valves was broken. Fine, arterial valves were fixable. Except … except …

Not brass. I couldn't use brass. Brass was good for sensory or intuitive magic and nothing else. Only silver bonded directly with organic matter. That was why several vital pieces of my heart were made of silver. But … we didn't have a real silver spoon left in the house. Worst of all, I'd melted and sold all my most personal spare parts just last week. I'd had to find a way to buy a new dress for this very meeting.

Mrs Dawes was talking at me. I stared at her and didn't hear a word. For the life of me, I couldn't remember why she was in our home at such a time.

She stood up, still talking, and pointed her fat finger right at my chest. We'd all heard a clonking noise that was terribly improper.

She demanded to know what it was.

Mrs Dawes wore a silver necklace. It called to me: one piece of silver to another.

'Necklace,' I said, very carefully. 'Give me your necklace.'

Someone's hand clutched my arm. It was Mother's hand—pale, with long fingers and neat nails. She knew I'd broken something internally, and she understood what it meant for me and for all of us. I stared at her in mute terror for my life, and her blue eyes widened. Her hair was a halo.

My brass heart told me exactly what she saw when she looked at me: she was thrown back to the day when I was nine years old and she found me bloody and unconscious on Father's underground workbench, with my original heart in a tray beside me. Father was so proud of what he'd achieved: England's first true fusion of steam and humanity. A triumph for Britain and for science!

Her hand slipped from my arm as she passed out.

'Necklace,' I said again stupidly, and held out my hand to Mrs Dawes like a beggar. My fingers were blue. Just one minor valve failure under pressure, and our family hung on the brink of social ruin. Again.

If I didn't get that necklace, I had less than an hour to live. My heart tried and failed to work.

Mrs Dawes took another step back, her hand at her throat. She stared at Mother but didn't move to help her. I remembered that long-ago day when my heart was brand new, and Father and I both tried to explain to a pair of horrified policemen how wonderful it was—how beautiful a gift. It was my blood all over the floor that day, but no one listened to what I had to say. I was just a girl.

Ambrose stepped between his mother and I. 'Emmeline, what is it? What's wrong? Are you unwell?'

I wanted to tell him, but I couldn't possibly expose my family's critical secret. Not after Mother bribed so many of London's elite to cover up Father's last days, both his actions and the law's reaction. Instead I shook my head at Ambrose, willing him to understand. Perhaps he could somehow guess that my heart needed silver, and needed it at once. Perhaps one day he could understand that my heart wasn't grotesque; it was engineering. Perhaps one day I'd tell him the whole story, when we were alone and he was in love with me.

His eyes clouded with confusion, and the link between us snapped. He took his mother's arm and walked to the door.

I lunged for Mrs Dawes and caught the life-saving silver necklace in my fingers, keeping her from leaving. She screamed in pain and sudden fear. I yanked with all my strength, and her scream strangled into silence. The clasp snapped and I fell backward. My skirts tangled around my knees, setting my crinoline wheels awry and showing far too much of my legs. I'd have burned with shame if I wasn't too busy trying to stay alive.

Running footsteps converged from all over the house—Henry, Mary, and my poor doomed brother and sister. I let the Daweses flee outside, and stumbled toward Father's laboratory.

My laboratory.

As I hurtled downstairs into the stinking dark, I heard Mrs Dawes bellowing at the top of her voice on our front step: 'Murderers. They're all murderers. Help, police! Somebody call the police!'

Chapter Three

'What do you need?' Arabella yelled down the stairs in a decidedly unladylike manner.

'Fuel!' I shouted back. The 'if you please, dear' was implied.

In three more steps I hit the damp cellar floor. My vision blurred around the edges, but it wasn't gone yet. I saw three desks overloaded with jars of metallic powder, loops of copper wire, Arabella's hairbrush (so that's where it was), and the broken cogs of at least three homemade rodent hearts.

One of my semi-mechanical rats scuttled out from under my feet, squeaking in annoyance. The others woke up all in a pile and immediately scattered under the benches, chittering frantically. They needed winding. I needed winding. No, that wasn't right. I wasn't thinking straight. Needed to fix one of my silver valves. Yes, that was it.

I stared at the rats' beady eyes and very nearly swore at myself in horror. All their hearts had silver valves. Given a little time, I could have cannibalised their engines to save mine. Why hadn't I thought of that earlier?

Jem tumbled into the laboratory bearing a bottle of my best glycerol. 'Arabella's in the kitchen getting backup coal, but I thought potassium would be faster—with this to bribe it into burning longer.'

'Good, Jem. We'll need all the magic we can get.' I handed him the necklace, and cleared my main workbench by shoving everything onto the floor with a crash of pipes and the tinkle of breaking glass. Fortunately Jem had already grabbed our jar of potassium, and it didn't smash with the rest.

He poured one individually-sealed section of the jar into the large crucible in the middle of the mouldy floor and added a puddle of glycerin, pulling back his bare fingers quickly. As it began to smoke he added our three remaining pieces of anthracite coal. He put the necklace into a second, cleaner crucible on top of the coal just as the potassium exploded into a brilliant tongue of fire.

I lay back on my workbench and positioned my operational periscope over my chest, ripping away lace and silk with my other hand. My fingers fumbled badly with the front and side ties of my steel corset, but at last the two leather-lined front pieces fell away and clanged onto the floor. I pulled up my chemise, exposing my bare chest, and hooked open my sternum access panel with one finger, staring straight up into the periscope mirror for the clearest view.

'It's melting already,' said Jem, buckling a leather apron around his chest and strapping on brass goggles with difficulty as he lay on the fetid floor to blow madly at the anthracite so the fire didn't fail.

'Please don't crack,' he said to the necklace, showing an unexpected sentimental side. 'Please please please just melt perfectly—and quickly. My sister needs you.'

The activated potassium knew its job, and was proving very helpful in lighting the reluctant coal. It would do all kinds of improbable things for a bit of glycerol. Potassium was easy to please, like an over-eager street urchin. I didn't trust it for a minute.

'What exactly am I making today?' Jem asked, dropping the emotions from his voice like so much scrap. 'Tubing, endothelium, or valves?'

Through the periscope mirror I saw my upside-down front boiler and tubing all intact. I pressed the emergency seals into place and lifted my entire secondary steam engine out of the way, hissing in pain as my fingers burnt. 'I have a feeling I need a new intake valve, maybe two.'

'Bigger ones, if you please,' said Arabella, appearing over me in goggles and a brass mesh-mask for seeing and breathing through my engine's jetting steam. 'She outgrew her arteries again. It wasn't completely that boy's fault after all.'

I handed her my front engine and she put it down somewhere beyond my periscope's field of vision. She grew taller before my eyes, and I thought I was hallucinating until I realised she'd utilised her Superior-Inferior Heels to get a better viewing angle on the failed valve. 'We're in luck—it's the right PA that's baked,' she said, her childish voice trembling in contrast to her steady hands as they took measurements of my metallic innards. 'It'll be easier to install than the left. Point one-two-five inches diameter, hinge drills at one-zero-one and one-two-two.' As she spoke she pulled on the gloves I'd made for her. Each finger had a blade, or tiny pincers, or a clockwork rotating saw. She hit her palm against the bench to turn on the glove's second and third fingers with a symphony of clicks and whirring.

'One-zero-one?' I said. 'So you're saying the silver bonded with my flesh well enough to alter its features, but not enough to grow in total area?'

'So it would seem,' said Arabella.

'Fascinating!'

I heard a clank and then sharp metallic plinks as Jem hammered and sliced and drilled the silver faster than he'd ever worked metal before. He muttered measurements and prayers in equal proportions as he worked, and I hoped the silver was in a malleable mood. Silver wasn't as easily impressed as potassium. I respected silver, and I hoped it understood. More than that, I hoped it cared whether I lived or died. Perhaps there was a way to test silver's potential for sentimentality without actually risking death. I made a mental note to do so at my earliest convenience.

The air stank of mould, coal, and burning sugar. 'Arabella?' I said, no longer able to see anything at all. If my vision was going, that meant time was running out. I had so many more theories to test! Oh yes, and I was meant to be getting married.

'What is it?' Arabella asked me.

'Some tepid water to cool the silver before it's installed would be terribly helpful, when you have a moment.'

I heard her gasp, and then nothing.

'Arabella?' I said. 'Jem? Are you still there?'

Something pressed down hard on my chest, and I fell helplessly into a swoon.

Chapter Four

I awoke fully clothed, with all my corset segments laced together and my blue silk dress sewn back into place. Before I sat up I automatically groped around beside me for the spare engine.

'Arabella replaced it for you,' said Mother, who stood at my side. 'Your decency was left to me.'

I sat up gingerly and checked my fingers. They were pink. 'Everything seems to be in order.'

'We did it!' Jem said loudly.

I grinned at him. 'Huzzah for brass and Britain!'

Mother sighed loudly. 'It really is cluttered in here. I don't know how you can stand it.'

'Really?' I glanced at the pile of smashed glass and twisted metal behind my main workbench. 'You're concerned about the mess right now?'

Harry appeared at the door, his face grey. The laughter between the rest of us died before he opened his mouth. 'I'm terribly sorry.'

'What is it?' I asked, sitting up to face him properly. 'It can't possibly be as serious as a valve malfunction.'

He shook his head without meeting my eye. 'The police are here, Miss Muchamore. What shall I tell them?'

Mother broke in: 'Tell them there's been a misunderstanding, and we thank them for their concern.'

'I already tried that, but they wouldn't leave. They have a description of the necklace. I beg your pardon, but I don't think the police are willing to keep our … legal proceedings … hidden a second time.'

I reached out for Mother, drawing her close to me. 'How long was I unconscious?'

'Only a moment,' she lied, barely glancing at me.

My eyes filled with tears. 'I've lost Ambrose forever. We're ruined.'

'No we're not,' said Arabella in a small voice.

'Yes,' said Mother, patting at her misbehaving hair. 'We are.' She took my face in two cold hands. 'My darling Emmeline, I'm so sorry. I should have thought of something useful to do long ago, before it came to this. It shames me that I let you bear all the weight of saving us.'

'Someone in this house had to value respectability over science,' I said. 'And it clearly wasn't going to be any of us.'

She kissed my cheeks, and we didn't cry.

'I have to go with them,' I said, pushing her gently away. 'Perhaps I can clear up this problem, but you must make me a promise.'

'Anything,' said Mother. 'It's time I did my part.'

Jem and Arabella stood on either side of her, their faces too grave for their years.

'Don't follow me. Whatever happens, let me stand alone at the trial, like Father did. Even if it goes badly …' My voice shook, and a short burst of steam through my corset's back vent almost made me lose control, 'We can't afford any more scandal. So for my sake, don't visit me. You can't help me anymore, but I can still help you.'

'That's not fair!' Arabella burst out.

I ignored her, picking up the half-empty jar of potassium to slip it into one of the hidden pockets in my skirt, checking as I did so that the inner seal was still holding.

Mother straightened her back. 'Just in case, we should pack you a bag. If the worst happens …'

I glanced at her. We both knew I'd never return. She was absolutely right. Even if my belongings were taken by other prisoners or by further misfortune or disgrace, I had to try to take something useful with me.

'Harry, have Mary pack my things at once—dresses, unmentionables, my good wrenches, and plenty of oil. Oh! And Father's broken pocketwatch.' He left without a word. 'Mother, you understand our financial situation, don't you? You understood all along.'

She bit her lip. 'There has to be something I can do.'

'Look after Jem and Arabella. You're the only one left who can.'

She straightened up, unconsciously activating her own pair of Superior-Inferior Heels for even greater height. 'You are a Muchamore, and no mistake,' she murmured. 'Come back to me safely.'

'When this is over, I will. I promise.'

I walked up the stairs to my arrest, knowing I'd made a promise I couldn't possibly keep. The guilt made me hate Mother for a moment, but only a moment. Then it simply became a part of me, with all the rest.

Three of the white clockwork rats leapt for me and buried themselves inside the pockets of my skirt. I didn't have the heart to shake them out. Father and I used to build their artificial parts together, but that was a long time ago now. He was dead because of me, and now the rest of my family had another scandal on my account. I'd worked hard to make up for my part in Father's death, but this new debt meant I'd left them worse off than ever. It would be impossible to help them at all from gaol, but at least I could separate them from my toxic influence.

Mary stood by the front door with my loaded portmanteau, weeping helplessly. 'Speak to Mother about your pay,' I told her. 'She knows everything, knew it all along.'

'Miss Muchamore!' she said, and dissolved into sobs. 'It ain't right, all this! And you're just a girl. You should tell the truth to the judge. He'll understand you had to do it.'

'Speak publicly about Father, and our lost money, and my heart? No Mary. That wouldn't do at all.'

'But—'

'Take care of them, won't you?' I said, despising the note of begging that crept into my voice. 'You mustn't let them come and see me, do you hear?'

I tugged the portmanteau from her limp fingers and walked out the open door. My fingers gripped the handle of the bag as if was all the home I had left—which of course it was.

Two policemen stood waiting for me, inhumanly tall in their varnished leather helmets. An air of quiet menace hung around them, and I realised we were the centre of attention for the entire street. It was eerily calm, with no sound but the endless dripping of the rain. Even the horses were silent, staring at the road with water running from their manes.

'Wait!' called Arabella. She hurried out of the door with my Probability Parasol and thrust it into my spare hand.

'Thank you.' I kissed her goodbye, knowing I'd never see her again. A part of me was selfish enough to hope she'd disregard all sense and decency and visit me in my cell. But I felt sure that when the first heat of grief faded, she'd be clever enough to know better. I'd carefully taught her to hide her true feelings—too well, perhaps. 'Now go back inside, for me.'

She shook her head fiercely, and for a moment I saw a little girl unwilling to lose yet another family member. Emotional displays were for the poor and the foreign—or so I'd thought. It appeared Arabella wasn't as receptive to my teaching as I'd supposed. I was both annoyed and grateful.

Steam hissed from my back vent and dissolved into the thin rain. Tears streamed down my cheeks, and I was grateful for the rain's disguise. Faithful British weather. I turned away from her deliberately and stepped into the police carriage without looking back.

Lace curtains twitched all up and down the street, and I wished Belgravia was as discreet as we all pretended to be. As the police carriage splashed off down the road, all the coster-mongers renewed their shouting in raucous chorus. Arabella's sobs followed me down the street. My fate was sealed, and if she insisted on maintaining her relationship with me, her fate was little better. I had to stop her maintaining her association with me—somehow.

The policemen sat facing me, their thick hands on their knees. One of them was old enough to attempt a moustache but not old enough to succeed. He cleared his throat. 'We're sorry, Miss Muchamore.'

'Thank you,' I whispered, then gasped indelicately as one of the rats nipped me on the leg, its teeth barely blunted by the layers of fabric. Suddenly I realised I'd completely forgotten to put on gloves. Mother would be horrified if she knew.

'Are you all right?' asked the young man.

'Quite.' I stared out the window to conceal my discomfort, drinking in the familiar view while I still could.

We rattled peacefully by Green Park, but as we turned the corner the view from my window filled with tiny shacks piled one on top of another up the hill. Above them all, high and dry for repairs, was a vast American clipper with its sails furled and its green copper belly glistening in the rain. Under the clipper's bowsprit, a pack of boys in short pants chased one another up and down across the bark and tile rooftops, shrieking with laughter as they ducked under strings of dripping washing and leapt over miniature gardens fenced in wrought iron. I wondered who Jem would have become if we'd grown up in that street instead of our own.

'Potatoes!' yelled a man at my window, displaying rotten teeth in a face like a badly tanned hide. 'Hot boiled potatoes, half a penny!'

I shrank back, and we passed him by. My heart ticked on, and I attached Father's unwound pocketwatch to my bodice before the policemen noticed the incongruous sound. Their faces weren't familiar to me, so I presumed they had no idea of my secret. I tried and failed to compose myself with silent prayer. God's presence gave me no comfort now. I'd left Him with my family in Belgravia.

'What's going to happen to me?' I asked the younger man.

'Depends if you're guilty or innocent,' the other said quickly, fingering his truncheon. 'Although, if you produce the stolen goods you may get mercy.'

'And if I can't?'

'With two witnesses against you, you'll be thrown in with the canting crew for sure. It's lucky you packed your things.'

Did prison wardens make a distinction between the gentry and the criminal class, or had I become a fallen woman so abruptly? Were fallen women still wearing metal corsets this season?

'Don't be so frightened,' said the younger policeman. 'You'll not dance the caper this week. No one likes to hang a woman, especially a pretty mort like you.'

It hadn't occurred to me that I might be executed for my crime. The new information wasn't comforting.

Outside the window I caught a glimpse of the elegant suspension cables of Hungerford Bridge. The notion of Ambrose reporting against me with his mother was almost too much to bear. I wanted to faint, but there was no time to waste. Minutes ticked by as I tried to think of some way to preserve Arabella's reputation now that my own was ruined.

We rode on past the neat stone arches of Waterloo Bridge, and I wished I'd had a chance to discuss its caissons with Ambrose. But he was Mr Dawes again now, and always would be.

I wrinkled my nose involuntarily. Even the rain couldn't mask the stench of human waste and tallowed industry rising from the Thames. I closed my eyes and tried to breathe as little as possible. Had Mary packed me a handkerchief? I didn't know. More importantly, how could I prevent Arabella's visits to me, her criminal sister? My strengthening desire to see her wasn't helping one bit.

We continued up The Strand in silence, and stopped on the wooden road outside the towering classical columns of the Old Bailey. Inside, a man I'd never met would decide whether to send me back home, to prison, or to eternity.

A crowd blocked the street, and at first I thought Mrs Dawes had gathered them in order to provide further humiliation for me, outdoing her own gossip-mongering reputation for this special occasion. It wasn't true, however; the crowd milled about Newgate Prison, wailing their grief or laughter as several hunched and blinking prisoners were escorted onto a queue of navy carriages. They were being sent away from sweet Britain forever. Some would already be marked as dead in the records, and the rest might as well be similarly dismissed. Rain fell unnoticed on their bowed heads.

The policemen hustled me inside the courtroom, where I was surrounded suddenly by polished wood and a dark sea of frockcoats. My blue silk was damp and one of my crinoline wheels caught in the fabric, making my skirts tip sideways. One of my policemen held a hissed conversation with a red-clad soldier while the other watched me. As I wondered why I was taken straight to court instead of a holding cell, I realised that my policemen had skipped the queue for me; saving me from prolonged disgrace as well as they could. My name still protected me—a little.

Before I could thank them for their pains I was hustled into the dock to defend my case. It was simple enough: I was accused of assault and theft and asked if I was guilty. Sickened at the possibility that Ambrose might be forced to testify in person against me, I admitted I had indeed snatched the necklace.

The judge asked me to produce the item and go free, but I was unable to either obey him or explain my disobedience. If I confessed publicly to the truth of my brass heart, our family name would be synonymous with mad science and bloody experimentation, regardless of my opinions on the matter, which had never counted for anything.

So I held my tongue, and I received the sentence of seven years in Brixton Prison with true British stoicism. Even my heart didn't give me away.

The judge asked if I had anything further to add.

I blinked in shock, recognising the hooded eyes beneath his

grey wig for the first time. He'd given me boiled sweets when he'd visited our home with a bevy of other judges. That was years and years ago, when men had gathered in our drawing room to discuss the discreet management of Father's execution. Not one of them ever listened to my defiant claims of health, but he had been kinder than the rest.

I had one chance to save Arabella.

'Your Honour!' I called out, and he motioned for me to speak. 'I've brought disgrace to my family's name today. Please send me away with those poor souls getting transported outside. Let London's good society know I'll never return, and let my family have no choice but to forget me.'

He paused in the act of lowering his gavel. 'Is this a plea for mercy or further punishment?'

'Both, Your Honour.'

He consulted with a brace of clerks, and I held my breath.

'Very well,' he said at last. 'There's always room for one more on those ships, which makes them a better place for our newest reprobate than the cells. Send her with them, on my order.'

After a flurry of paperwork, two soldiers took me out the great doors into the wet chaos of the street. I realised what I'd done and began to shake. Would the judge mark me down as transported, or deceased? Some chose the latter description, and it was true enough. Leaving London was death, as far as I was concerned. Arabella couldn't find me in Hades, and that was all that mattered.

In the privacy of my own mind, I admitted I was scared. I didn't want to go. Not to gaol, not to some distant shore. I didn't want that living death; forgotten entirely yet still alive. But it was too late to change my fate now.

Three clockwork rats dug their claws into my legs through my crinoline underskirts. I hoped they didn't damage the cloth. There was no chance I'd be able to buy another.

One of the soldiers hauled my portmanteau. I tried to smile at him in thanks, but he wasn't looking at me. He shoved the crowd aside, using my goods as a battering ram. Since it was half-filled with scraps of metal and the steel Probability Parasol (designed to protect its bearer in the probable event of a gentleman becoming overly familiar), it worked handily.

In moments I was crammed into an overpopulated carriage that stunk of fish and sweat. I was a brand new member of the dirty, hideous criminal class that any lady knows to loathe and fear. Did that mean I loathed and feared myself?

With a muffled crack of whips my journey to unknown lands began.

Chapter Five

'I'm Lizzie,' said a pale face in the stifling dark. 'From the fish-gutting girls. And more recently from the King's Head Inn for my pickpocketing skills. What are you in for?'

'I suppose I'm a thief,' I said, becoming dizzy as the air in the carriage was used up by too many throats.

'Perfect!' she said, and I wondered if she was quite sane. I'd been crammed into a carriage with a madwoman. Given our mutual destination, it was entirely possible she was dangerous. She bounced on her sliver of seat, making the thick-set fellow beside her grunt in anger. He was much more likely to be dangerous, now I thought about it. Lizzie might be a criminal, but she didn't strike me as dangerous to anyone but herself.

By necessity, I carried my portmanteau clasped in both my arms, standing on its end on my lap. As the lack of oxygen grew worse, I felt my valves open wider to compensate. Arabella and Jem had done fine work, and I had a feeling Mrs Dawes's necklace enjoyed its new position in my heart. Silver had excellent taste, and expressed itself by functioning well or badly depending on whether it liked its owner.

'I'm going to be rich, you know!' Lizzie said.

'Congratulations?'

'Don't you know where we're going?'

I shook my head, realised she couldn't see me in the crush, and answered in the negative.

'We're shipping off to Australia! There's gold lying on the ground if you know where to go. The whole country's made of it. We're the very last packet of louts lucky enough to be sent to the Eastern end of the continent!'

'Oh, how … fortunate for us.' Definitely mad as a hatter. I couldn't help liking her for it.

'You understand! Excellent! As soon as we're there I'm going to run away to Bearbrass City, then walk from there to the gold-fields. All I'll need is a sharp eye and I'll be a rich lass before I know it!'

'Bearbrass?' I repeated, scouring my mind for the little Australian geography I knew. 'Isn't it officially called Melbourne?'

'That's the one! You're a right blue-stocking, aren't you?'

'But we're not being sent to Victoria, are we?'

She laughed merrily. 'Van Dieman's Land is close enough, innit? Closer than London! But of course the bits and bobs of gold in Van Dieman's Land aren't enough for the likes of you and me. No, it's Victoria for us. We'll walk there in a week or two, won't we?'

Something about her gap-toothed smile and inclusive pro-nouns drew me in to her delusion, despite her much lower social station. I could tell her that Van Dieman's Land was an island some other time. 'I'm Emmeline. Emmeline Muchamore. Pleased to make your acquaintance, Lizzie.'

The carriages took us to the docks and soldiers loaded us onto a drenched mongrel of a steamship. Its wet sails looked like linen blown in knots around a washing line, and it sported a pathetic row of fake gunports in peeling black paint. A single cold central funnel marked the location of an unlit steam engine lurking below. Other prisoners staggered aboard behind us, brought by soldiers from the prison hulks at Woolwich. They smelled like a tannery, and I tried to hide my gagging.

Prompted by rifle butts and swearing, Lizzie and I submitted to having our legs chained together and numbers stencilled onto our backs. I hoped viciously that the paint wouldn't stick to silk. We climbed down a ladder to the engine room with difficulty, working together as well as possible. I had Lizzie and my bag, and that was all the cheer left to me. Fortunately Lizzie didn't require my help in maintaining her own high spirits, as I felt too low to answer her with civility. This was our ferry to Hades, and it was as grim as its destination.

The engine was a crowded mess of pipes and pistons, with a single great round boiler hunched on one side. Both walls were bulkheads, with a single small door each. A pair of chained convict men crawled through the door on the opposite side, and Lizzie bent double and led our own way through the thick oak barrier into the female berth. We didn't rank high enough for human-sized doors. Instead we were made to crawl like rats. My palms turned black and slick with what I hoped was merely engine grease.

I blinked, hoping my vision would clear, but there was nothing to see except a windowless twilight. Water dripped through from above, and Lizzie dived into one of the lowest bunks for shelter. At least the water from above was cleaner than the water on the floor, which strongly implied that chamber pots were all too easily overturned at sea.

'Isn't this wonderful?' Lizzie grinned. 'Off on an adventure to gold and glory!'

I squeezed her hand, keeping a tight hold on my portmanteau with the other. Some of the other hundred or so women had luggage too—anything they'd managed to keep, or that their family had given them before they left. None were as nice as mine, or as heavy, or clinked as much. Several of the women stared at me openly, and others pointedly avoided my eye.

An odd part of me felt hopeful despite my belly's ominous cramps and the distinct flavour of vomit and worse in the air. Lizzie's optimism about escape and riches was infectious. Besides, the stink and darkness of the hold was reminiscent of my laboratory, and my heart felt better with the comforting bulk of the boiler squatting on the bulkhead's other side, ready to be lit when the sails weren't enough to keep us moving.

I explored a little inside my portmanteau and found Mary

had packed smoked ham and fresh bread rolls for me. The other women stared at the food with unconcealed desperation, so I shared it all out at once, beginning with those from the hulks. Somehow, I wasn't hungry.

'You're all right,' said one.

'Thank you,' I said, and hesitated before adding, 'So are you.'

My rats tickled my ankles with their whiskers as they ran into a hole in our bunk. As long as nobody looked close enough to see the clockwork heart engines strapped onto their backs, they'd do very well on board ship.

'Bing,' squeaked the last one.

'You're welcome,' I said.

Lizzie jumped. 'Did that rat just talk to you?'

'Certainly. They're part tin, and you know what tin is like.'

'Oh!' She fingered a heart-shaped tin locket on a chain around her neck. 'Did you make them?'

I admitted that I'd made two of the clockwork engines, and she exclaimed in delight. She sounded much younger than she appeared, and I couldn't tell if she was older or younger than me. Her hand in mine was raw and splintered as a block of wood, but the skin of her face and neck was a translucent white. I supposed she'd gutted her quota of fish under some kind of shelter.

She saw me glancing at her locket. 'Mam gave it to me when I was young. She taught it to hum lullabies. Want to hear?'

I saw the brief flash of real sadness in her wide eyes, and said a reluctant yes.

Like most tin, the locket was a terrible musician; out of tune and shrill. Being able to make noise was a rather vulgar form of magic, but evidently tin had its uses for some. Lizzie soon fell asleep, pulling unconsciously on the iron chain linking our ankles. I lay down beside her, dangling half off our narrow bunk, and wondered how I'd fallen so far in a single day. Ambrose rose unbidden in my thoughts, and I pushed him away with an effort.

We didn't leave port for several hours, but at last the engine creaked and popped and turned over, and we crawled away from London. The other women treated me as a block of wood, holding their conversations above or around me. My obvious wealth had been forgiven thanks to my largesse with the food, but they weren't willing to befriend me as Lizzie had. The feeling was mutual.

I wondered if anyone had told my family where I was. I hoped no one had. Soon I'd be erased from London's memory and as good as dead. If Lizzie was right, I could escape from my Australian placement, get rich, and send gold to Mother. That would be worth my coming back to life. I hoped there was some tiny glint of reality in Lizzie's dreams.

Soon the rumble of the boiler was as familiar as the sloshing bilge on our floor. After a few days we stopped vomiting, and the smell began to fade. The soldiers removed our chains, presumably to prevent the strengthening magic of the iron working in us for too long. Iron had a straightforward magic, and needed only the touch of human skin to activate.

By then Lizzie and I knew the names and personal histories of every convict woman on board, all of whom shared our cabin, our chamber pots, and the frequent music from Lizzie's locket. They didn't mind me, and I did my best to hide my revulsion as their lice and filth inevitably became a part of me. I wasn't part of Society anymore, and I was reminded of that fact every waking moment. Nonetheless, some habits are hard to break. I spoke like a Belgravia lady still, and the lack of clean water never stopped bothering me.

My rats came and went as they pleased, looking sleeker by the day. Evidently they'd found the officers' food stores. I convinced them to sneak us a few rations when they could.

Some of the other women were ill, and I privately vowed to help them in any way I could. It would have been a great deal easier if their bodies were made of brass and steam instead of flesh, but the rats and I did our best. It was better than simpering at an endless procession of men, like in my old life. I didn't have to pretend anymore, which was oddly satisfying.

The women repaid me by leaving my portmanteau alone. Even criminals had manners of a sort.

The captain ordered us to have two hours' exercise per day. We took the air in a wooden-walled area on deck, in company with the smelly contents of the male convicts' berth.

I glanced at them, and saw not one worth a second glance. When I said as much to Lizzie, she giggled at me and looked over my shoulder. Sure enough, one of the ruffians had slid up to us and heard every word. He was short and dressed in rags, but I clearly saw the thick cords of his muscles through the fabric of his shirt. His jaw stuck out in front of him like a battering ram, and he kept as tight a hold on respectability as he could, wearing a stained and partially collapsed top hat. He introduced himself to Lizzie, ignoring me.

His name was Markus Dunne. I was perfectly happy to remain unacquainted, but Lizzie immediately introduced us to one another. Neither one of us made any motion to take the other's hand.

'Miss Muchamore,' I said stiffly.

'Mr Dunne,' he said, and turned back to Lizzie.

From that first hour on deck, the mass flirtation began. I watched in awe as the rags of my companions were draped ever more strategically, and the men's eyes strained ever more desperately to stare at us without seeming to. For my part, I stayed away from the men as much as possible, despite Lizzie's urging. Since I had no recourse but to be my own protector, I carried my Probability Parasol at all times. If nothing else, the steel's connection to me would make me physically strong, which could save me if a fight broke out. Steel and iron both strengthened the one who carried them, but steel was more effective.

Lizzie wasn't so preoccupied with personal space. Dunne continued to monopolise her, and she showed no sign of being averse to his attentions. I tried to raise her standards beyond him, but she only laughed. He had a sort of reckless handsomeness that I supposed might appeal to the lower classes. Eventually I was forced to accept that we were a party of three—for now. I didn't like him and he didn't like me, but we endured one another in order to keep Lizzie's company. And I had an idea.

'Lizzie,' I hissed. 'Mr Dunne!' They came closer to hear me. 'Listen! What do ships do when they meet?'

'Crash?' said Dunne.

'No,' I said. 'They exchange mail.'

Lizzie nodded several times. 'Thrilling! But … why's it thrilling?'

'Because we can use it to get to Bearbrass, without having to stow away on a ship after we escape.'

'How do you mean?' asked Lizzie, who still didn't quite believe in Bass Strait.

'We'll use my rats to plant a letter addressed to our captain, saying there's a labour shortage in Bearbrass and they'll pay more for his load of convicts than they'd pay at Van Dieman's Land. If we date the letter as if it was meant to arrive before we left London, he'll take it as an order. Mr Dunne, you should write it.'

'Oh Emmeline, you're so clever!' said Lizzie. 'But how can we get the letter to the capta—'

Dunne reddened and strode to the other side of the exercise area without a word. Judging by the set of his shoulders I'd offended him—again. I'd no idea the low-born were so sensitive.

'What's wrong with him now?' I asked Lizzie.

'You didn't realise? Markus and I can't write letters, nor read. You'll have to write it.'

'Oh! A masculine hand would have been so much more convincing. How unfortunate.'

'Don't worry, he'll forgive you. He's so sweet.' She smiled and unconsciously touched her chest where her locket used to be.

For the first time, I noticed a piece of leather cord twisted around her ring finger. Evidently she and Dunne had reached an understanding, and exchanged the small tokens they possessed. My heart audibly skipped a beat, and Lizzie gave my prominent pocketwatch a look of concern.

'I'm all right,' I said, and was faintly surprised when she believed me. But her eyes were on Dunne.

For her sake I stepped away quietly, and let her join Dunne for their short time together under the sky.

Chapter Six

In recompense for our continuing good behaviour, the captain allowed us to stand on board, back in irons and heavily guarded, when we landed at Gibralter. There was another ship there from London, and Lizzie, Dunne and I took our chance, carefully instructing my best rat, Bobby, for his crucial task. He scampered off, binging happily, and when I saw him next the letter was gone. All we could do was wait, and hope.

For two weeks after leaving Gibralter, we all ate a fresh orange every day. We passed the long hours below deck betting on rat races between Bobby and the rest, and paying one another in orange pips. The pips rapidly became an obsession, and I heard more than one hardened criminal crying herself to sleep after gambling away her entire stash. Then, the following day, the games began again.

As we ate our last orange, one of the female rats passed, trailing a long strip of paper from its back claw. I snatched at it, catching the paper as the rat scampered off. There on the sliver of paper I found fragments of my own handwriting. Bobby had taken our forged letter and made a nest. Stupid tin! It was my turn to cry myself to sleep.

I wrote a new letter and wore it tucked between my chemise and corset, hoping we'd get another chance. It wasn't likely, but Lizzie, true to her character, was certain luck would favour us. I bit my lip and managed not to comment on our luck thus far in life.

As we passed into the deadly heat of the tropics, the captain switched our exercise time from afternoon to night. I considered reducing my number of crinolines, but bravely resisted. Although

I was a fallen woman, I hadn't fallen as far as that. I felt ludicrous sometimes, wearing my full fashionable quota of petticoats in the gaol-hold of a transport ship in the tropics, but as my gentle perspiration reached an unbearable quantity I comforted myself that I hadn't changed so much after all. And at least I had a handkerchief to carefully dab at my forehead so my own sweat didn't sting me as it dripped unendingly into my eyes.

During the long days in our cabin I prepared Lizzie as well as I could for the necessary six-weekly maintenance of my heart. My front engine had never been intended for regular use, but only as an emergency backup. I could barely reach my primary motor, since it was accessed through the centre of my back. Luckily I didn't open the conversation with my pride in my father's ingenuity, since she burst into tears of pity the instant I overcame her natural disbelief.

We warned the other women to look away, and I talked Lizzie through the process of opening the latch in my back and checking for flaws in the metal, or in my flesh. One woman stood by to assist. Since she had killed her own son, I assumed her stomach was strong enough that she could step in if Lizzie failed.

I was wrong. When the murderess had finished throwing up and the other women were pressed as one against the farthest wall with their eyes closed or turned away, Lizzie continued with her gruesome task.

'It's not so bad,' she told me through gritted teeth. 'Sorting out your innards isn't so different from gutting fish. Except … fish don't move. Or clank. Or rust.'

'You're doing very well,' I told her, and it was true. Only Jem and Arabella had assisted me before, and they had the ignorant adaptability of children. Without them, I was not able to function unless Lizzie helped me. I tried not to think of all the unfortunate fates that could befall either one of us at any time. Lizzie didn't strike me as a girl who should be relied upon on pain of death. On the other hand, she was all I had.

Night by night, Lizzie and Dunne and I watched the Bear and the Big Dipper slowly wheel away beyond the horizon, replaced by a jumble of unfamiliar stars. On the day the sextant reading told us we'd passed the equator, even Lizzie stood quietly facing north, wondering aloud whether we'd ever return to familiar seas and a British sky. Every one of us would give up an ocean full of gold for one day at home.

The captain took away our exercise privileges for two weeks while we passed through storms off the horn of Africa, and Lizzie expressed her longing for Dunne's company by engraving horrific attempts at portraiture into the wood of the bunk above ours. That may or may not have explained the new rash of seasickness.

At last the sun came out again, and our daily exercise resumed. Lizzie burst into semi-permanent song. She wasn't any more talented than her tin locket, but I didn't care. There was fresh air again, for two hours a day under the magnificent sweep of the sails and the thick cloud of the smokestack.

One night I was awoken by a sharp nip on the cheek. I sat up carefully, and realised our ship's sea anchor had been thrown. We had stopped, and that meant we'd met another ship. Bobby was making up for his earlier lapse. Tin wasn't as stupid as it seemed. Through the bulkhead wall, the boiler's rumble was lower than usual.

If it truly was a passing ship, the forged letter had to be delivered. My rats had already gnawed a considerable hole in the wall between our cabin and the engine room. Together they and Lizzie and I tugged and dug out more of the old oak.

'What if they catch you?' Lizzie whispered. 'What would I do without you?'

A horrid part of me felt delighted she still needed me, despite Dunne's attentions. Of course that didn't mean she depended on me to keep her body alive, which would have made our relationship more equal.

'I won't be caught,' I told her. 'Just stay quiet, and we'll be changing course to Bearbrass before you know it.'

I crawled on my belly through the ragged hole into a hot mass of pipes, and carefully stood to my feet. Usually the boiler room held four sweating stokers, one pair each to guard the men's cabin and our own while keeping the engines burning. But the meeting across the waves was too good to miss, and one lone soldier sulked in the centre of the room, poking savagely at the red mouth of the boiler with his back to me. The others risked flogging for leaving their posts, but I didn't blame them.

All around me a tangled mass of pistons and pipes gleamed and rumbled, each moving part turning and clanking and wheezing despite the relative steadiness of the deck under my feet. I didn't care to walk along the narrow track past the redcoat, regardless of his lack of attention. That left only one way out—climbing over the engine.

I wasn't caught yet; that was good. For Lizzie and her shining dreams, I was willing to risk the little freedom I had left. Delicious smells of oil and coal and hot iron filled my senses, and I felt my heart lift. Maybe I really would be able to escape some day, and even find gold to send back home. I didn't need to marry well after all. That was a weight off my mind. I was ruined, imprisoned, lacking any gloves whatsoever—and I was freer than I'd ever been. My future was a blank for the first time, and I felt sure I could make it more interesting than the original.

The engine was a gleaming cornucopia of brass, copper and iron. Brass and copper were always especially inclined to help me, not that the pistons wouldn't crush my fingers to paste if I wasn't careful. Judging by the close communion of the soldier and the thick iron boiler, he'd have absorbed enough of iron's strengthening magic to overpower me without trying. Still, I'd been wearing my steel corset exclusively for months just in case my physical strength was important. Since I wasn't planning on fighting the soldier, all that mattered was using what strength I had to get past him.

There was nothing for it. I unhooked my crinoline wheels and passed them back to Lizzie. They wouldn't be any use to me now.

The engine was like a piece of music; all I had to do was make it a duet. If I could find my way inside its rhythm, all would be well. I stepped on an upward piston and quickly across to an immobilised crank, then another piston higher up. As the second piston threw me upward I grabbed hold of two copper pipes and hauled myself higher. Timing my leap to coincide with one great turn of the engine I jumped successfully and lay on my belly between two tall cylinders.

Each cylinder shuddered as the pistons inside were caught between natural steam pressure and the helmsman's desire to keep still. Since I was there and the engine was in pain, I manually opened each release valve and used my fingernails to scrape off the rust beginning to blossom there. Feeling better about the engine's efficiency, I crawled across the supporting strut, perspiring terribly in the steam, until I was close enough to reach over the narrow pathway and touch the access ladder leading up to the deck.

The sky through the hatch was cloudy, and the light beneath it was still the orange of boiler fire rather than the white of moonlight. That was a good sign. With my head bare and my red hair gathered at the base of my neck I could be a man, unless someone saw my silhouette. I braced my slippered feet against a row of rivets and leant across the gap to catch hold of the ladder with both hands. Precariously balanced there, I froze as the single stoker chose that moment to pace up and down the narrow section of path below me. He tripped over an oil can and swore like a cutter, dropping to his knees to pick it up before all the oil flowed out.

I took my chance and swung across the empty space above his back. The second my feet touched the rungs I climbed upward until my eyes were at the level of a grown man's knee. Looking all around, I didn't see anyone close to me—just a line of booted legs facing the water at the starboard railing. I pulled myself out, lying on my belly on the deck. Below me, the male convicts suddenly clamoured for attention, distracting the single guard. Dunne knew what I was doing, and for once we had the same goal.

The whole ship danced with the shadows cast by lantern light. I crept out on my hands and knees and lay down in the shadow of the exercise barrier.

For a moment, I was safe. It was as far aft as I'd ever been allowed to go. The sheep set aside for the last month of our voyage bleated plaintively from beneath the deck, one bulkhead closer to the soldiers' and officers' quarters than my own.

A shout of laughter from the railing made me cringe in terror. The other ship's captain had come onto his deck, and he called across a greeting in a broad American accent. I wanted very much to sit up and gawk at him like the rest. Instead I crawled through the unlocked barrier door with my head down, hoping to hear news of mail from Australia. If he'd sailed from India or Java our forged letter would be suspicious, and might even be traced back to my infamously well-equipped portmanteau.

A footstep thundered close to my head as one of the men, impatient for a better view, ran aftwards to peep at the exotic American from our quarterdeck. I crawled forward a few more feet, and my hand touched hessian. My breath caught in my throat as my fingers explored the hard corner of an envelope visibly sticking out from within the fabric of the bag. I'd never truly expected to succeed.

Pulling my own letter from my corset, I shoved it in amongst the rest. The vast majority were made of thick handmade paper, a consequence of life in the colonies, and I wished my own wasn't made of such fine quality.

It was odd the bag was so full. That was a great deal of mail for one convict steamer that wasn't even expected to cross the

American ship's path. But that was something to think about later. As I withdrew my hand, it brushed against an envelope of very fine machine-made paper, and I pulled it out without thinking.

My mind said I should crawl back to Lizzie at once, but the magic sixth sense of my heart told me otherwise. The brass parts had often given me knowledge that I couldn't possibly have guessed any other way. For some reason, I had to read the letter.

Unfortunately, the shadow that hid me also blinded me. I laid the envelope on the deck and slid it into a patch of lantern-light so I could read what was written there. It was addressed to a woman in Sydenham, London. For a second I thought it was a mistake, and then I realised the Americans had simply slung across all the mail they possessed. It would be sorted by someone on my ship, and the rest would be thrown back. So that was why the bag was full.

Other than that intelligence, the address meant nothing to me, except that I needed to hurry before the designated sorter approached. The address of the letter-writer made me thank my instincts. It was sent from Government House in Melbourne; the same building as my own letter's false origin. No wonder the paper was the best quality in all Victoria.

Leaving propriety behind—I was a true convict now—I pulled the flap open and drew out the letter.

My dear sister,

The children are well and my devoted Governor Hotham is succeeding in his brave attempt to bring about some reconciliation between the best gentlemen of our circle and the most civilised of the natives. It is my special task to teach the native women and girls how to attire themselves properly, but I am having mixed success. The poor creatures try to please me, but their understanding is so lacking I am quite at a loss. At best, they will wear one or two crinoline underskirts, even to a ball. When I try to explain the importance of undergarments they look at me as if I'm quite mad.

Some disagree with my husband's visionary policy to focus our industry entirely on this country's plentiful metal; trusting trade to supply our other needs. I know he's done the right thing, and minor issues such as drought or the lack of a successful wheat crop will soon sort themselves out. These days, tin is cheaper than cotton, and even aluminium can be seen here and there in daily life. This colony will be mighty indeed, if we continue to harvest its greatest bounty. Metal is everything.

I do not wish to complain, but all Melbourne is very nearly deserted due to the allure of nearby gold. Governor Hotham has been forced to take on convict servants in our household once again, and they are woefully lacking in every particular. Last week our governess announced that her paramour was about to become rich, and she had no intention of bowing and scraping to us any longer.

Those were not her exact words, dear one.

I stopped reading, my heart ticking fast with a new hope. Perhaps Lizzie's golden dreams weren't mad after all. Surely if I could gain the post of governess to the wealthiest children in the colony it would give me privileges and freedom beyond the norm.

Restraining myself from the luxury of further thought, I resealed the envelope as well as I could and returned it to the bag. As I shuffled backward through the barrier door, a man snatched up the mail in front of my very eyes. I had not a moment to lose before the ships parted and all our British redcoats returned their attention to their work.

The hatch was still open, not six feet from me, and I could only hope the sullen fellow left on guard was still talking to Dunne. I crawled across the last empty section of the deck, meaning to escape back into my cabin, when a strong hand caught my arm in an unmistakably iron-strengthened grip.

'Well!' leered the one unlucky stoker. 'Miss Emmeline Muchamore, caught in the act of escape. It seems Dunne was telling the truth about you.'

Chapter Seven

The soldier dragged me into the portion of the lower hold set aside for the worst miscreants, and locked me inside a wooden cage with a wet and stinking floor. It reminded me pathetically of my old laboratory, which I hoped Jem hadn't blown up since I left. I took shallow breaths and tried to tell myself I really was at home. My eyes filled with tears at the thought.

There was no light, and no bunk or seat, nothing but iron rings fixed into the wall. I held onto the rings for balance and listened as the boiler's rumble increased. We were on our way once more. Two redcoats guarded me, facing away and maintaining a military silence. The hour of lax discipline had passed.

It was clear from the smell that the brig had been used to house animals—frightened animals—before it became my dwelling. I didn't dare sit down.

At some point the blackness turned to an eerie grey as sunlight filtered through the decks. I could tell by the quality of the light that my cage was below the water level.

My stomach rumbled, and I guessed it was breakfast time. I wished I'd worn my Superior-Inferior Heels, so I could have stood above the muck.

Three men entered, relieving my guards. One of the new men was the captain himself. I'd never seen him at close range, and I tried not to stare. His mouth wore hard lines, and his skin was red. Evidently he'd been at sea since he was Jem's age. He stood sharply upright, and I trusted him implicitly before remembering that he was not my protector, he was my gaolor.

'Miss Muchamore, do you confess to an attempt to escape, a charge laid by Mr Dunne and supported by second lieutenant

Fitzwilliam's capture of your person on deck?'

'Yes,' I said, relieved Lizzie was not implicated. 'I mean, no. Not trying to escape. I was just … I wanted some fresh air.'

His eyebrows shot up. 'You confess to breaking out of your cabin, then?'

I hesitated, but there was nothing for it. 'Yes sir. I freely confess to being on deck, sir.'

'Who helped you?'

'No one, sir. The oak has been gnawed through by rats, sir.'

'How did Dunne know to alert the guard?' he asked.

I thought carefully before answering. 'He's engaged to Lizzie Box. The three of us told tales of adventure to one another to keep our spirits up. We were never serious, but I went a little mad last night and made a real attempt to have a few minutes' freedom. Spontaneously. Dunne made a lucky guess.'

'If that's your story, so be it. Did you carry any weapons in this "spontaneous madness"?'

'I carried nothing but the clothes on my back, sir.' Which was perfectly true. 'Oh! And a pocketwatch. I'm sure you can hear the ticking. It was my father's, so I carry it everywhere.'

'Very well. You'll remain here for the duration, with solitary exercise every second day. As per his request as informant, Dunne will receive training to assist on deck with sextant readings.'

'Yes sir. I …'

'What is it? Speak up.'

'I'm concerned about my personal effects.'

'My man will check the manifest and have all that belongs to you brought … here.' He glanced about only briefly, but it spoke volumes about the low ceiling and filth.

When a man brought my things, I rigged a hammock from some spare crinolines and was able to rest and sleep. My heart was running low on fuel, but the rats managed to sneak me slivers of ship's coal without alerting the soldiers, who were polite enough to avoid looking in my direction except when they changed shifts. Even in the brig, being a fine lady gave me luxuries that would not be given to anyone else on board. I hoped Arabella still possessed that level of protection. It hurt to think of her trying to visit me in prison and finding no record of my existence, but I'd done the right thing. When I freed her, I freed myself as well. I would not be in the brig forever, and I was determined not to waste my social freedom languishing as a convict. My life was more my own than it had ever been, and iron bars and the seven seas would not hold me down.

The soldiers talked to one another as if I wasn't there, and they were almost as pleased as I was that we were changing course—to Bearbrass. My first attempt at changing my destiny was a success, other than the unfortunate side effect of landing me in the brig.

I soon realised my rats had begun to breed. The little fully-organic babies came to me with piteous squeaks of woe. It was clear they wanted to be like their parents. I utilised my precious coal to heat and shape some simple mechanisms. Luckily Mary had remembered to pack my portable toolbox. When I explained to the rats that I couldn't install their young hearts without silver, they produced several small silver tokens that I assumed were stolen from the guards. Since I'd stolen silver myself so recently, I could hardly refuse them.

The new generation was different, however, as I personally observed when one of the little ones was caught by the ship's cat atop a crate of flour. I caught my breath in sympathetic pain, but my sympathy was misinformed. The cat yelped and fled.

My rat skittered away, leaving black scorch marks on the wood. Apparently my rats had evolved a method of defending themselves. The magical qualities of tin continued to surprise me. Perhaps it was the combination of silver and tin that deserved further experimentation. Perhaps someday I would have a chance to run those experiments myself. Perhaps I was far enough from London Society to publish my findings under my own name for the first time. Once I was free, of course. Something about the stinking dark gave my imagination wings.

After three days, my personal guard was permanently relieved and I was visited only at mealtimes. But I heard a scratching overhead, and guessed Dunne was making his way down to me the only way he could. I checked my Probability Parasol was in working order and looked forward to our meeting. Somehow, I didn't think he was breaking out of his cabin to beg my forgiveness.

Tick, tick.

Three hours later, Dunne stood before me with bleeding fingers from his hard work. He brandished Lizzie's precious locket and a short spear he'd whittled out of a broom handle. It was the first time I'd seen him without his ruined top hat, and his outthrust jaw was now heavily bearded. I wondered how I'd ever considered him handsome. Now that I examined him with more attention, I saw the burning hatred in his eyes. He'd hated me from the first instant he saw my fine clothes and soft hands. I felt better now I understood.

'What did you say to Lizzie?' he demanded.

'Nothing,' I answered truthfully, and made the best use of the new vocabulary she'd taught me during the long voyage: 'You thick-necked brandyface.'

'Then why does she want her locket back?'

I smiled, feeling lighter now I knew Lizzie had played no part in my betrayal. Better yet, I didn't need to be polite to that ruffian any longer. 'Because Lizzie and I are friends, you fat-headed, splay-footed, goat-faced dog.'

He cursed and reached through the bars for me, stabbing out with his pathetic wooden weapon and trying to grab me with his other hand. I stepped neatly aside and brought down my Probability Parasol on his outstretched left arm. Lizzie's locket dropped from his nerveless fingers.

Tick, tick.

Picking it up in one hand, I dropped it in my hammock and

stood tauntingly close to the bars, knowing a man who hated me so passionately had little room for reason. He thrust out his spear, and I grabbed his right arm and bent it back against the bars without bothering to take his weapon. I pressed the release catch on the parasol and let the upper part fall away, leaving the concealed flick-knife of the handle in my hand, the blade of which I held against his exposed throat.

Tick, tick.

'Listen carefully, you sour-faced mongrel.' I was breathing fast, but I didn't feel afraid. Applying my newfound way with words left me light-headed with a kind of power. 'If you show the least impertinence to me or to my friend Lizzie, I will come and find you, and I will slice you open like a medical experiment. I have more friends on board this ship than you will ever have, and when my fortunes return you'll still be wearing irons and breaking rocks. Now crawl back to your cabin before I call the redcoats to have you whipped until there's nothing left of you but skin and blood.'

He shook with rage, but when I let him go he dropped his wooden tilter and turned away. When he climbed on a crate and reached up for the ceiling hole he'd made, I thought I was safe.

Tick, tick.

He climbed back into the men's cabin, his bare feet black with filth as they wriggled out of sight. But then his head reappeared through the hole. 'Don't tell the redcoats what I did today,' he said, 'or I'll tell the world exactly why you always carry a watch.'

He vanished before I could think of a reply.

Tears sprang to my eyes, but I dashed them away, telling myself I was still in control of my fate. He wouldn't tell my secret, and I wouldn't tell the redcoats to check the compromised floor of the men's berth. Everything would be fine. Why did Lizzie have to trust people so easily?

I used half my water ration to clean and polish Lizzie's locket. She was a true friend, and together we'd find gold. No matter what.

Chapter Eight

When the engines finally shut down inside Port Phillip Bay, I was placed back with the other women while we waited to be taken ashore. Lizzie and I greeted one another warmly, and I returned her locket. We both noticed the scents of eucalyptus and hot iron drifting across the water and down to us.

'How long do you think it'll take us to escape?' I asked her.

The smile dropped from her face. 'No, Emmeline.'

'What do you mean?'

'This is all my fault!' Her voice shook, and she gestured down toward my personal prison. 'I have such silly ideas, and I always put such trust in them.' She touched her locket unconsciously, and I remembered the way she'd gazed at Dunne in the moonlight. 'It's time I grew up and paid for my mistakes. In a few years I'll have my ticket of leave, and then I can earn my own money. Who needs gold, anyway?'

'Oh,' I said slowly, knowing that I couldn't simply wait for my seven-year sentence to finish. Arabella would be a grown woman then, and past my help. Our charms blossomed and expired too fast for the luxury of patience. Besides, there was little point in my being free from the bounds of Society only to serve as a convict. 'In that case, I shan't involve you in any more schemes.'

'Good luck, Emmeline! I feel sure the world has wonderful things in store for you.'

'And you, Lizzie.'

At last the quarantine officers declared us safe and the ship's engine rumbled one last time, taking us closer to Sandridge Pier. Our whole cabin hushed in anticipation, and we straightened the remains of our skirts and pinched colour into our cheeks to make ourselves presentable for our intake interview. It would determine whether we were given good work or immediately put in prison to pick oakum or sew clothing for the military.

The soldiers brought us up on deck, and my eyes smarted in the sudden harsh sunlight. I smelled saffron, sweat, pitch and burnt cinnamon. The other women worked hard on smiling, but I was unable to stop myself. This new horizon was mine. It just didn't know it yet.

All around us other steamers, clippers and merchant traders bobbed on the wavelets, knitting an endless web of masts and lines in the sky. The yells and crashes of men unloading stock drowned out the lapping of the waves, a noise drowned out in turn by the rattle of cogged iron wheels against the railway that ran all the way along the pier in front of us. It was moulded into square crenellations and was so new it gleamed. The crenellations fitted the teeth of the wheels so that not an inch of power was lost to friction. It was a beautiful design, and an expensive one.

Before we could make sense of our surroundings, the soldiers loaded us into an open carriage and a steam locomotive hauled us toward Melbourne Proper. The city was full of smoke and movement; red roofs intermingled with shingles and bark and even canvas and tin tents. A wide river curled and frolicked down the hill toward the sea, and miniature falls sparkled in the light. In amongst the bustle scores of hunched and greying trees whispered amongst themselves, and I wondered why nothing was truly green. Even the grass on the far hills was the colour of new-minted copper. I understood why common people called it Bearbrass instead of Melbourne.

More redcoats took us to a low wooden hut where a portly man interviewed us one by one. He consulted a list and assigned us to our places of labour. I lied offhandedly that I was a governess, keeping my heart from venting steam with an effort. He glanced up at me for the first time and asked me in French what I intended to do in Australia.

'Je vais enseigner aux enfants,' I said, 'si je suis admis.' *I will
teach the children, if I am allowed.*

He made a mark on his sheet, and I was hustled with my possessions into another cogged cart and steamed away before I
could farewell my one close friend. I wasn't sure if I'd passed the
interviewer's test or not.

For a moment I wished I'd lied that I was a fish-gutting girl like
Lizzie. We might have been cast together a little longer. But that
was a test I certainly would not pass—one glimpse at my hands
showed my station. I turned and waved back at the thronging pier,
hoping Lizzie might see me, though I could not see her. One day I'd
find her and thank her for being the sunshine that lit our voyage.

The smell of eucalyptus made my head spin, and I paid attention to my new journey. All around me on the wide streets I saw
evidence of more cogged rails in the process of being laid, and
women in the latest fashions promenading arm in arm with their
friends or walking as close as they dared to dashing sweethearts.
The men favoured iron or tin waistcoats instead of steel, and one
man sported a high iron collar that caused him to look down on
everyone around him. I had half expected dirt roads and medi-
eval huts, and I tried to conceal my astonishment. The city was
almost as big as London, but it sprawled languidly in the sun
instead of standing cramped and tall.

My Probability Parasol was a great aid against the glaring sun,
but I soon longed to be back below decks—or anywhere under
cover. Australia was a furnace.

I wondered whether Bearbrass had a steady supply of imported
ice, and decided that it probably did. If it didn't, I pitied the free
settlers almost as much as I pitied myself. Even the thick clouds
of coal smoke flowing from chimneys and basements here and
there quickly dissipated into the endless blue glare above.

A sudden patch of green turned out to be the Botanic Gardens.
They were small and stunted compared to Hyde Park, but I spotted real imported elms and oaks casting real patches of shade.

The park featured a lake with a simple arched bridge. I longed to alight from my rude cart and cool myself in the deep shadows by the water, but instead the railway ended suddenly and I found myself loaded into an ordinary carriage which took me due east, accompanied by a basket of fresh fish that ogled me with blank white eyes.

The carriage slowed beside a long wooden fence lined with soldiers, and turned into the curved white mouth of a bricked entryway. There was no mistaking Governor Hotham's residence. My heart beat more quickly, and I pulled out my unwound pocketwatch to divert attention in case the driver heard the ticking. We halted on a circular drive beside a stand of silver birches, and I realised no one was going to help me down from the carriage. I clenched my parasol and found my own way, keeping my skirts and wheels under control with a supreme effort.

The building itself was a glaring white edifice in the Italian style, with white-painted wrought iron trim and a square belvedere tower in the centre that reminded me unpleasantly of the face of Newgate Prison. A pair of soldiers hustled me inside the arched doorway at the base of the tower and abandoned me in the foyer with the slack-jawed fish and my heavy bag, pausing only to announce me to a passing maid.

Every surface shone as if strewn with diamonds. It took me a moment to realise that the doorknobs were made of lead and thus possessed of a magic that cast any who passed by into an ecstatic appreciation of their surroundings. Mother often used leaden paints in her pictures, and I sometimes found her drooping with artistic fervour if she spent too long around its beautiful poison. I shook off the magic with an effort of will. It was an attractive home, but it was also my prison. I needed to study it in order to break free.

Not one of the uniformed staff rushing by spoke a word to me and I wondered if now was my one chance to escape. I rubbed the manacle marks on my wrists, and told myself to flee at once. But the house was clean—so very clean—and I was desperately thirsty. I didn't even know where the goldfields were located, except, presumably, somewhere to the north. But how would I get there? And how would I escape the dozens of guards placed all around the perimeter fence?

The crystals in the chandelier high above me clinked softly in the breeze from fast-opening doors. Evidently some major social event was about to occur. I longed for Mary, who always understood exactly what was required of her. Now I was the servant, but no one required anything at all.

A maid carrying a heavy tray of fresh vegetables tripped over my portmanteau, hitting me so hard we both tumbled to the carpet. 'Oh miss!' she blurted out. 'I'm so—'

She halted, narrowing her eyes. I felt like a bug under glass as she looked me up and down, observing the fine lace and silk at my throat, and the rim of filth around my hem. She stepped to the side and saw the white number stencilled on my back. For a moment, I'd forgotten what I was.

'You're a convict,' she said flatly, and paused again to examine my face. 'A new one. I thought we'd seen the last.'

'I am the last,' I said. 'There will be no more transport ships to Melbourne, and Lady Hotham requires a governess.'

She laughed aloud, as if I'd made a great joke. 'Best set you to work dressing them for the ball, then.'

I quashed the urge to demand to be taken to my quarters, or given a drink. Instead I took up my luggage and listened carefully as she directed me to the children's dressing room, stacking the dead fish atop her vegetables as she spoke. I felt a rush of air behind me and my brass heart told me not to look around. But I had to know.

There in the doorway was Dunne, and his out-thrust jaw was

tight with tension. His beard was trimmed and his black hair slicked down, probably with spit.

'Morning miss,' he said to the girl beside me, with a mockery of a bow as he took off his pathetic top hat. 'I'm your new ostler. Before I start, let me help you with those runaway foodstuffs.'

To my horror, the girl flushed with pleasure. She bobbed a lop-sided curtsey, and I knew I'd just lost any hope of an ally. Worse, Dunne had seen me—how had he followed me?—and could blackmail me into giving him anything he wanted. My family was oceans away, but the truth about my heart was so explosive it would still destroy their lives. As if Father's execution wasn't punishment enough. I felt my chance at real freedom, at having a life of my own, fading fast.

Dunne slid his gaze over me, making my skin crawl, and bestowed a simpering smile upon the maid. I opened my mouth to tell her how he'd treated Lizzie, but Dunne touched his chest above his heart with one stumpy finger, and I bit my lip. With a sinking feeling, I took my bag and climbed the stairway, flanked by the accusing stares of dozens of oil-painted faces.

Chapter Nine

I knocked on the closed door of the children's dressing room, careful not to touch the leaden doorknob so I wouldn't be distracted by the magic's gilding effect.

'What?' shouted a child's voice.

'Je suis Mademoiselle Muchamore,' I said, feeling my stomach drop in anticipation of further rudeness. Images of neatly-dressed children with faces eager to learn surfaced in my mind and I dismissed them with an effort. 'Je suis votre gouvernante.'

I heard hasty whispers, followed by the same voice. 'Speak English and we'll let you in.'

'Please may I come in and assist you?' I said carefully.

'Hurry up.'

I walked inside to a room strewn with silk, satin, fur, lace and muslin. Three children sprawled on piles of freshly-pressed dresses and trousers, scowling. Two girls and a boy. All messy-haired, all barefoot, all pouting like infants.

'Turn around in a circle,' said the boy. 'Let's take a look at you.'

'Have you chosen what you wish to wear?' I asked, instinctively keeping my eyes low, as if he was an animal that could fly into a rage if provoked. Shame filled me in an instant.

'He *said*, "Turn around",' said the middle child, a girl who was already showing signs of plumpness to come.

I placed my bag on the floor and described a drab pirouette.

'Will you be an obedient governess, one-five-three?' said the boy, crushing a cotton skirt between his fingers.

'Your dutiful servant.' I curtseyed, loathing myself and my blank face.

The younger girl laughed and clapped hands stained with red

fruit juice. 'One-five-three! One-five-three!'

I had answered to my number as if it was a name. The humiliation made me want to shriek. 'Would you like me to fetch you a drink?' I whispered.

The middle girl narrowed her eyes, spotting my ploy at once. 'No. You have to stay here.'

'Yes, Miss,' I said, crushing the grandeur of the Muchamore name beneath my soiled feet. 'Have you chosen what you wish to wear?'

Five hours later, I'd successfully negotiated three abominable children into their finery, and handed them into the care of another maid, who I knew instinctively would be rewarded for my efforts. For the first time, I understood why Jem and Arabella's nursemaid had seemed so pleased to be prematurely released from our service.

When they were definitely gone I subsided onto the floor, my lips and mouth dry and thick as paper. A few maids had dropped in to check on my progress, but no one had offered me a drink or asked my name.

I lay back, delighted at the once-familiar sensation of thick carpet under me. The ceiling was beautiful, divided into deep moulded rectangles with rosettes and filigreed linings all around. Music drifted up from downstairs, and I understood the ball had begun. Others were dancing, smiling, flirting with their paramours, and, worst of all, sipping tea or ginger beer at the same time. For me, the world still swayed gently, as if I remained locked in the brig waiting two days for my next glimpse of sky.

I sat up and smoothed down my skirt. Regardless of the circumstances, I was a Muchamore and there was no call to be untidy. As I decided to find my own tea, I discovered new strength and stood to my feet. I swayed a little, but didn't stumble. That counted as a victory.

It appeared no one would give chase, or indeed notice, when I did escape. All I had to do was get past the boundary guards.

I shook myself and heard the clunk as my crinoline wheels fell into place on the carpet. The rats popped out of my pockets and scuttled into hiding under a newly-wrinkled pile of pink dresses. I wished I had the self-preservation instincts they did.

Tea.

I exited the children's room and stood looking down over a banister. A woman swanned past, her wheels creaking fashionably, and paused to slap the side of her corset with a muffled clank before entering another gilded doorway. Evidently she had an itch in her ribs, perhaps caused by a badly-placed fold in her chemise. Three more women floated past, giggling, and I realised I overlooked the stretch of hall between the ladies' retiring room and the main ballroom.

Suddenly embarrassed by my attire, I slipped back into the children's room and searched through my portmanteau for a clean dress. Of course there wasn't one; I'd worn my best blue silk for the intake interview, and it had been ruined by the clouds of coal and dust and pools of stagnant water all around the docks. There was nothing for it; I left it on, descended the stairs and stood at the doorway of the ball, gawking like the underling I was.

I recognised the governor and his wife by their fine dress, but there were far more gentlemen than ladies—a chronic colonial problem, by all accounts. The room swirled with brilliant colour as those who could find a lady partner paraded her about the room. I caught the occasional alluring flash of wheels from beneath their skirts. In the far corner, the three horrid children sat on wooden chairs, still scowling. Surely Jem, Arabella and I were never so unpleasant. I quashed an unbidden memory of designing my Superior-Inferior Heels with a particular rat-faced gentleman of twelve in mind. That was a long time ago. Perhaps now that I no longer needed to marry well, I could spend my time putting my inventive skills to better use. I felt my heart lift. Of course, I needed gold first.

One woman stood facing the dancers with her back to me, her

neat shape perfectly silhouetted by the lamps. A bundle of glossy black curls spilled down her back from beneath her bonnet, and fine lace outlined her neck. I sensed she was wearing a brass corset rather than steel—a wise choice for a ball, since brass tended to make one sensitive to the prevailing mood. That was far more useful than strength, no matter what men thought.

As I watched, she stepped forward and addressed a tall gentleman in impeccable tails.

'Ah! Poor Officer Dry.' She spoke in a perfect London accent, and I congratulated myself on gravitating to someone who showed no sign of being a mere colonial. 'It must be the heat.'

'Pardon?' he said, apparently too startled to greet her properly.

'I presume the heat has afflicted you or, being a gentleman, you would have asked me to dance.'

Stifling a gasp at her daring, I crept closer to eavesdrop more readily. It was true she was the only woman left standing. I wondered how such a gross oversight could have occurred.

'Or,' said the woman, 'you are overcome with shyness, well aware you are not a true guest at all, nothing but a well-scrubbed guard.'

As I moved closer, drawn by her impertinence despite myself, I saw her face for the first time. She was not British at all! There was no mistaking the smooth face and dark skin of one of the Australian natives. I'd seen pictures, but I'd never seen a native properly dressed who didn't look like an ill-fitted doll. This woman's bearing, manner and accent were all flawless. Her only digression from the highest London fashion was that her crinoline wheels were maintained well enough to be silent—a choice I applauded. But how could she exist?

I remembered Lady Hotham's letter, and presumed the native was here to benefit from her civilising influence. She appeared perfectly civilised to me, so perhaps Lady Hotham was succeeding after all.

Officer Dry's face reddened with fury. He fingered his hip as if he was accustomed to carrying a firearm and wished it was still available. So she was right, he was merely a disguised guard.

'Or am I mistaken?' the native woman continued sweetly. 'You *are* wearing a gentleman's attire this evening, rather than your police uniform. Perhaps the clothes are borrowed?'

'My suit belongs to me,' he sputtered, 'and to my father before me.'

'I see! The … acquisition … of a fine suit can be a risky business. Forgive my ignorance—until now, I had not been aware of the type of ship your father sailed when he arrived on these shores.'

Officer Dry's face shifted from red to purple, and I feared he would collapse from lack of breath. I didn't blame him.

'As you can see,' the woman went on smoothly, waving a slender white-gloved hand in the region of her face, 'neither I nor my ancestors have ever travelled the waves. Voluntarily or otherwise.'

Officer Dry recovered himself with an effort, and lowered his voice to spit words for her ears only. 'Your people are nothing but savages, and I won't permit their continuing existence on my land!'

The girl lowered her hand, resting it on the yellow silk of her skirt. 'Is it your land, Officer Dry?'

He opened his mouth to insult her further, and I could bear it no longer.

'Sir! Restrain yourself!'

He glared at me, letting his gaze slide down my body until it reached the filthy hem I wished I could hide. His eyes were cold and grey. Without acknowledging me, he turned on his heel and stormed away. Neither I nor the native woman rated high enough for a civil bow. I was breathless with fury.

She swirled around to face me, as graceful as the other fine ladies dancing with their gentlemen. 'Good day. I don't believe we've been introduced. My name is Matilda Newry.'

'That's not a native name,' I said, and cursed myself for speaking my thoughts aloud.

She shook her head, smiling. 'My father is British.' She motioned to a tall man bent almost double as he attempted to elicit a smile from the governor's children. He was clearly an eccentric, but he was also the only man dressed as richly as the governor. With enough gold, a family could get away with a great deal. 'A fact that I choose to remember on some occasions, and forget on others.'

I was surprised at the expression in her dark eyes, since I'd expected to see a hint of tears after Constable Dry's violent threats. Instead I saw delighted laughter, only barely restrained. She enjoyed making trouble.

'You shouldn't speak to me,' I told her, feeling my heart tick more firmly than it had in weeks. 'I'm not a lady like you, just one of the help.'

'How terrible for me that we're already speaking, and I can't think of an excuse to break away.' She led me by my ungloved hand to a low table set with drinks, and pressed one into my hand. 'Call me Matilda, and then we shall be so close I'll be doomed never to escape the acquaintance.'

'Emmeline,' I said, and took what I hoped was a ladylike gulp of juice. 'Emmeline Muchamore.'

She nodded to herself. 'You'll do.'

'I will? What for?'

She took my hand in hers a second time and turned it palm-upward. 'I thought as much.'

'Pardon?'

'You're not one of the help, not with those hands. Although the burn marks are rather interesting, if you don't mind me saying so.' Since she was taking my empty glass and passing me another, she could say anything she liked and I'd forgive her. 'You've spent a good deal of time working metal, haven't you? Now, the only reason someone so ill-accustomed to servanthood would try to claim it is that you're new to Bearbrass.'

'I arrived today. And if there's any doubt remaining in your mind, I can assure you it was by ship, and it was not by choice.

Feel free to examine the number on my back, if there's any doubt.'

She shrugged. 'Do you think I'm at this ball getting snubbed by choice? Neither of us is in an enviable position.' There was a hint of tears in her eyes, after all. 'How would you like to run away?'

'Very much,' I said, squeezing her warm fingers, which were as smooth as porcelain through the fine silk of her gloves. Whatever else she was, she was a lady. 'I simply don't know how.'

'I do, but I'm far too recognisable around here. With my face, I can't travel alone. Perhaps together we'll both have a chance at freedom. There's a picnic this Saturday at the Cremorne Gardens. Be ready to leave, and I'll be ready to take you. Wear that dress, and don't try to wash off your number.'

'How are you imprisoned? You're no convict. Whatever it is, can't your father help you?'

Her eyes turned hard. 'Do you want to be free or don't you?'

'Forgive me, please! I'll do whatever you ask.'

She smiled a lighting-flash of a smile, joyful and deadly, then floated away across the polished wooden floor to stand attentive at her father's side. Her posture was perfect, her dress immaculate, and yet she'd just promised to throw in her lot with me. I didn't know what such a woman could possibly want, but I felt certain she'd get it somehow, whether I liked it or not.

Chapter Ten

When the ball was over and there was nothing left to do but clean, I was interviewed in passing by the housekeeper and permitted to stay. It was clear I would be expected to clean as much as anyone else, regardless of my supposed status as governess.

She herself was thin as a rake, a shape that spoke of an admirable work ethic in someone who reigned supreme over the entire household staff. I would have loved to hire her for myself, but working beneath her was daunting. If only I could have stayed invisible. Worse, my cleaning knowledge was minimal at best. While other servants made beds with fresh linen and gossiped about Dunne, I sweated over the hot kitchen sink, scrubbing at a stained pan until the copper bottom peeked through. When the cook noticed my poor work, she sent me elsewhere. I found myself on hands and knees in the ballroom, extracting sticky remnants of food from the carpet thread by thread with a combination of my bare fingernails and a cleaning solution that made me retch.

The next few days passed in a haze of screaming, hair-pulling, jabbing elbows, and the occasional mercy of more gut-churning household cleaning. The one compensation was that Dunne worked outside and I worked inside. I saw him once from a second-floor window, and hoped that would be all. There are times when the intuitive knowledge of brass is less than welcome.

As the picnic drew closer, however, the distinction between inside and outside servant blurred, and Dunne was able to corner me by a staircase. 'When I escape I'll need food,' he said. 'So you'll be speaking of me very favourably to your kitchen staff.'

'I understand. Please let me go.'

'Tick tock.' He smiled.

With little choice in the matter, I brought him up in conversation while washing dishes—cast iron this time—and made sure to mention he'd assisted with navigation on board ship, a privilege given to no other convict. All I could hope for was that my word was worth so little the conversation would not be repeated. My hopes were dashed when three other servants were reprimanded for having a shrieking fight over which of them was likely to marry Dunne. His reputation was solid from that point onwards, and he was given far greater freedom of movement than he deserved.

Since my own supposed escape attempt was well known, it was very difficult to keep my boilers filled without being observed. The supply of clean water was oddly precarious as well. Apparently the governor prioritised the manufacture of new railroads, and the resulting water shortage extended even to his own household. I didn't like to think how the rest of Bearbrass fared. Even my rats looked less glossy when I saw them darting under curtains or behind newly-chewed holes in skirting boards.

When the children had had their required allotment of history, geography, French, Latin, English and mathematics, I was sent to the kitchen to assist in the picnic preparations. The household staff ate nothing but leftover quail from the ball while still cooking full fresh meals for the governor's table, and preparing for the next big event.

Officer Dry recognised me as I refilled his mug of tea at Friday luncheon, and he seized my wrist in a painful vice. His knuckles were criss-crossed with scars. This was not a man who required a pistol to fight. 'I've got my eye on you,' he said.

Keeping my eyes fixed on the floor, I murmured, 'Yes, sir,' and backed away before he decided to have me sent to the Female Factory. One of the other convict maids had told me that Van Dieman's Land had a prison just for female convicts who tried to escape. She'd served three years there before being allowed to work amongst the free once again. When I asked if she planned to attempt another escape, she shuddered.

I spoke to no one of my own plans, and hoped Matilda could be trusted long enough to get me to the goldfields. In my dreams, I saw the hunched and silent lines of the Female Factory workers endlessly sewing military uniforms for the outside world that so many of them would never see again. I hoped Matilda wasn't an idle socialite who pretended to have troubles only in order to make sport of me. But my heart told me there had been real desperation behind her laughing eyes. I simply didn't know what she was desperate for. My heart told me I had another fall ahead, and that Matilda was a greater danger than Dunne and Dry combined, but the road with her was the only one open to me.

Other servants brought live fowl, sheep and a cow to be butchered for Saturday's event. In the kitchen I pounded bread dough and churned butter until my arms and back burned. Down the stairs in the cellars I checked vats of milk and wheels of cheese, and counted and recounted the wine bottles. Back up in the children's room I conjugated verbs, drew maps of Europe, and pulled spitballs from my hair. No one ever addressed me by name. At best I was called 'Miss'. The children only ever used my number, and I had no choice but to obey. I vowed silently to escape before the fury in me faded to acceptance.

Saturday arrived, and a queue of straw-filled carts pulled up in the round drive. I felt horribly self-conscious in my stencilled dress. The children slipped away, knowing I couldn't keep them still, and I set to work with the other servants loading half the pantry into straw-lined baskets covered in white muslin cloth. After that we stacked boxes of plates and bowls and glasses and cutlery. Then we piled the carts high with tablecloths and whole tables, saucepans and griddles and firewood. Apparently we hadn't finished cooking, despite the mountains of foodstuff already prepared.

After the cellars disgorged themselves into another cart we

filled every tiny gap between the larger items with parasols, cush-ions, cloaks and spare shawls in case some lady guest felt a chill. It didn't appear likely, since I was yet to see rain in Australia, and the heat was unrelenting.

When there was a lag in orders, I raced back up to the servants' quarters and grabbed my portmanteau to slip in with the picnic luggage. My rats came scampering at my whistle. Some settled down in my bag, and others curled up in my pockets. The little ones were growing fast. Hopefully no one would inquire as to why my skirt had several unexpected bulges with no correspond-ing flounces. A set of crinolines could only hide so much.

The children appeared from elsewhere in the grounds and climbed inside their carriage already dressed. Since they seemed to know what they were about, I pretended not to have seen them. By then several more carriages and barouchettes waited along the path, and the drivers entered a rather hazardous period of adjustment as the carts and carriages passed one another on the gravel drive. At last the first bullock-cart lumbered out of the curved white gateway and the rest of the household managed to cram itself successfully onto horses or into carriages. The gover-nor rode a white charger, and I saw his wife exchange a few words with him in front of the house's square central tower. She nodded at me in passing, and I curtseyed back, oddly disappointed with her appearance at close range.

I had expected a great personage, ramrod-straight and majes-tic. Lady Hotham was perfectly ordinary, especially considering her plans to reform an entire continent of natives. I could have passed her on the street and never known who she was. She was very light on her feet, however, and it took me a moment to realise why. When I figured out the answer, I was properly impressed.

One of the segments of her corset was made of real aluminium. It was as costly as gold, and in its own way even more astonishing. Aluminium was very difficult to extract from naturally-occurring bauxite, but its magic had the effect of neutralising the weight of any object it was built into. Lady Hotham and all her finery weighed slightly less than a feather.

I spotted Dunne assisting a gentleman with his horse and hastily looked away. He approached me all the same, and doffed his ragged top hat with ironic insolence. 'I heard all about your chat with that darkie at the ball,' he said, and smirked as I recoiled. 'Whatever foolishness you have planned with her, I'll tell the boss all about it. She'll be even easier to find than you.'

'Why do you hate me?' I burst out.

'I could ask you the same thing.'

'Because of you, I was thrown in the brig.'

'You made my fiancé leave me.'

'I did no such thing! She left because you betrayed our trust.'

'You hated me from the first instant we met,' he said.

'We're hardly the same class!'

'Oh, but we are. It's time you realised that.'

He walked away, neglecting to bow. It made little difference, since I was speechless. It was the single greatest insult I'd ever received, and it was quite true. I was no better than him. My heart ticked loudly as he stopped to chat with a soldier, and both of them glanced back at me at the same time. The number on my back felt bigger and whiter than ever.

At that instant the tides of the departure resumed, taking me with them. As governess, I was handed into the final carriage with several giggling kitchen girls. Dunne hadn't picked a favourite yet, and they thrilled with anticipation. I prayed God would forgive me for aiding such a man.

Drivers cracked whips all up and down the line, and we set off. We drove in our long procession toward the Yarra River, but reached our destination before I had time to become uncomfortable with the kitchen girls' sidelong glances. They didn't know whether to admire me or scorn me for having fallen so far in social position. It mattered little, since I would escape shortly—or so I hoped. I stepped from the carriage on the driver's arm, and gasped in delight.

The Cremorne Gardens were beautiful, and very like their namesake back home. All around I saw mercifully shady trees and elegant promenades punctuated by bright flowers. Before I could quite convince myself that the Yarra was at least a little like the winding Thames, I heard my name called and the moment vanished in a flash. I hurried to obey.

Governor Hotham's children demanded entertainment. I did my best, somewhat distracted as I searched for my self-appointed rescuer—or betrayer—to appear. Disappointingly, the park was largely empty save for the general household, several dozen guests, and a small complement of guards. The weather was hot as a boiler room and I wished there was some small sign of coming rain, but the sky was an upturned bowl, flawless and cruel.

All around me the smells of hot roasted potatoes and frying oil drifted by, making my mouth water and my skirts twitch suspiciously. I hoped the rats maintained their self-control—they'd need it if they ever wanted to be wound up again.

One of them grew suddenly hot—I was almost certain it was involuntary—and I let out a yelp before hastily rearranging myself. I patted down that section of skirt with unladylike vigour, and felt the sudden fire in my pocket subside. Judging by the cheery *bing!* from within, the rats were impervious to the heat they created. I only hoped they didn't set anything else on fire.

'Where were we?' I asked the children, with the brightest tone I could muster.

After my peculiar exertions, they were momentarily speechless.

The eldest rallied. 'You were telling us a story, and it was very dull.'

'Shall I continue?'

'If you must,' she sneered.

Several carriages drew up at once from a new direction. They disgorged the wide skirts of several fine ladies, who turned to the next carriage and twittered their greetings. The gentlemen accompanying them were very sweaty indeed, but stood heroically tall and stiff in their fine steel or brass waistcoats.

I lost the thread of my tale and began again, unable to stop searching for Matilda. Perhaps this was her game, letting my heart strain for a second meeting that would never come.

There were a few fractionally less resplendent individuals in the park, who seamlessly integrated their parties into the greater whole. No one seemed to mind. On the edges of the growing picnic I spotted a shabby group of natives, barely dressed, and wondered what they were doing in such fine surroundings. All the proper ladies pretended to see straight through them onto the bright flowers elsewhere, so I followed their lead and chose not to see the jarring note to our picnic.

Despite my careful lack of interest, the natives sidled closer and closer. Suddenly I recognised Matilda, and my stomach lurched. She slouched and grinned foolishly, dressed in something very like an undyed calico sack. It barely covered her knees!

She motioned for me to close my mouth, and I stared in horror at the children. Surely they'd recognise her and know something was amiss. But they followed their elders' example and carefully failed to notice the natives. Without her fine yellow gown, Matilda was invisible. The youngest of the children prodded me sharply, and I realised I'd fallen silent.

'Hide and seek!' I blurted out. 'What shall I count up to before I come and find you?'

'A hundred,' said the eldest.

'Twenty,' said the youngest, since it was all she knew how to count up to.

'One hundred and fifty-three,' the middle one said, neatly spiting both her sister and myself.

'One-five-three it is! Off you go then, quick!' I closed my eyes, willing the children to play along instead of starting a new fight. 'One … two … three …'

I heard running footsteps and opened my eyes. The children were gone. Matilda crouched beside me and shoved a black fabric parcel into my hands.

'Put it on as soon as you can,' she hissed. 'Everything's ready.'

The fabric was smooth in my hands, and heavy. It was silk.

'The ostler knows about you and me.'

'In an hour it won't matter. Hope you don't mind missing luncheon.'

'My things—'

'Where?'

'In the second cart, under a pile of shawls.'

Matilda turned on her heel and ambled away without another word. I saw large crescent-shaped scars on the back of her legs, and wondered again what kind of person she was beneath the bravado. She moved like an animal, as jerky and alert as if the whole world hunted her.

Perhaps it did.

Chapter Eleven

There was no time to lose. I walked to the rotunda for a little modesty, half-heartedly calling the names of the children in the sing-song manner my own nursemaid once called me. The guards glanced at my stencilled back and glanced away again. It was all they saw of me. So much for my famous blue eyes.

I reminded myself that I had absolutely no desire to be recognised. My life was different now. I tried to breathe normally, but my heart vented steam in both directions. The back of my bodice dripped with condensing water, making me hotter than ever.

'Don't notice me,' I murmured. 'Don't look twice.'

The copper-coloured grass was so dry it crunched underfoot, ruining the illusion that I was back in London. This park was newer, too. Some of the earth was still loose, yet to be rained on since the trees were planted. I consoled myself with the observation that Matilda remained unrecognisable among the ragged natives. Was it the natives she wanted so badly to escape, or was it the other side of herself?

Before me, the rotunda stood in solitary splendour, momentarily forgotten in the bustle of cooking, gossip, and servants assembling furniture and finery. The weathervane was perfectly still. I saw windows in the cupola, but no way to get up into it. The ground-level windows were elegantly rounded in a trinity of open circles at the top, putting me in mind of Arabian Nights. Luckily, no one was inside yet.

It was empty except for baskets of wine and cold meat, which would not remain unattended for long. Less fortunately, there was absolutely no shelter from observant eyes. I crouched behind the tallest pile of baskets and unwrapped Matilda's silk parcel.

Handling the silk made me calm down and I stopped venting steam. That was something, at least.

The package had two pieces of fabric. Matilda had packed a shawl inside the silk, which I wrapped around me at once, hiding the unmistakable number on my back. The main bulk of the parcel was an uneven rectangle of fabric, heavily flared out into a curve on one long side and buttoned down one of the short ends. Since it could only be some kind of skirt, I fastened it around my waist, and found it fully concealed the powder blue of my dress. I felt sure I looked very odd indeed, with a dress in two colours, one of them woolen and one silk—and wearing a shawl despite the heat.

Matilda was nowhere to be seen. Was she preparing a trap for me, or fleeing her own? No ordinary woman would dress like she was dressed, not if she had a choice. She was unpredictable, and that frightened me.

I straightened my new skirt as well as I could and stood up just in time to see my youngest charge fast approaching. Too late to duck out of sight, I waved and said a belated 'Found you!'

'One-five-three!' she said, and burst into sobbing gulps of rage. 'I'm thirsty!'

'It's all right. I'll fetch you a drink.'

'Now!' she screamed, and I saw heads turn toward us.

'Yes,' I said hastily. 'Right now.'

I glimpsed a stoppered glass water bottle in amongst the wine and breathed a sigh of relief. 'Here you are!'

She shook her head slowly, taking deep breaths for maximum volume. 'I … want … lemonade!'

Matilda's group sidled away toward the line of carriages, and I hoped I understood what they were planning. 'It's in the carriage. I'll go and get you some right away, and in the meantime you can hold on to this bottle of water, all right?'

She pouted at me, but it was too hot for another bout of screaming. Hopefully she had the sense to drink the water once she realised I wasn't coming back.

The very thought of her futile anger gave a spring to my step as I strode away. I straightened my back in an effort to avoid looking like an escaping convict in motley garb.

One of the carriages was not like the rest. It was wider than any one-horse carriage I'd seen before, and had wicker sides and an odd semicircle seat-back behind the driver, swathed in silk instead of leather. The great mass of silk continued downward, filling the entire front half of the carriage. Unlike the other carriages, this one's driver sat on his seat as if he was ready to depart. He wore a black woolen chambergo with the wide brim pulled low over his eyes. It was instantly clear he was hiding something.

But there was nothing for it, because Matilda headed straight for him. She hopped up the wide iron steps without waiting for assistance, and her native entourage peeled away into the trees as if they'd never seen her before. The driver shot her a glance and a nod, and I saw a flash of teeth from under his hat.

She picked up a length of brown fabric from the single forward-facing seat and draped it around her waist, cinching it in tightly. In one quick wriggle she hoisted her hessian rags over her head, revealing a proper bodice of brown-dyed wool underneath. In another moment she'd fixed a bonnet to her hair, sat up properly, and was the picture of respectability. I thought I was going mad, because I suddenly smelled fine Chinese tea.

Matilda waved a hand for me to join her, and I climbed inside without assistance. The stairs were the sturdiest I'd ever encountered, but it still felt odd. How could anyone nearby fail to notice what was happening? Matilda had effectively appeared out of thin air. I noticed she'd turned her dark face away from the picnic, and thus looked like any other fine lady. But surely her disguise was too simple to actually work?

For some reason, the entire carriage smelled strongly of refined coal, like burnt toast—that, and Chinese tea. My heart was very pleased about something, and I knew there was some unusual metal built into the structure.

'Good afternoon, Emmeline,' said Matilda. 'Your bonnet, please.'

I passed it to her without a word.

'My apologies,' she said.

'Pardon? Why?'

'You need to crawl under there,' she indicated the pile of silk, 'and keep your feet where I can cover them with my skirt.'

I understood the extent of my disguise at once, and buried myself up to the hips under the thick silk. It was surprisingly heavy, lined with rubber varnish for some reason, and I was extremely hard-pressed to breathe. Fortunately my heart made the usual adjustments. I felt Matilda's feet arrange themselves around mine, and knew I was nothing but another patch of black silk in the mass.

Less fortunately, I was effectively blind as the carriage jerked into motion. I braced my hand against the floor to try to steady myself. My finger touched leather, and a few moments later something bit me; my bag had been smuggled away safely, and the rats were still inside. We were free, in a manner of speaking.

My life was in Matilda's hands, and those of her faceless driver.

Chapter Twelve

The peculiar carriage rattled and bumped and creaked for what felt like an age. Then someone tugged at my skirts, and I burrowed desperately into the silk nest. A hand reached down and squeezed my ankle. I recognised Matilda's smooth palm and realised she was signalling me to come out of hiding.

She half-guided, half-pulled me out. I emerged panting, and knew my hair was ruined. Luckily, my daily wrestles with the Hotham children had taught me to keep my composure despite such trials. 'What happened? Where are we?'

'None other than Collins Street,' Matilda announced happily. 'Home of the great and the greater still, and a school of Venus or two, just to balance it out.'

I saw sandstone walls on three sides. 'This is Collins Street?'

'No,' said Matilda, pointing at the far end, where there appeared to be an impromptu parade of fine ladies and gentlemen, carriages, barouchettes, horsemen, and urchins crossing perpendicular to us. 'That's Collins Street. Take off the black overskirt, if you please. Do you have a differently-coloured shawl in that bag?'

I unbuttoned the first of my improvised disguises as Matilda helped herself to my portmanteau, giggling at some of the less typical items. 'Ah!' she said, draping a white shawl around my shoulders. 'This will do nicely.'

'But that's the best piece of lacework I own!'

'Exactly. People will see the shawl instead of your face. And the white stencil will blend in nicely.' She pushed my hair down roughly, jabbed in three pins, and fixed a new bonnet on my head. 'Excellent. You're a little red-faced still, but the look of a lady hasn't left you, despite your week at the governor's brattery.

If anyone's searching for you this far afield, they won't recognise you, not even if they meet you face to face. But I doubt they'll come here. Who would search for an escaped convict on Collins Street?'

I sat on the seat beside her, and noticed that it was nothing but an iron box with a padded lid. A single leather strap held it in place. As I sniffed experimentally, I discovered it was the source of the smell of coal. Why would a carriage have a hollow seat filled with coal?

'Comfortable?' asked Matilda. 'We've a long way to go yet.'

'I—'

'Excellent!' She raised her voice for the driver. 'A snail's gallop, Patrick, if you please!'

'Aye,' he said, and set the horse moving toward the crowd.

My heart sank. The companions were so familiar with one another they could only be lovers. Worst of all, I suspected they were yet to be formally engaged, yet they were clearly accustomed to meeting without a chaperone. Matilda was above him in every way. He wasn't even English, but Irish. I didn't want to see another friend betrayed like Lizzie. My heart skipped a beat at the thought of my old friend, and I hoped she was happy.

We pulled out into a crowd as self-consciously fine as any in Hyde Park or Kensington Gardens. I clutched Matilda's hand in terror at the sight of a full regiment of redcoats, and she squeezed my fingers. 'When they look at us, they see two fine ladies taking the air. What escapee in her right mind would come here?'

'I ... suppose that's true. But what if we're stopped?'

She shrugged. 'You'll be gaoled and Patrick hung. My fate's worse than either, and you don't see me complaining.'

'And what fate would that be?'

She raised one eyebrow. 'That's a story for another day. We're fine ladies, so shouldn't we talk about fine gentlemen? Or the finest gossip?'

'How can I gossip when I don't know anyone's name?'

'Excellent point. We'll have to look pretty then—what else is there?'

I heard what sounded like a laugh from the driver, quickly stifled into a cough.

The street crawled with soldiers, and I felt very exposed. Then a gentleman in a brass and leather waistcoat smiled at me, and I realised that, for a moment, I was myself again. I was Miss Muchamore, somehow unfallen and unruined, riding in a grand carriage and letting the world admire and envy her. My body relaxed instantly, and my ticking heart grew steady.

Several cabs stood ready for passengers outside two- and three-storey shops and offices all along the wide street. Many of the buildings featured elements of the classical style, and a white-washed church boasted elaborate Corinthian capitals on all its columns. It wasn't anything as majestic as Saint Paul's Cathedral, but it wasn't stained black with coalsmoke either. The colony wasn't inferior in every single particular, just most of them.

A merciful breeze appeared, and I lifted my face to bask in it. Matilda said something in another language. It sounded rather like she was swearing.

'Aren't we being ladylike?' I reprimanded her quietly. 'Wasn't that the plan?'

'Only until the wind picked up.'

'Good. It's here. I assume this means we'll be heading out of Bearbrass before we're all arrested?'

'Yes and no. The wind's meant to be heading south-west. This,' she waved her hand about, 'is precisely the opposite.'

'At least there's wind at last. That's something worth having.'

'Quite right.' She sat up, smiling sweetly at a little girl who stared open-mouthed at the fine native parading herself and her white companion down the street. 'Patrick! Head for Batman Hill.'

'Told you so,' he said.

'Oh, hush.'

He turned the carriage in a wide arc made wider by the unusual girth of its construction.

'We're going back along the same street?' I asked quietly, trying my utmost to keep my smile from becoming a rictus. 'There are a great number of people here, and someone is sure to notice you—us.'

'Don't worry your pretty little head,' Matilda said happily. 'This is the last street of Bearbrass you'll ever see.'

Chapter Thirteen

We stood perfectly still for some moments. Two carriages tried to overtake us at once and almost collided.

'What are we waiting for?' I asked.

'The horse,' said Matilda. 'He needs to … well, you know.'

'Now?'

'I certainly hope so.'

Before I could decide she was mad and take my chances with the redcoats, the horse let fly with a gushing torrent. I didn't know where to look, and settled for gazing directly upward. At last the horse was finished, and the driver snapped the reins. The carriage set off toward the Western hill and the sea at a steady pace, but gradually picked up speed until we overtook other people. Soon the horse broke into a canter, and the carriage wheels rattled furiously.

'Matilda …' I said.

'Would you mind assisting me?' She stood upright, wobbling only a little, and dug her fingers between the padded lid of our seat and the iron beneath. When she drew out a slender pack of metal sheets, I forgot everything else.

'But … where did you get all that?' I asked.

She smiled and chose not to answer. 'It's very shiny, isn't it? Hard to manufacture, but worth it, don't you think?'

'Yes!' I swallowed, trying not to show how much I wanted to touch it. The silvery sheen of the aluminium was unmistakable, even though I'd only seen it a few times before. Father had held aluminium in the highest regard, and I didn't blame him. Too bad it cost as much as gold, or my heart would have been made from it and I'd have been as weightless as Lady Hotham.

Matilda passed the sheets into my hand as if they were nothing special. She tugged at the pile of silk at our feet, and quickly located a series of square pockets arranged in a circle. 'Pass me one sheet?'

I gave it to her, marvelling at how light it was. She slipped it into a silk pocket and buckled down a double-stitched tie to seal it inside. We repeated the operation until twelve pieces of aluminium lay inside the silk. The aluminium reacted to some magic-activating trigger in the silk pockets, and the mass of silk billowed as it tried to float into the air.

'Over here,' said Matilda, and kicked away several folds of silk to stand on the left-hand side, where the carriage's forward seat should have been. She took hold of the back of the driver's seat with both hands, and I saw that it was a full circle of iron, as tall as me but wrapped tightly in silk. I mirrored her on the other side, and together we lifted the heavy circle, and a pile of cloth with it. The air of our passage began to fill it from the open front, and the silk responded with gleeful billows. Suddenly our carriage was three times as tall: a mass of fabric and air. People stopped and stared. So much for our cunning costume changes.

'Now!' called Matilda, and the driver slapped the reins against the horse's flanks. It leapt into an outright gallop, pulling the carriage at breakneck speeds. The silk expanded rapidly, rising up in an elongated sphere above and behind the carriage. All at once I saw what it was: a giant hot air balloon. A giant hot air balloon with wheels. I didn't care anymore about whether we were caught and I spent the rest of my days in the Female Factory. It was the most glorious contraption I'd seen in my life, and it was worth any price.

The iron circle let in more of the incoming air and the silk envelope rose higher, almost lifting the iron. Matilda abandoned her post, leaving me to steady the metal ring on my own. She unbuckled the iron box of our seat, turning it lengthwise and flipping back the lid with a crash of colliding metals. It was full of high-quality coal.

She struck matches one by one, trying to light a fire inside the seat. It was impossible in the increasing wind of our passage.

'In my bag!' I said, grasping the urgency of our situation. 'The jar!'

She dived underneath the writhing silk and emerged with my potassium, holding it out to me. I threw it directly into the box of coal, smashing the glass. The potassium didn't react to the exposure at first, and I felt the strength in my arms reach breaking point. But then a flame burst out, and another, and the refined coal came to life. The nightsoil stink of it made me cough.

Matilda stood under the monstrous silk, battling to keep the fabric from falling in the fire. 'Turn it!' she yelled at me.

I turned the ring horizontal so that it was directly over the fire. The aluminium-enriched silk responded to the hot air by leaping upward instantly, tugging the iron with it in a sudden reversal of the law of gravity. Heavy chains linked the burning chair with the iron ring, and I could only hope the burner was attached in turn to our carriage.

The driver reined in the horse, and we found ourselves standing still between two large churches, both built of multicoloured brick with neat white edging on the corners. A woman stood open-mouthed not three feet away from me, clutching her parasol in a death grip. Strangely calm, I admired the Roman arches and tall gothic belltowers of the churches, and wished I could simply join the congregation—either congregation. Or just take a closer look at the elegant joins between the bricks. What had they used for cement?

What would happen to a church if it incorporated aluminium into its structure? Someday, I'd be rich enough to build a scale model and I'd find out.

The iron ring tore itself from my grasp, and I stood under a gaping black maw of silk and fire. It reached all the way to heaven.

'Watch out!' said Matilda, and the iron box lifted itself off the wooden carriage floor.

I dodged it, almost falling from the carriage, and gaped with dozens of other observers as the iron box pulled its cables taut. 'We're going to fly,' I said quietly. 'Up there. We're going to fly away.'

'Excuse me, Miss,' the driver said at my shoulder.

Something huffed hot breath on my arm, and I turned and shrieked at the long white face of the horse, still wet with sweat. The driver pushed back his hat, exposing wicked green eyes.

'Stand with Matilda if you want to survive this,' he said.

Matilda pulled gently on my elbow, and we stood where the rear seat used to be. Now, the seat floated in the air just above our heads.

My rescuers' horse whuffled in annoyance, then continued into the carriage, hopping up with both back legs at once.

The driver stood on Matilda's other side. 'Here's hoping your friend's heavier than she looks, or we won't be steady at all.'

'Oh,' I said quietly. 'We're taking the horse, are we?'

'Why else would we wait for him to, you know,' said Matilda.

'And the driver's coming too, I suppose.'

'Naturally.'

'Oh … good.'

Nothing happened. The man stood on his toes and thumped the side of the burner. I heard coal tumble into a new position, and hoped it was enough. My potassium had burned away, leaving us with no more magic tricks.

A pair of redcoats approached from the east at a run, led by a man wearing a top hat but no coat. The man pointed right at us. I heard his voice rise, cutting through the delighted chatter of the crowd. 'That's her! She's the convict!'

It was Dunne.

'We may have a problem,' I said, and was surprised to hear that I wasn't screaming. 'When shall we be able to take off?'

'We're flying already!' said Matilda. 'Don't you see?'

I looked back at the street beside us, and found I was looking down. All the people had transformed into upturned faces, pale against their fine clothes. Some of them clapped delightedly, and others stared back and forth between us and the redcoats, suddenly unsure of themselves. The open windows of the taller belltower of the church were directly in front of us.

'We're flying,' I repeated, not at all sure it was true.

On the ground, Dunne shook his fist. He jumped up and down in rage. I laughed out loud and waved merrily. We were really free!

Beside him, the two soldiers put their rifles to their shoulders—and fired.

Chapter Fourteen

I screamed at the report of the guns. The horse tossed its head and kicked out with its back legs, shattering the wickerwork. Matilda clapped her hand over my mouth. I stared at the gaping wound in the carriage's side and didn't move.

The driver wrapped his arms around the horse's sweat-drenched neck, whispering words I couldn't hear. Its eyes rolled back in its head, showing the whites.

'Are we hit?' I asked, pulling Matilda's hand away. 'Did they get us?'

'We're fine,' said Matilda, using exactly the same tone on me as her paramour used on the animal. 'Everything's fine now. We're too high for them to reach.'

I looked down onto a child's model of Bearbrass, split in two by the elegant ribbon of water, and knew she was right. The sun glinted off shining new railways leading from the harbour in all directions, and even the beginning of a track out of Bearbrass.

The horse whinnied and subsided, and the driver produced a lump of sugar, which it snuffled at happily. He turned to me, 'Are you going to spook Barry again, or are you quite finished, Miss—?'

'Miss Muchamore,' I said faintly, and immediately wished I'd sounded firmer. 'And you are?'

'Patrick O'Connell,' Matilda cut in. 'Don't mind his rough talk, he's not what he seems.'

I held out my hand. It was only fair, since I owed him my freedom. The sooner I could get through the niceties and get rid of him the better. 'Pleased to meet you, Mr O'Connell.'

'Call me Patrick,' he said. His hand was rough with calluses and residual sugar, but his handshake was as firm as any I'd known. 'I hate to be mistered.'

'All right,' I said reluctantly, feeling my life pulled into orbit around his. But it was too late to back away now. Besides, I had nowhere else to go. May as well embrace the depths rather than trying to fight my fallen status. 'My name is Emmeline.'

'Tea?' he asked.

'I beg your pardon?' I said, perking up at the magical word.

'Would you like some tea?'

'I … yes.' It was the first time anyone had offered me tea since I'd sat in my old drawing room with Ambrose and Mrs Dawes. Now a half-savage Irishman was my best protector.

His manners left a great deal to be desired, and his right cheek bore a grey scatter of gunpowder scarring. But other than that, his face was oddly peaceful, as if he belonged in a garden overlooking wooded hills on a misty day—or amongst the clouds, which after all was where he was currently located. Perhaps he wouldn't be as awful as he seemed, although his beard was so thin I wanted to get a damp cloth and rub it off.

Matilda helped me into a sitting position on the floor, as far from the horse as possible, which was still close enough to touch. I pulled my knees up under my chin and wondered where Patrick planned to purchase tea in mid air.

He climbed onto the horse's back and pulled up the lid of his own seat; it was a rectangular box too, but made of wicker instead of iron. One by one he produced a blackened tin pot with a wire handle, two tin mugs, and a small pack of tealeaves. So I hadn't imagined the smell of Chinese tea, either. He unfastened the lid of a second pot and refilled the first before putting its lid back on and placing it inside the coal burner at one end. As it heated up he added more leaves to the pungent mixture, sitting astride his horse the whole time. Reaching into his seat once more, he produced a handful of oats which the horse ate from his hand.

When the tin pot binged to say the tea was ready, he slopped some of it into a mug for me and I stood to receive it, carefully looking only at the wooden floor so I didn't frighten myself.

'It will taste somewhat of coal, I'm afraid,' he said. 'Do you take sugar?'

'Yes, thank you.'

He took it back and crumbled a thick clump of sugar into it, stirring it with a twig of wicker he broke from the jagged edge of the hole. I sipped it hesitantly and relaxed. It really was tea, sweet and hot and redolent with wonderful smells. A hint of coal in the taste was hardly going to deter a science experiment such as myself. In fact I rather liked it and wondered how to rig our kitchen to get the same effect before remembering I was unlikely to be mistress of a proper British kitchen ever again.

Matilda adjusted her makeshift skirt to ensure it was decent, and then shared her tea with him, refilling it from the pot until there was none left. They didn't insult my standards of hygeine by offering me a second cup, for which I was grateful.

I lifted my eyes cautiously to the outside world, expecting to be terrified. The ride was oddly quiet, interrupted only by Barry's hopeful whufflings toward Patrick. A vast expanse of land rolled out beneath me, golden with grass at Bearbrass's fringe, and green where the thick forest began. The trees stretched out as far as I could see, shadowed here and there with the rise and fall of the land.

'Do you like it?' Matilda asked, suddenly shy. 'I so hoped you would.'

'You've flown before,' I said, knowing the truth as I spoke it aloud. 'And so has Barry.'

'Naturally, though I confess, not this far.'

I relinquished my mug to Patrick and he put it away, producing a package of rather squashed lamb chops, long since gone cold. To my surprise I was hungry. I ate my share as neatly as possible without the civilising influence of cutlery. The tea and lamb chops served to convince me that none of it was really happening—I wasn't flying, I wasn't at the mercy of an Irish brigand, and I wasn't truly in Australia at all. Except I was. My chains were gone, along with the Hotham family. I was literally flying free. Nothing else mattered, except the one thing that always mattered. Money.

'Are the goldfields this way?' I asked idly, admiring the detail of leaves as we drifted low enough to see them clearly.

'What do you mean?' said Patrick, and his voice was suddenly strained. 'Matilda said you needed a safe place, so I'm taking you to my father.'

'No!' I sat up sharply. 'I'll be no use hidden away in a wattle and daub hut on the outskirts of some filthy town.'

Patrick turned away, stiff-backed. I realised my error and would have apologised except Matilda motioned me into silence. In the forest below, I saw individual leaves and brief flashes of smaller plants between the trees. I smelled sweet flowers and, as always, eucalyptus.

'We all need gold, Patrick,' said Matilda. 'We've nothing but fiddler's money left, and it just won't do.'

'You said you'd bring money!'

'Oh.' She patted absently at her skirts. 'Father showed some unexpected wit and confiscated my entire cache.'

Patrick gaped at her a moment. 'All of it, all those months of saving—gone?'

'Every farthing!' she said. 'I am sorry, Patrick, really I am. So, goldfields then?'

'I'll not visit the diggings for all the gold in the world,' he said fiercely, apparently unaware of the rustle of the carriage wheels as they hit the fringes of the taller trees. Since the others were used to flying, I tried not to show my fear. Presumably they knew what they were doing. 'Regardless of your reduced circumstances, all we really need is food and water and shelter. My father has all of those.'

'He doesn't have Shauna,' Matilda said quietly, unconsciously soothing Barry with one hand as he whinnied in fear. The ground came closer and closer. Barry and I were the only ones that appeared to care. Several kangaroos broke from the trees and bounced away, looking as if they were flipping their tails up and down. They looked even more ludicrous in real life than in pictures, and I wished I could have examined their movements with my father. Ideally from ground level, since I was perilously close to squeaking in terror.

Patrick's hand on the wicker edge of the carriage turned white as he clenched the rim. He didn't react as sharp-edged silver leaves whipped against his skin. 'I will take care of her—myself.'

'If you think I'd abandon her for a second, you're mistaken.'

'Stop bickering!' I said, unable to remain stoic a moment longer. 'We're going to crash!'

My companions looked around for the first time, and their mouths dropped open in a manner that would have been comical if we weren't already on a level with the trees. Matilda blew madly on the fire, and Patrick used his forgotten tin mug to rake the coals into the centre of the burner. Apparently we had been in true danger for some time, and our peril was increasing by the second.

It was no use. A branch snapped off on the carriage's side, and Barry tensed to leap out. I wondered if I should do the same, but I didn't want to leave the others to die. Patrick wrapped both arms around Barry's neck, abandoning the burner to save his horse.

Matilda gasped for breath and blew again. She wasn't laughing this time.

I hitched up my skirts and grabbed two rats in each hand. 'We're going to die!' I yelled at them, hoping I was correct about their survival mechanisms, and threw them straight up into the balloon.

The largest of the four flew up, up into the dark, chittering with rage. It exploded in a burst of blue and yellow flame. Another parped loudly, flailing its claws until it hit the varnished inside of the balloon and held on, tail quivering. The other two fell right back down into the boiler, where they ignited the grey coal in moments, then leapt off the box onto my shoulders, making me hiss in pain before they cooled back down.

Matilda stopped her puffing to swear, and this time I understood every word.

Patrick gave Barry one last pat and released his hold. Thanks to my panicked rats, we headed upward again, clearing the treetops easily and flying almost due north.

'Where's my parasol?' I demanded.

Patrick retrieved it from between the horse's long legs, handing it to me handle-first. I pressed the buttons to release the flick-knife. 'Your box needs vents to burn this quality of coal,' I said, and crouched underneath the burner. Given the weight restraints, I was willing to bet the iron was paper-thin, and my steel was a match for it.

It was. I made three small punctures and directed Matilda to blow on the coal from underneath until a good draft was established. They should have built a grate into the box in the first place.

'Well,' said Patrick slowly. 'She's not the innocent and pathetic creature you described to me, but I suppose at least she's useful.'

I stared at him, suddenly furious. Far better gentlemen than him had described me as elegant, refined, even beautiful—but useful? That was all I was to him. Worse, it was his justification for my presence. As if I needed a reason to be welcome. It appeared Matilda had embroidered my distressing circumstances a little in order to engage his sympathy.

He knew nothing of the gentlemanly arts, and I wondered if perhaps Lizzie was right; I should have given up my family's future and earned my way with years of ordinary toil. But it was too late now; my fate was intertwined with the fate of a red-letter man from the criminal class, and with a mad native woman who still hadn't told me what she was fleeing from.

Chapter Fifteen

Patrick informed us that the wind was taking us north. It so happened that his family lived several miles upriver, so we were heading for them whether we wanted to or not. Matilda sulked, and I discovered that a balloon basket was not a good place to observe a lovers' quarrel between the other occupants. We flew almost directly above a river, catching the wind as it funnelled through the valley.

The sun set and we drifted downward—on purpose this time. Matilda sidled closer to Patrick, and the two of them stood with their arms touching, looking out across the wide emptiness below. It seemed their fight was over. They didn't need words. I felt a pang of jealousy but stifled it at once. Silly to be jealous of colonials conducting a foolish tryst.

'Tomorrow,' Patrick said with quiet satisfaction, 'we'll visit my father.'

'I don't know why I put up with you,' said Matilda affectionately.

'The balloon's mine, and you're nothing but a passenger. A dishonest and a non-paying passenger, which is a great shame.'

'I'm your family!'

'Yes, that's why *I* put up with *you.*'

She threw back her head and laughed, which made Patrick smile and Barry mutter horse-threats under his breath.

'Um,' I said, 'isn't the ground rather close?'

'Aye, that it is,' said Patrick. He tugged on a pair of ropes, but if anything the ground came up faster.

'Stop that, you larrikin,' said Matilda.

'It's not intentional.'

I held on to the wicker sides, which suddenly felt very fragile indeed. The tussocks of grass and low, spiky bushes rushed past at an alarming pace. I'd felt safer high in the air.

Matilda passed me a pair of brass goggles, and the cool circles of metal reminded me of the quiver in Arabella's voice as she repaired my heart the day I was arrested. I reminded myself that I was in the process of saving her and put the goggles on. They sharpened my vision, which only made our descent more frightening. The gusting wind yanked off my bonnet and cast it away. Grass seeds sprayed my face, stinging my cheeks and plinking off the glass of the goggles. So that's what they were for.

'We're all right,' said Patrick, holding on to Barry with one arm and poking at the last remnants of the fire with a stick. He wore goggles too, but Matilda's face was bare. She'd given up her pair for me. I wished I'd thought to refuse, so I didn't have yet another item on the long list of services owing. 'Almost there now. It's not so—oh!'

I saw it at the same moment, a sudden ravine right before us.

'Move!' said Patrick, turning the horse's head so that its nose pressed me against the fragile wall.

Barry harrumphed, and awkwardly turned all the way around, almost crushing Matilda in the opposite corner. He faced the jagged hole in the wicker, and I had a sudden terrible premonition of Patrick's idea. The horse now faced exactly backward.

Patrick slapped Barry hard on the rump. Barry snorted in annoyance. Patrick slapped him again with a wild Irish yell, and Barry gathered his slender legs and leapt from the flying carriage, thudding onto the ground and galloping away.

'Ah!' said Patrick with enormous relief. 'He's all right.'

He'd forgotten entirely about the danger to the three of us.

We slid across the ground, slowing down as the long grass slapped against the undamaged side of the carriage, hitting the wheels side-on and showering us with dust and grass-seeds. Matilda covered her eyes with her hands. I watched in paralysed horror as the lip of the ravine loomed right before us, so close that for a moment it looked like we might skim over it without suffering any harm.

The leading wheel slammed against the rock on the opposite side, and the entire carriage tipped over, spilling Patrick and Matilda and I in a very improper tangle on the sharp grass. Still flying, the carriage moved over us, and one of my crinoline wheels caught between the pieces of wicker.

'Matilda!' I shrieked, all dignity forgotten.

She and Patrick grabbed my hands and tugged, but the wheel was stuck fast. I was dragged along the ground, scrabbling helplessly for purchase and half-buried in my own crinolines.

'No!' Patrick yelled. 'Push her!'

They shoved me bodily back into the carriage and away.

I flew over their heads, a solo passenger in a balloon skewed at such an angle that it strewed smouldering coal over much of the wooden floor. Now that I was upright, I was the balloon's prisoner, and my skirts were ablaze. I kicked at the carriage, trying to get free.

One of the chains was caught on something.

'Help!' I cried, smothering the closest flames with handfuls of cloth.

My rats dived out of their nooks and crannies and pulled the embers apart with their tiny front claws. I stamped out the rest, and fell sideways as the carriage bumped to a sliding stop. One last patch of flame was crushed by a tumbling fold of black silk, and I released my pent-up breath. At last, I was on the ground!

Something pressed on my shoulder and I realised the rest of the balloon's envelope was collapsing. I pushed it up with one hand and hauled the iron burner lid back into place before the flammable outer layer of silk touched the embers within and reignited.

Before I could escape, the black shroud covered me, pushing me to the floor and then hovering over me like an overanxious mother bird, unable to either fall or rise as gravity and aluminium fought one another's influence.

'Emmeline!' yelled Patrick. 'Are you all right? Say something!'

'Emmeline!' yelled Matilda. 'You're fantastic! That was enough to make a dog laugh!'

I pushed feebly at the vast pile of fabric, and felt a hand grip mine. It was tough as untanned leather—Patrick's hand. He pulled me out slowly, looking monstrous in his goggles. We both pushed them up onto our foreheads, and at last I stood on solid ground, trying not to pant excessively as I took in breaths of clear air once more. I'd gone through two balloon crashes, a fire, and a near-fatal dragging in the space of five minutes—but I was British. I smoothed my hair and glanced about for a new bonnet.

Sadly, my attire had to wait a little longer. The three of us packed the silk back into its former position inside the carriage, then Matilda reverently placed the aluminium sheets back where they belonged. They lay quiescent, waiting for their next opportunity.

'Keep the goggles,' Matilda said to me. 'The magic makes my eyes itch.' My heart assured me she was lying, but I accepted it with minimal guilt. The goggles reminded me of home.

Without a word, Patrick set to work repairing the damaged wheel. He soon blunted his knife on the hard native wood, and I considered offering him the use of mine. I didn't, however. He was both intelligent and brave, which made him powerful. If he became an enemy, I wanted my Probability Parasol close by. Some gentlemen are uncomfortable with the idea of a lady who owns a rather sharp knife, and I didn't care to have him claim it for himself.

'Would you look at that!' he said, and held up a crushed ball of lead shot. 'They managed to hit us after all.'

'Can I see it?' Matilda asked, confidently holding out her hand. 'Imagine what Father would say if he were here!'

Patrick passed it to her. I wondered if the lead's innate magic was strong enough to make the dead land all around us look beautiful to her. She sniffed it and threw it away into the grass. I wished I'd asked to keep it—one more piece of scrap metal, just in case. It could hardly make my portmanteau any heavier.

She climbed up into the sadly holed carriage and retrieved a thick piece of layered tin from inside Patrick's seat. It was the same size as my bag, and almost as heavy. She hauled it to a flat stretch of dirt, with the peaked end facing up the hill. When she saw me staring, she motioned me over to look.

I arranged myself as well as I could on a nearby rock that looked a great deal more picturesque than it felt. She reached under the upper end of the tin, pressed a hidden switch, and jumped back. The tin whirred for a moment, then snapped up on four jointed legs like a demented side table with a thick curved top. It whirred again. I chose not to examine it more closely—yet—but watched in delight. It shrieked as tin scraped on tin, and grew several feet long. The front peak snapped into position and I saw it was a cylindrical shape with two triangles at the top—like ears—and an open maw that revealed a series of cranks and switches.

'It's … a horse,' I said. 'A retractable tin horse.'

'Bing!' it said happily.

My rats sprang into existence in the grass, and rushed to investigate. They sniffed its legs, bit it experimentally, and allowed it to bend its head and examine them in turn.

'Bing,' they agreed. 'Bing, bing!'

'It seems they have a new friend,' I said.

'Just wait,' said Matilda. 'We're not done. Tell your … things … to back off for a moment.'

I did, and the rats obeyed.

'Not enough,' said Matilda, and we repeated the operation until she decided the distance was sufficient for her purpose. She stepped forward and tripped a second, smaller switch inside the horse's mouth, then fled.

The horse shot up a foot higher, and spread out wide. It splayed its spindly legs, and its layered back unfolded, piece by piece, until it reached all the way to the ground. The head drooped, and kept drooping until the open mouth just touched the ground. Then the neck folded out into a flat sheet. I found myself looking at an oval-shaped dome with one open side at what used to be the tail end.

'It's …' I said, 'um …'

'A tent,' said Matilda happily. 'Do you have this kind in England yet?'

'We should, but of course we don't have Governor Hotham telling us to abandon food production to speed up mining, so metal costs a normal amount.'

She shrugged. 'They do tend to rust, but they double as pack-horses.'

'Can you ride them?'

'Not if you want to ever sit down again,' she grinned. 'I only tried *that* twice.'

'Twice?'

'I assumed it was mere bad luck I broke my leg the first time. But of course if they could be ridden all the soldiers would have them, instead of the usual flesh and blood type. Thankfully, that failing is great enough to make them useless to the powerful, and twice as useful to folks like us.'

'Speaking of horses—where's Barry?'

'Probably off to the O'Connell's farm, where he knows he'll get better food. He will be more handy tomorrow, and I bet he knows it.'

Patrick materialised beside us. 'Water or fire?' he asked Matilda.

'Either,' she said.

'I'll fetch water then,' he said, and stumped off with the second billy can. We were no longer within sight or sound of the stream, but my heart knew exactly where it was. Even in Australia, I'd never be lost.

Matilda and I gathered dead wood off the ground. The native

trees smelled like medicine, and the wood was rotten in the centre. My Superior-Inferior Heels kept getting caught in the undergrowth, but I didn't care to take them off and risk further injury. Somehow, there still wasn't time to fetch a fresh bonnet.

Now that I was within the trees, I saw that my original impression of nothing but silver-green gum trees was incorrect. There were trees with oval leaves in pale blue; others with grey leaves pointed like spears; black trunks bleeding red sap; others peeling away like snakes sloughing their skin; and large bushes with sprays of soft spheres in brilliant yellow. Altogether the bushland was red, orange, black, green, silver, gold, pale blue and purple. But I still longed for proper shade. It was bad enough that I'd lost my hat, while Matilda still looked pristine. She appeared to relish being barefoot despite the rocky ground.

'Have you ever been in love?' she asked.

I paused just as I picked up another wide sheet of bark. An image of Ambrose's eyes flashed into my mind—that exact moment when life came into his face because of something I'd said. Of course I'd never see him again, and I couldn't even hate him for what he'd done. How infuriating. But I'd gathered from reading that the greatest love stories began with mutual hatred, so perhaps we'd had a chance after all. 'I didn't have time. Have you? Is that why you—' I felt my eyes turn to the section of bush where Patrick had wandered off.

She picked up another piece of wood, and I realised the conversation was over. I struggled to see her as a lovesick girl, but perhaps a forbidden romance really would be reason enough to flee Bearbrass. It didn't explain the fear behind her eyes, however. There was something more.

We decided to try to use the rats to light the fire, but it seemed cruel to frighten them, particularly with the new possibility of total combustion. Instead I picked the youngest and placed her on the tinder. 'Can you heat up please?' I asked.

'Bing,' she said. 'Parp.'

I sat back on my heels. 'You're not sure?'

'Bing.'

'Well, do your best. No one's going to hurt you.'

She crouched down, and her eyes glowed red for a moment. A wisp of smoke drifted from her back, and for a moment I thought we'd succeeded. Then her eyes dimmed and she toppled on her side, fast asleep. I placed her carefully on a soft patch of new grass.

'Matches, then,' said Matilda, and fetched their tin to get started.

Patrick reappeared soon after the fire outdid the last feeble light of day. The hatefully unfamiliar stars grew visible overhead, and I was careful not to look up.

He poured some of the river water into a mug and placed the billy over the flames. I couldn't help noticing the water was the colour of tea before he added the leaves. Perhaps all of Australia's water was dirty. How suitable, since the continent was peopled almost entirely by convicts.

I wondered if Officer Dry was tracking us, and how well his search was progressing so far. At least I'd left Dunne far behind me. That was one good thing.

Patrick threw in a handful more tea leaves, and mixed flour and sugar with the remaining water to make a kind of bread. He and Matilda discussed the state of the river, and whether the narrower stream was a sign of coming drought. I felt my eyelids droop, and drank more tea to stay awake. We ate the damper hot and smeared with jam, and then Matilda and I crawled inside the horse tent to sleep, while Patrick remained by the fire.

Neither of them knew my secret, and I intended to keep it that way, but I needed fresh coal and clean water, and I needed them before the sun rose.

Chapter Sixteen

I awoke with a rock sticking into my back in the exact same spot where the edge of my corset had rubbed against me the previous day. The flickering firelight no longer shone through the chinks in the tent, and Matilda was gone from my side. Perhaps she and Patrick were together. The thought made me rather uncomfortable, but at least they were distracted.

I crawled out of the tent and stood up. The night was full of the ominous rustle of eucalyptus leaves. For a moment I thought it was raining, but of course it wasn't. I spotted a lump of man-shaped darkness where I'd last seen Patrick, and I didn't risk waking him—or them—by going closer.

The ground underfoot snapped and crunched as I stepped on tinder-dry sticks and weeds. Something howled from the nearby forest, and something else answered it. I shivered and tightened my grip on my Probability Parasol. Australia had roaming packs of wild native dogs, close relatives of wolves. But there was nothing for it—my heart was now scraping rather than ticking, and I had to refuel. The coal part was simple—I simply chose the best pieces from the burner, rubbing the black stains from my fingers onto my skin until they disappeared. Water was another matter.

Fortunately the intelligent brass of my heart worked as well as any compass. After an hour of walking, I heard running water and proceeded more slowly, wary of dusk animals that could be dangerous when interrupted. I had no desire to stumble across the native dogs.

The water didn't sound right. Something was moving, making irregular splashes and sighs. I crept closer, widening my eyes until the night air dried them out and I had to blink. This night-time creeping was well outside my experience, and I longed for the more civilised hazards of a ballroom.

Crouched behind a spiky Banksia bush, I peered through the leaves and saw the river. It shone silver in the moonlight. The dark hump of some wild creature emerged from the water, shaking its shaggy head and spraying bright drops in all directions. I froze, and then it laughed.

Matilda dunked herself one more time, then walked out of the river toward me, not realising I was there. Her hair was very long when it was wet. It stuck to her chest, curving around her breasts.

She was completely nude, lined with crescent scars from her neck all the way down to her feet, including her breasts. I wondered what horrors filled her past, and was frightened to think. My etiquette books didn't begin to cover the situation, and I held my breath as she strode past without seeing me, singing to herself in another language.

She wasn't like me at all. Scars aside, she was flawless and unafraid of anything the night had to offer, and if she'd seen me watching her she'd have greeted me as if nothing was wrong. I wasn't sure whether to admire her or take her aside for a discussion of ladylike behaviour. So much for Lady Hotham's civilising influence.

When I was sure she was gone, I found the fastest-running part of the water and refreshed both my boilers. The back boiler was very difficult without an assistant, but I took off my clothes and managed it in the end. Unlike Matilda, I glanced around anxiously every few seconds, and crouched low in the water, afraid to be seen. I missed Lizzie's stoic assistance, and hoped she was happy wherever she was.

When I crept back to our domed tin tent and lay down next to Matilda, she was dressed in her chemise to sleep. Her hair was still wet, however, and I flushed in the darkness.

In the morning Patrick brewed more tea, carefully preserving the dregs from the previous night for added flavour, and we ate the hard leftover damper. I was very stiff, and longed for my bed back in London.

Matilda loaded the tent with an enormous amount of fresh coal and ordered it to turn back into a horse. It parped at her—evidently none of us had slept well—but scraped and screeched into the correct form. A flock of giant white and yellow cockatoos responded by swooping in circles around us before flying off, screaming as they left. The sound chilled me, and I remembered how I'd thought of Australia as Hades. It wasn't so far off after all. Except of course that Governor Hotham had prioritised mining over all other industry, and as a result even an outlaw could afford a device that would boggle the minds of any member of London Society. Little wonder the colony was low on water when driven by such greed. Since I wasn't currently thirsty, it seemed a worthy sacrifice.

Only Patrick was cheerful, whistling as he strapped my bag and parasol firmly onto the horse's back.

'Parp,' it said, and flicked one metal ear.

Patrick loaded the horse with more coal and slapped it on the tin rump. It lurched into a jerky pendulum motion, with a great deal of movement and very little forward progress. I wondered how long we would be walking, but didn't show my weakness by asking. Instead I detached my increasingly irritating crinoline wheels, slipping them into a pocket with two sleeping rats. I set my Superior-Inferior Heels to their lowest setting. Matilda walked barefoot, equally impervious to bindi grass and modesty. She wasn't even wearing a corset!

We walked north, with thick brush on our left and tall grasses on our right. I rarely heard the water, although I sensed it lay parallel to our path. Every so often a cloud of dust rolled across us, making my eyes sting and staining the yellow grass red. I put the goggles back on whenever I saw more dust coming, and kept them on my forehead the rest of the time, just below the brim of my one remaining bonnet. The leather strap of the goggles cut into the back of my neck.

'What's your father like?' I asked Patrick, wondering what manner of man I was about to meet.

'Honest,' he grunted, stopping the tin horse to tighten the straps yet again. 'No matter what anyone says.'

'Is he a … did he choose to come to Australia?'

Patrick grunted a reply that could have meant almost anything, but clearly meant I should stop asking questions.

'He was a swing rioter,' said Matilda cheerfully. 'That's why he was brought here. When Mr O'Connell sees a machine where a human should be, he burns it, or smashes it, or blows it up.'

'Ah,' I said. I focused on walking and on keeping my pocket-watch visible. Hopefully Mr O'Connell would never find out that I was both human and machine—and secretly proud of it. I tried not to think about the possibility of being blown up. There was plenty for me to stoically ignore in this ragged colony, and I consciously drew on Mother's skills. Burrs stuck to my stockings, but I didn't mention the scratching. Tiny sharp rocks made their way into my shoes, but I didn't stop to shake them out. The dust made me cough, but I didn't curse and rail as I increasingly longed to do. I was beginning to understand why fishwives made such a racket on sunny days.

Matilda, clearly choosing to neglect her crinolines along with her shoes and stockings, had abandoned her bonnet for one of Patrick's wide-brimmed blank hats. She occasionally took it off to fan herself, and as far as I could tell was genuinely enjoying the walk. I definitely had a duty to civilise her, but I hadn't the faintest notion where to begin. Maybe if I waited long enough, the right words would come to me. In the meantime, it was hard enough to hold onto my own decency, let alone to inspire it in another.

When the sun was directly overhead, we topped a rise and Patrick motioned for us to hold still. The horse parped, annoyed at stopping when the journey was nearly over. Below us lay a ragged shelter, propped up by trunks of wood and open to the elements on the northern side. It was surrounded by tilled soil and the fragile plants of a new holding.

'Trouble?' Matilda asked Patrick.

'Maybe. No sign of Barry, which means Father's hidden him. He must have a reason.'

'So that's a yes, then.'

Patrick untied the straps on the tin horse, and Matilda tipped it over on its side, below the level of the grass. She told it to stay quiet, and that we'd come back to it soon.

It didn't answer, which presumably meant that it understood. The smoke and steam from it eased off, and it was still.

Patrick passed me my portmanteau, and I struggled to hold the weight of it off the ground.

'Perhaps you should leave it here,' he said.

'No.' I remembered myself and added, 'Thank you.' He moved toward me as if he was about to take the heavy weight off my hands, but he didn't. I knew he was an Irish Catholic, but even that was no excuse for his stubborn refusal to treat me properly. All the tea-drinking had almost made me forget what he was.

Kneeling beside me, he dug his fingers into the dust and pulled a thick section of grass upward, exposing a concealed wooden trapdoor. 'Ladies first,' he grunted, as surly as if he knew what I thought of him.

Matilda stepped down onto rough dirt stairs and I followed her, trailing my fingers on the wall so I didn't fall. My thumb touched a thick piece of twine and I jerked away by reflex, not knowing what it was. Patrick came in after us, letting the grassy trapdoor fall back into place with a thud. It instantly cut off all light.

'You did bring the matches, didn't you, Patrick?' Matilda said.

'You were supposed to. You always have the matches.'

'Do I?' she said. 'Ah well. Shall we take hands?'

'No need,' said Patrick. He scrabbled against the wall, and I guessed the string was attached to some signal at the other end. 'Now we wait.'

Matilda subsided on to the earthen stair with a rustle of her one remaining skirt. I sat a little lower down, feeling ill from the heat and the long walk. Patrick stood. The only sound in the darkness was his steady breath, and the low tick of my heart. My eyelids drooped with exhaustion.

I saw a will-o'-the-wisp in the distance, and at first I thought I was seeing things. It danced and flickered like a flame behind smoked glass, coming closer by the moment. I reached for Matilda's hand in the darkness, but my fingers only brushed against the dusty cloth of her skirt. The close air grew suddenly alive with the stink of rotting fat and fire.

We all heard the soft snick and thunk of a pistol getting loaded.

Chapter Seventeen

'Who's there?' Patrick called out, and his voice was steady.

'Is that you?' replied a man's voice.

'Yes, Father—with Matilda and another lady.'

'Miss Muchamore, I presume.' The Irish voice came closer, and I saw a wild mass of beard within the circle of the lamplight, shockingly dark against a stained white shirt. 'Where's Mr Dunne?'

'What!' I'd stood to my feet, but the shock of that name almost threw me back to the ground.

'They say a Mr Dunne is with you,' said the voice.

'He was never with me!' I said. 'Never! Don't tell me he's escaped too?'

The man stopped and raised his candle high. It stunk of burning tallow and clay, and its light reflected against the cloud of black smoke hovering around him. 'You'd best come into the house. Barry's safe at Joe's. I was expecting you to come, but I didn't know if the coppers would arrive first.'

'Joe'll be good to him,' said Patrick. 'I don't suppose we'll get him back?'

'Not likely.'

'Well, all right.'

I wondered at Patrick's mild response to the loss of an animal he clearly loved, but I didn't comment. Perhaps the reason his face seemed so peaceful despite the powder scar was that nothing in the world provoked him into strong emotion.

We followed Mr O'Connell the rest of the way down the steps and through a long tunnel with a slick clay floor. At last he passed his pistol and the jam-jar candle to Matilda and opened another hatch. There was no room to turn around, so he led the way into the low corner of his house. We left my sundries in the tunnel and followed after him.

The house was not as poorly made as it appeared. Although the thatched roof was low it was sturdy, and the back wall was made of stones cemented together so not a breath of wind could wriggle through. I followed Matilda's lead and sat on the floor with my skirts spread out about me. Two rats immediately poked their noses out, and I pushed them back into hiding before Mr O'Connell saw them. I didn't like to imagine what a swing rioter would do if he saw that science was now able to successfully fuse organic matter and machinery. He was wild enough to blow up my rats, and I didn't like that idea at all.

'Shall I let the neighbours know Mr Dunne is no friend of ours?' he asked.

'Please,' I said, flipping open the lid of Father's watch and pretending to check the time. It was a nervous habit when I met new people. 'But why did you think he was?'

He leant forward and pulled up another hidden panel in the floor, producing a piece of paper decorated with three faces— Patrick was one, Dunne was another, and the third was a girl. A chill went through me as I recognised someone's drawing of my face. The chill vanished into annoyance when I realised they'd given me a most unbecoming scowl, and completely failed to capture the elegant curl of my hair. Anyone can draw a woman's hair perfectly well with minimal effort, so there was no excuse for that tangled fuzz.

I was surprised out of my reverie when Patrick—slouching, abrupt Patrick—read the paper aloud without stumbling: 'Wanted! The ballooning bushranger and his two escaped companions: Emmeline Muchamore and Markus Dunne. Five pound reward for any information leading to their capture.'

'Only five pounds?' said Matilda, wrinkling her nose. 'On your behalf, I'm insulted. I'm willing to bet my father had a hand in this. He has a spiteful side, despite how gullible he can be.'

'You're a bushranger?' I said to Patrick.

Patrick ignored both of us. 'I suppose Mr Dunne escaped in the confusion, and someone assumed he was one of us. How do you know him, Emmeline?'

I swallowed, tasting dust at the back of my throat. 'He travelled on the same ship as I did, and hated me from the start. When he betrayed me to the officers in exchange for greater privileges, his fiancé left him. He blames me.'

'Where do you think he'll go now he's free?' Patrick asked.

'Not to Lizzie, I hope. Actually, I'm sure he won't think of her. He'll aim for the goldfields and riches.'

Mr O'Connell shook his grizzled head. 'If that's so, he's in for a shock.'

'What do you mean?' asked Matilda.

'First, there are more trappers on the goldfields these days than there are guarding the prisons. Second, unless he's got a good lot of shiners already, he'll not get more gold out there.'

'How is that possible?' said Matilda. 'People go to the goldfields to get money, not to spend it.'

'The Rum Corps trades in licences these days—no licence, no gold. And the licences are worth more than most diggings.'

'Doesn't the governor intervene?' I asked, feeling my heart sink. So much for Lizzie's dreams of gold lying about on the ground. I should have known better than to let that lovely image take hold in my mind.

'The goldfields are too big and too crowded for any but the military to move freely,' said Mr O'Connell. 'That, and the hundreds of poor souls living on hope and dirty water. The redcoats would chalk Mr Dunne as soon as look at him.'

Matilda and I exchanged a glance. I cleared my throat. 'Sir … I also mean to find gold. And Matilda's fortunes are lost too.'

He closed his eyes briefly, and the ticking of my heart was like a death-knell. 'What would two ladies like you do with more gold?'

'That's the problem. I don't have anything but what I'm

carrying, and my brother and sister and mother have nothing but their walls and roof. If I don't want the Muchamore name turned to mud I need to send them gold, and I need to do it quickly.'

'And you, Matilda? What would your father say if he knew you were here?'

'I'll not go back to Bearbrass,' she said with sudden vehemence. 'I'd starve first.'

Mr O'Connell sighed, and passed his pistol to Patrick. 'You'll be needing this then.'

I stared, wondering if he'd realised my secret and decided to kill me. Matilda placed her hand on my arm and squeezed. They were all in on it—Dunne had betrayed me in Bearbrass, and I'd been brought out into the bush to die.

Patrick slid the pistol into his belt.

Matilda grinned at him. 'I knew you'd join us when you understood.'

'What can you possibly mean?' I asked, embarrassed at the shaking of my voice. Was I going to be killed or not?

Patrick avoided my eye. 'I'll not let ladies like you wander those cursed lands alone.'

'Oh. You mean … oh.'

I saw tears in Mr O'Connell's eyes, but he excused himself to fetch lunch.

'Thank you,' I said, wondering how long I could keep my machinery secret, and what would happen if either man found out. Nonetheless, Patrick's presence in my near future was reassuring. So was his gun, although I would have preferred to be the one carrying it.

Mr O'Connell started a fire in the stone hearth built into the back wall, and took day-old mutton from a mesh cage hanging in the shade of a Peppercorn tree outside. When the fire was built up, he cooked slices of the meat in a thin stew. There was more onion than meat.

'No matter which gold town you land in, you'll want to find

Seamus Keneally and James Scobie,' said Mr O'Connell. 'They're good men, and they'll send word around the rest of the goldfields that you're to be kept away from the law.'

'Thank you,' I said again, feeling foolish.

The rest of our dinner passed in silence. I should have been in my element—steering conversations among company I despised was a specialty of mine back home—but in the face of natives and Irishmen I was tongue-tied.

'Well,' Mr O'Connell said at last. 'Come what may, I'm pleased to meet any fine lady of my son's acquaintance. He has a knack for meeting them, especially when they're in need.'

I flushed, wondering if he meant to insult me.

'Oh, stop your gammon,' said Matilda. 'I didn't make him come to my rescue that day.'

I realised the mockery was aimed at her rather than me, and resolved to find out how the incongruous pair had met. Mr O'Connell seemed surprisingly tolerant of their relationship. I wondered why. He even let Matilda borrow a full outfit that evidently belonged to his wife.

'Oh!' he said to Patrick. 'To think I almost forgot. Your mother wrote a letter.'

'And it reached me?' he said. 'All this way?'

'Aye. Don't doubt the bush telegraph, son. The news of your most recent rescue arrived here half a day before you did.' He delved into the secret compartment in the floor and produced a handful of papers. 'I can't remember which it is.' He shoved the pile into Patrick's hands, and I realised Patrick was better educated than his father.

Patrick sorted through the letters with a private smile, passing them in handfuls back to his father until he found the right one. He walked outside to read it in private.

The three of us looked at one another awkwardly.

'Is Mrs O'Connell calling on friends?' I asked, presuming she was in Bearbrass.

'My Shauna is at the Female Factory in Van Dieman's Land,' said Mr O'Connell, turning his face away as if to check on the fire, but I saw the set of his shoulders belying his pain and fear. 'Did Patrick not tell you?'

<h1 style="text-align:center">Chapter Eighteen</h1>

Patrick walked back inside the mouth of the shelter, holding the letter open in his hand. His face was blank with shock. 'It's … I don't know what to do.'

'Shauna drew me a picture,' said Mr O'Connell. 'I gather she doesn't want to be rescued.'

'How could you tell from a picture?' I asked.

'She drew the whole place, all shut in by hills and then shut in a second time by windowless stone walls so high there's no sun at all, and then she drew herself inside the yard with that impudent smirk on her face.'

'That's more or less what she wrote,' said Patrick faintly. It seemed he could show emotion after all. 'She said … she said—' He turned to the letter and read a line of it aloud: 'Don't break me out just yet, dear. I'm busy.'

Mr O'Connell laughed a great laugh, making me jump.

'Sounds like her,' said Matilda.

'Aye,' said Patrick, recovering himself. 'That it does.'

'You plan to break your mother out of the Female Factory?' I asked, not knowing whether to consider him a lunatic or a hero.

'Aye, when she'll have me. And when Matilda and I have the resources.'

'I'll help,' I said, surprising myself. 'When my brother and sister are taken care of.'

Patrick glanced at me and raised one eyebrow. 'Why would you do that?'

Suddenly there were tears in my eyes. 'I want to be more—more than finding gold and marrying well. I want to have a life that means something. If you'll let me, I'll start with helping your mother out of that vile place.'

Patrick met my eye and stared until I blushed. Whatever he was searching for, he found it. 'Thank you.'

'How long has she been in the factory?' I asked, hardly daring to say its name aloud.

'Three months,' said Mr O'Connell.

'Three months too long,' said Patrick. 'But it seems she's made herself comfortable in her own way.'

'I pity the warden,' said Mr O'Connell. 'Do you think—'

Suddenly Patrick cocked his head to one side. 'Did you hear that?'

Mr O'Connell stood in stages, grunting in pain. I caught a glimpse of a flogging scar on his calf, and quickly looked away. Only the worst miscreants were whipped so thoroughly that the scars extended down the legs, because the back was too ragged to take anymore without killing them.

He stood at the open door, and I forgot his past in the more immediate threat. We held our breaths.

A thin cry drifted on the still air. 'Coo-ee!' The second syllable was a high-pitched shriek. I shivered at the eerie sound.

'That's Joe's boy,' said Mr O'Connell. 'It's a message.'

'Time to go?' asked Patrick.

'So it would seem.' The two men shook hands gravely, and Mr O'Connell opened the hatch for us to depart.

I descended first, holding the unlit tallow candle in its jam jar. It was cool underground, and I felt relieved despite the new danger.

'Get comfortable,' Patrick whispered. 'We'll stay close until Father tells us it's safe to move on without being seen.'

'Will they find our tin horse?' I asked.

'No, they're coming from the opposite direction.'

From above, I heard Mr O'Connell clearing away all traces of our passing.

The darkness closed in, and I shivered again. 'Patrick, are you really a bushranger?'

'It's just a misunderstanding,' he said.

Matilda giggled, muffling the sound with her hand. 'You've "misunderstood" yourself quite a few fine stallions, though. And you and your parents have dug quite a handy entrance hall.'

'I only meant to borrow them,' he mumbled, 'at first. They like a good gallop every once in a while. Especially Barry.'

'You've stolen Barry, what, four times now?' said Matilda.

'More or less.'

'Ah,' I said. It was a relief to know he didn't have his father's violent tendencies—not yet—but I felt uncomfortable to hear Matilda speak of his crimes so lightly. 'At least they can't transport you for your sins.'

We heard voices above us and stopped speaking.

Patrick carried my bag a little way down the passage, and Matilda and I took the hint and followed him, shuffling on until the distant crack of light around the hatch was thin as a hair. The clay underfoot stuck to my shoes, but it smelled clean and cool. We stood still and waited, but it was only a few moments later when the hatch opened. I felt the other two relax, and Patrick took a step forward. Then the man at the hatch spoke.

'What's this then?' said Officer Dry.

Chapter Nineteen

The grim image of the Female Factory rose up in my mind, filling me with terror. My heart ticked far too loudly in the small space, and it seemed impossible that Officer Dry could fail to hear me and catch all three of us. My brief moment of freedom would cost us dearly.

'If my son had been here,' said Mr O'Connell from his hut, 'he'd be long gone by now. But do feel free to search the … er … cellar, if you can spare the time from your very important pursuit of that bushranger.'

The three of us held our breath.

'I don't care to ruin my uniform on a whim,' said Officer Dry. 'William, you go.'

A soft voice answered him, but we were already scrambling farther back in the tunnel, stepping on our skirts and bumping into the walls. I considered dropping the unlit candle so I had both hands free, but I realised it would reveal our presence close by. A horse whinnied outside the hut, and the sound carried clearly. I tried to breathe softly, and concentrated on keeping calm enough that my heart didn't start clanking outright.

Officer Dry and his man exchanged words behind us, and when I glanced back I saw someone climb awkwardly down after us. He was a native with a shaved head and hands like shovels. We slowed down suddenly, anxious not to make a noise and give ourselves away.

I realised we couldn't possibly outrun him in the dark, not when he'd certainly see us open the hatch at the other end. But we couldn't give up now. Despite Mrs O'Connell's good cheer, I feared the dark hopelessness of the Female Factory above all else.

So we crept on into the black. I said a silent prayer for mercy, but I wasn't sure if God listened to convicts on the run. It had been a long time since I attended church back in London.

The man behind us moved out of the pool of light and stood waiting for his eyes to adjust. I thought he'd light a candle, but he didn't. That would have kept him blind to our faint outlines against the blank walls. I silently cursed his good sense.

He walked toward us with even steps, not even hurrying. I couldn't tell if he'd seen us yet, but it didn't matter. We had to keep moving—carefully, awkwardly—for as long as hope remained.

So we tiptoed onwards, straining our hearing for the soft shuffle of his footsteps coming ever closer. Then the footsteps stopped.

'Patrick. It's me, William,' said the soft voice. 'I have you fair and square, so let's not fight.'

Matilda spoke suddenly in her other language. It sounded like birds calling.

'All right, Matilda,' said the voice, but it was sharper now that Matilda had revealed herself. 'I'm listening, which is more than you deserve.'

Matilda spoke again in the strange language. I caught Patrick's name and my own, and the note of pleading in Matilda's voice.

'This is my life now, thanks to you. What do you expect me to do?'

Matilda answered.

'But how can I trust you to keep that promise, after what you've done to me?'

'I never promised myself to you, or to any other!' she said loudly, then stopped cold. She resumed speaking in the other language.

'All right,' said William. 'Until the full moon. After that, you'd better find me—or I'll find you. You know I can.'

She whispered something else I didn't understand, and William walked back toward the light. He climbed up and out, and closed the hatch.

'Why on Earth is William working as a tracker now?' Patrick asked. 'He used to be so proud. What did you do to him?'

'Nothing!' she hissed. 'Now hurry up and let's get out of here. We need to find four shares of gold, not three—and we've got less than two weeks to do it.'

'Nice negotiation,' said Patrick sarcastically.

'Better than you would have done,' she retorted, gasping as she stumbled across the first step upward. 'You don't even speak our language.'

'And I suppose he spoke in English for my benefit,' said Patrick.

'It's simple manners to speak in your opponent's language,' Matilda retorted.

'Exactly.'

'Oh,' said Matilda in a small voice. 'He sees me as British now.'

'Never fear,' said Patrick gently. 'I've never thought such a thing of you, and I never will.'

'What precisely do you mean by that?' I asked.

Matilda giggled, her spirits restored. 'You know what you are, Emmeline? Fun.'

'And fond of something extremely heavy,' said Patrick. 'What on earth is in this bag?'

'Clothing,' I said quickly.

He shook the portmanteau, and we all heard metal hitting metal.

'Oh … parts. A few minor parts,' I said. 'For the rats.'

'Anything useful?' Patrick asked.

'Yes,' I said. 'Grease.'

'How is that useful exactly?'

'We can get that tin horse going without drawing attention by making a racket.'

'I was right about you,' he said with a smile. 'You are worth your weight.'

We climbed to the top of the final set of stairs.

'William will lead the troopers the other way,' said Matilda. 'We're safe, for the moment.'

'Time to get back to the balloon and on our way,' said Patrick, pushing open the hatch. He stood up slowly, blinking, with one hand on the pistol at his hip. 'It's safe. They're gone. And I bet they took my horse too.'

'Joe's horse,' said Matilda.

He shrugged, neither agreeing nor disagreeing. I made a mental note to do a daily inventory of my things. Not much would be useful to him, but you never know what a perpetual thief will do.

We hauled up my things and climbed onto the grass. I sighed at the thought of the hike back to the carriage, but there was nothing for it. We greased and loaded the horse, and started walking.

Chapter Twenty

The carriage was running low on coal, so after walking most of the day through bushland we had to go back into the pallid trees and gather as much wood as we could carry, several times over. I found an entire dead tree, bleached grey and hollow, and together we cut it up into manageable pieces. As we gathered, we had to keep glancing around in case Officer Dry had come to search in our area.

It was difficult to keep my mind on the job. My heart was beating quickly, happily—and I knew why. For the first time in my life, I had a chance to make a life for myself, instead of pretending to obey the rules of society to save what remained of my family. My future was terrifyingly broad. I wanted to build things. I wanted to turn my back on all I'd been taught about the importance of proper manners and true British superiority. I wanted to change the world. Matilda and Patrick—and the unsinkable Mrs O'Connell—were my family now.

Before I could be truly free, I had to find gold. In the meantime, I still needed to keep my secret. I chose the best pieces of the remaining coal and hid them in the deepest pocket of my skirt when the others weren't paying attention.

When we'd amassed a pile of wood as big as the horse, we still didn't leave. There was absolutely no wind to push us on our way. I longed for a regular carriage and a good macadam road. We made a meagre dinner, drank tea, and waited until the stars came out. Patrick volunteered to keep watch, and Matilda and I crawled inside the expanded tent to sleep while we could.

I woke up when the horse-tent dripped grease on my face. There wasn't enough room to move out of the way, unless I wanted to ruin my clothes forever, so I went outside.

The stars were very bright, far brighter than in London. I kept my eyes downcast, not wanting to be reminded how distant my family was from me now. A part of me wished I'd sent them some message telling them where I was. I didn't even know if I'd been officially recorded as transported or simply deceased. But I'd tell them everything gladly the day I sent them a pile of gold. In the meantime, I hoped Arabella was all right without me.

Patrick stood by the fire, holding one finger up against the nonexistent breeze. He sighed, then saw me and bowed. 'Are you unwell, Emmeline?'

'No, thank you. But I can't sleep. Would you like to sleep while I keep watch?'

He shook his head. 'I can't sleep either. They may have taken Father, on suspicion of harbouring me.'

'But they have no reason to think he's guilty! William protected him at the same time as he hid us.'

'Doesn't matter. Police officers are powerful here. A little piece of Britain to invade us over and over again.'

'Please,' I said, and felt my voice catch. 'Don't speak about Britain that way.'

'My apologies. You seem so decent I forget where you're from.'

'I'll never forget where you're from!' I said, and bit my tongue.

'Ireland?' he said, and I realised he was grinning at me across the rippling flames. 'Is that what you mean?'

'What else could I possibly mean?'

'I've never set eyes on Ireland, myself—though I'd like to, someday. It seems no one told you I'm a currency lad.'

'What does that mean?'

'It means I was born here, in Australia. Australian-made currency is worth less than British sterling. So you're sterling, and I'm currency. You see?'

'I'm … sorry?'

'This is not such a bad place. It's rarely so dry for so long. The smelting works and railway pumps everywhere are draining all the lakes and streams, but we'll get more rain in spring.'

'It never seems to rain here.'

'It will,' he said, sounding sure. 'But if you can loosen your laces a smidgeon, the distance to rainy old England won't hurt so much. Try not to think of Australia as a prison, it's no prison to most of us. You British call Australia the end of the world, but you're mistaken. It's the beginning. The sun rises here, after all.'

'If only it would rain, just once.'

'It rained a little just now, but you missed it.' He blew on the fire and it flared into life, warming my face.

'Do you think …' I hesitated, wondering why I was asking such a question of a Catholic—and a man living in blatant sin. But my heart was ticking loudly, demanding an answer. I had to know just how far I'd fallen, and if there could be redemption. 'Do you think God is here, too?'

Patrick let out his breath in a long huff. 'Sit down.'

'Excuse me?'

'It's all right. Just sit down and focus on the stars.'

My throat tightened, and I wished I'd never spoken. But I didn't want to be impolite when I was the only representative of proper manners for a day's walk in any direction. I found a relatively clear patch of ground and sat there, glad I'd chosen a brown woollen dress to sleep in. Gritting my teeth to hold in the inevitable tears, I looked up.

The moon was more than half full, and the stars felt like a million staring eyes. Patrick lay down on his back so close by me I smelled the sweat on his clothes, but it didn't smell bad. My heart ticked loudly. Patrick didn't seem to realise he was being too familiar, or to notice the effect he was having on me. He lifted his arm and pointed to the sky. 'Do you see it? Do you see the cross?'

Five stars shone in an unmistakable cluster. 'I see it.'

'That's ours,' he said. 'The Southern Cross. Who put it there for us, if not our Lord?'

'Yes,' I said quietly, and my heart stabilised at once. A light breeze ruffled my hair.

'Ah,' said Patrick. 'We have wind at last, enough to be going on with. Would you mind waking Matilda?'

'Not at all,' I said, feeling my heart tick happily at the thought of flying once more. The odd closeness with Patrick meant nothing. I certainly wasn't in danger of falling for a colonial, and Matilda's paramour was certainly faithful to her. 'What direction are the goldfields?'

'Anywhere but south,' he said, and tested the air with a wet finger. 'It seems we're going west. Perhaps we'll make it to Castlemaine by morning.'

I shook Matilda awake, and discovered that she grunted in a most unladylike manner when awoken at midnight. She walked off to the river for her ablutions, and Patrick and I stacked the burner fire, ready to be lit. He warned me that it would be more difficult to take off without a road to help us gather air before we lit the burner. Reminded of my vulnerability, I took the opportunity to slip several more pieces of coal into my pockets for later. I tried not to think of it as stealing, but it was difficult to think of another word for my actions. One of the rats was awoken by having coal dropped on its head, and parped indignantly. I started guiltily, but no one else heard it or saw what I did.

We packed up the horse tent and loaded all our things into the hollow driver's seat. The aluminium made the balloon's envelope hover over the carriage in a half-hearted mass, and it took all three of us to get the fire burning well enough to inflate the balloon without setting it on fire. My arms ached by the time the balloon was finally light enough to lift the burner from the floor. But it was mere minutes later when we lifted up into the night sky like another bright star.

The wind gusted and lagged, playing havoc with our directions. Patrick had enormous difficulty figuring out our heading, and I was sorely tempted to tell him we were drifting a few degrees south, but still mainly west. But I couldn't tell him how I knew without revealing the truth about my heart.

Together we built up the fire to try to find a steadier breeze higher up. He mentioned that greater altitudes had often helped him alter speed and direction in the past. I couldn't help remembering his earlier assurance that he was unable to steer the balloon in any way—the assurance that had taken us to his father. He wasn't as straightforward as he seemed. I was glad I hadn't given in to the temptation of sharing my mechanical secret. Having met his father, I knew where his stubborn streak came from. It would ruin me all over again to let him know I wasn't entirely made of flesh; not since my father installed my heart when I was nine years old.

As we flew, I saw scattered fires in the distance.

'Is that Officer Dry and his men?' I asked.

'Not likely,' said Matilda. 'There are too many fires for that. I think it's a tribe, although it wouldn't be mine—not this far north.'

'Can they see us?'

'Almost certainly. They'll tell William they saw us, too. He speaks all the languages I do, with the exception of French and Latin. He'll inform Officer Dry, if only to stay close to the promise of gold.'

'How many Aboriginal languages do you speak?' I asked, trying to distract myself from the thought of Officer Dry riding swiftly on our trail.

'Five—and a half. I grew up in the tribe, playing with all the other children as if nothing was different about me.' She turned away, feigning fascination with the fires. 'Mother and I lost a great deal when Father moved us to Bearbrass. She tried to give it back to me by negotiating for a marriage with William. Amazingly, she managed to hide her plan from Father. I didn't know she had any will of her own left.'

'Is that why you ran away?' I asked. 'Because of William?'

'Oh, no,' she said. 'That was because of the other one.'

'The other … fiancé?' I asked.

'Father chose him, and virtually bribed his parents to take me. They'd fallen on hard times, and needed to shore up the family name with wealth, or none of them would last the year.'

'I've heard of that happening,' I said, pitying Matilda's second suitor.

She sighed, and I knew I was about to finally learn the truth of what she most feared. 'If Father ever catches me, I'll be married within a week.' She shuddered, and I knew she was thinking of what her marital duties would require her to do. Perhaps the Female Factory would be a gentler fate—or perhaps not.

'Was he horrible, the man your father chose for you?'

She prodded the fire, showering both of us with sparks. 'His face and body are pleasant enough, if you like that sort of thing.'

'Then why didn't you—' I stopped, remembering our pilot. 'Um. Well.' Once again I found myself wishing I could step out of the carriage for a moment. She had given up her society life for love, then. I wasn't sure whether to despise or admire her, and I certainly didn't know what to say, or why she and her lover had taken me with them.

Luckily, she slumped before my eyes. She truly was exhausted. I hoped she'd lost concentration before my horrifying gaff.

'Patrick,' I said. 'I didn't mean to—'

He collapsed into me, sliding helplessly down my skirt onto the floor.

'Patrick!'

Both my companions lay prone at my feet. My heart scraped from one beat to another before self-correcting the level of oxygen flowing into my blood. We'd flown too high! The air was too thin to breathe. I cast manners momentarily aside and knelt on the wood to vigorously shake Patrick.

'Wake up!' I shouted at him. 'We need to get lower, quickly! Which of the ropes must I pull to release the hot air?'

He didn't respond. His breathing was shallow, and I feared for his life. Matilda's eyelids flickered, but she was utterly limp.

'Well,' I said, straightening up and casting around for inspiration. There was nothing to see but stars and air. 'This won't do at all.'

Chapter Twenty-One

Hot air rises. That was enough scientific knowledge to be going on with. I peeked into the burner and immediately regretted it as my eyes watered in the sweet-smelling smoke. My goggles were on my forehead, so I strapped them on and took another look. It was no use: every piece of wood blazed merrily. Patrick had stacked the fire with admirable skill, the wretched fool.

I dived for my bag and searched for the welding gauntlets Mary had so thoughtfully packed for me. They were nowhere to be seen, although I did find a double-ended adjustable spanner that I thought might be just the thing for stabilising the tin horse a little. Presumably I could fashion a similar spanner to steady the back legs. If I didn't, the pendulum rhythm of the movement wouldn't work at all. Of course, the second spanner need not actually be a spanner, if I could just borrow a welding torch and melt down the spare brass scraps lying wasted at the bottom of the bag.

Gauntlets! I threw aside four spare crinolines, a sewing kit, and the white lace dress Mother had ordered our tailor to make for me after Queen Victoria's wedding. Had Mary thought I'd be getting married in prison? My pocketwatch caught in the lace, and I called it a brandy-faced dog before recalling that, whether they were conscious or not, I was in company. Our likely doom was no excuse for vulgarity.

The left gauntlet tangled in one of the larger flounces of my future wedding dress. I ripped it out with savage desperation. As I rummaged through clock parts, brass curtain rings, and spare bloomers, I touched something like a metal finger. It was the second gauntlet.

I fastened the first gauntlet tightly to my hand. The other hung loose—Mary or Arabella had always assisted me in the past.

There was nothing for it. I sprang up and grabbed the burning logs one by one, casting them over the basket's side like fiery comets plunging to Earth. One by one they fell away, sputtering out of flame in their plunge to the ground. When the wood was gone I scooped handfuls of charcoal and embers and threw them out of the carriage in sparkling bursts, each one quenched by the flow of air before they set the ground alight. In minutes, the fire was completely doused. But I didn't know how long it would take for the air already in the black silk envelope above me to cool. It was suddenly very dark. I glanced up at the Southern Cross and said a prayer, knowing God would hear me. After all, I was uncomfortably close to the heavens now.

Tugging experimentally on the ropes, I was utterly unable to see what was happening, but hoped that Patrick and Matilda weren't done for. Or myself, for that matter. I was alone in the darkness, and all I could see were more stars grinning at me with white teeth. Were we descending? Or was it my imagination?

'Mmph … urrr,' said Patrick.

'Excellent,' I said. 'You're beginning to recover. That means we're falling. Good. Except …'

I grabbed fresh wood and threw it into the burner, seeing nothing but shades of black and grey below. 'Matches! Now!'

'In mmmm pocket,' said Matilda.

'Plss … 'scuse mmm,' said Patrick. 'Can't mmm.'

I bent down and fumbled with Matilda's rough woollen skirt. After what seemed an eternity, my fingers closed on a tin box smaller than my palm. I brought it out and struggled with the clasp. It snapped open suddenly, spilling matches everywhere. I groped in the box and found one remaining match stuck in the lid. Bending over the burner, I realised I didn't know where Matilda kept her tinderbox. But I knew where my Probability Parasol was, propped in the back left corner where the seat would be if it wasn't being used elsewhere.

I grabbed it and pulled out the knife, sighing only a little as I sawed off a thick wad of my own hair and dunked it in my grease tin. Cramming the hair between two branches, I lit the match and touched it to my orphaned red curls. It caught at once, and I coughed at the toxic stench. But there was no time to lose if I wished to avoid crashing into the continent Patrick was so peculiarly fond of. I wrenched leaves and twigs off the piled branches and carefully fed them into the fire. The leaves caught and curled like paper, and the twigs soon followed suit.

'The rope with the yellow ribbon,' mumbled Patrick, trying and failing to rise. 'Let it slacken.'

I laid a small branch on the embryonic fire and squinted at the ropes until I found the correct one, and untied it from its hook so it dangled in my face. The fire burned steadily, but I could once again hear the whispering of the trees below. We were perilously close to disaster, and I hoped there were no mountains in our path.

I built up the fire and blew on it, enlisting the rats' help. Two of them scuttled about inside the burner, apparently impervious to the heat (although their fur burned with a choking stench), while the other three scampered up the ropes into the balloon to heat it from inside. I made a mental note that they'd already learnt to regulate their own heat. Good news.

Patrick stood up, clutching the edge of the basket to hold himself up. 'I'm fine. I can help. What should I do?'

'If it's not a bother, can one of you explain why I can't move my arms?' Matilda asked.

'You can talk fluently, but can't move your arms?' I said. 'How does the rest of your body feel? I've never met someone who survived such severe oxygen deprivation before. This opportunity is unparalleled! Oh, and can either of you tell if we're going to crash?'

'I hope not,' said Patrick. He struggled over to poke at the fire with a spare branch. 'Matilda, we flew too high. The air was thin, and we passed out. Emmeline just saved us all.'

'Oh,' I said, flicking a stray ember from my right gauntlet back into the fire. 'I suppose I did.'

'Why didn't you pass out when we did?' Patrick asked me.

'I'm sure I don't know. Must be because I'm so useful.'

He raised an eyebrow, but when I didn't respond he turned and helped Matilda to her feet.

Somehow, none of us felt like sleeping. Also, the smell of burning hair and fur was making us cough. The sun rose slowly, turning the sky grey and leaving the land black. As it spilled over the horizon it lit up a hundred tin horse-tents scattered all across a wide golden field. Low hills rose from the horizon, blue with distance. I spotted a few white canvas tents among the shining throng, some sandstone or brick buildings, and several bark lean-tos.

'That doesn't look like Castlemaine,' Patrick said.

'Clunes, maybe?' said Matilda.

Long black gashes marked the ground around a gravelly rise, with wooden frames at each end attached to steam-powered pumps and sifters. 'Those are definitely mines,' I said, 'but I don't know what type.'

'Let's land before we get too close,' said Patrick. He took handfuls of dirt from his seat and scattered them onto the fire to dampen it. If only I'd known where to find the soil when it mattered most.

The vast majority of the population below us lived in tents and lean-tos. I wondered how long they had been camping there, and whether the water pumped out of the shallow mines was clean enough to drink, or was simply poured away into the dirt ready to be pumped back up again another day.

We landed with barely a bump, and packed away the balloon as the sun rose.

'I saw a road that would suit us,' said Patrick. 'But I can't get the carriage there without help.'

'We can work,' said Matilda. 'Can't we, Emmeline?'

'Certainly.' I wondered if my voice sounded as hollow to them as it did to me. Grubbing about in the dirt was the last thing I wanted to do. I cast a hopeful glance around me, but no nuggets of gold appeared helpfully at our feet.

We unpacked the horse and hitched it to the carriage. I made some basic improvements to the legs, but longed for my laboratory. The others voted to have me riding at the reins since I was the smallest, and my modifications to the horse made it look a tiny bit like a giant robotic spider, which bothered them for some reason.

Since we were entering a town, I insisted on dressing properly. Now that we were leaving the bush, perhaps I wouldn't have to endure the rips and smudges of tree branches and dirt. So I ducked behind the carriage and put on the blue silk that highlighted my eyes so well. The stencilled numbers glared with my guilt, but I wore my white shawl and felt reasonably presentable—by colonial standards. Matilda reluctantly donned a couple of crinolines and her brass corset. She still didn't bother with shoes.

I settled the rats inside the driver's seat and slipped the brass goggles into my pocket with my few spare pieces of coal. My one remaining bonnet was sadly flattened, but I wore it anyway, carefully pinning up my hair to disguise the ruined left side.

Patrick led the way, swiping at the grass and bushes with a stick to check for overlarge stones. Matilda ran back and forth at the carriage's rear, doing her best to brace it with her arms so it didn't fall into the many burrows and depressions in the ground.

The tin horse was still incredibly jerky. I was bumped and bruised from sitting in the driver's seat before we reached the dirt track on which a steady trickle of humanity was travelling—all in the same direction as us. Patrick spoke to some of them, asking if they knew Seamus Keneally or James Scobie. No one knew anything certain. Almost all of them were on foot, with a few ragged horses and here and there an ox-cart bearing a mixture of people and luggage.

I heard the light clop of a well-bred horse and wondered what respectable person would be travelling such a road. Could it be

Officer Dry? I turned and saw a fine two-horse carriage trotting toward us, throwing great clouds of dust into the people behind it, who doubled over coughing. Those in front scrambled to get out of the way of the vehicle before the horses trampled them.

The man driving the carriage clutched his whip in both hands, eyeing the crowds for signs of trouble that never came. It seemed not everyone poor turned out like Dunne; my heart certainly sensed no danger from the throng.

In the forward-facing seat of the carriage two women reclined side by side. Judging by their looks, they were mother and daughter. They faced two gentlemen in the opposite seat, both of whom wore top-hats of exquisite silk at the most fashionable height.

One of the women leant forward, and the gentleman facing her directed the driver to stop beside me. Between us, we completely blocked the road. A dusty family stopped in the road behind us, their heads bowed. The children held hands, but didn't speak. Others simply walked around us, through the dust. None so much as looked at me, although one nodded companionably to Patrick as he moved to climb inside. Matilda remained at the back wheels.

'Good morning,' trilled the older of the two women. 'I'm afraid we're yet to be introduced, but under the circumstances …' She waved to indicate our pathetic surroundings. 'My name is Mrs Southwell. My husband, Winston, and my son Hugh. And this is my eldest daughter, Hyacinth.'

'Good morning,' I said, understanding her desperation for suitable acquaintances. 'My name is …' I remembered suddenly I was an outlaw. '… Ellen Mills.' I turned to introduce Matilda, but she shook her head at me.

'We're hosting a dinner tomorrow evening,' Mrs Southwell continued. 'Nothing fancy. Perhaps you would care to attend.'

'That sounds delightful.' I meant every glorious syllable.

She gave me a complicated series of directions through the tent city, and ordered her driver to continue on.

Patrick took the reins and Matilda and I moved to the single seat.

'What was that about?' I asked her.

'You just made a friend—a rich friend. In part, because she assumed Patrick and I are your servants. Don't you see how useful that will be?'

'I used to have dozens of rich friends.'

'As did I,' she said. 'But they were my friends, so I wouldn't steal from them.'

'Is that what we're going to do?' I asked, with a pang of guilt at the coal in my pocket. 'Are we thieves now?'

'I already was,' said Patrick. 'Although I'm happy to change my ways if you can pay for a licence honestly. And before you ask, no, we're not selling any part of this balloon. It was a gift.'

'From my father,' said Matilda. 'Who was terribly upset when you didn't take it and go.'

'Irrelevant,' said Patrick. 'I earned it fair and square rescuing you from that gang of thugs.'

'Two thugs,' she said.

'Exactly. Two thugs is a gang. And since it's mine now, I'll not give up any part of it.'

And so we continued down the road.

The road widened and merged with a margin of flattened and dying grass bordering one side of the vast tent city. All around us, people simply walked around the fringes of the other tents, and then set up their own or just collapsed on the ground and built a fire for their breakfast. The air was full of the scrape of expanding tin horse-tents and the crackle of new fires catching hold.

We wobbled and jerked farther inside the tent city, narrowly avoiding the scattered tent ropes, fires, and the occasional small child.

'It's not so bad,' said Matilda.

'Aye, and nor's the Female Factory,' Patrick said drily. I was too aghast to speak.

A red-headed woman burst out of a rusted horse-tent at our left and flung herself at our carriage steps. 'Mr O'Connell!' she cried. 'They told me you were here. Is it really you?'

Patrick slowed down the horse and stood up to let her see him more clearly. 'Aye, that I am.'

She slumped in disappointment. 'I'm sorry, I was expecting another gentleman. A friend of my husband.'

'The only other O'Connell I know is my father, Michael,' said Patrick.

'Oh,' she said quietly. 'So he hasn't come back to Ballarat, then?'

Patrick stepped down to meet her face to face, while our horse jerked doggedly onwards. 'What is it that's distressed you? Any friend of my father is a friend of mine.'

She lifted her head and saw something in his face that made her speak her piece. 'Those blasted limeys killed my husband, and I don't know what to do.'

Chapter Twenty-Two

Patrick responded instinctively, as I now realised he always did. He reached out to hand her aboard before the carriage stopped moving. I yelled at the horse to stop. It parped indignantly at my brusqueness and snapped itself up into its smallest shape.

'You'll help me?' asked the Scottish woman, her blue eyes brimming with tears.

'Of course we will,' said Matilda, as if it was the most normal thing in the world. 'Do you want to bring your tent?'

She shook her head. 'It's long past moving, but I've two children.'

'Fetch them,' said Patrick. 'They can sleep in our tent tonight.'

She bobbed a frantic curtsey and hurried back to her tent. 'Aline! Duncan!'

Two young children scrambled out and the woman pushed them up into the carriage. The girl giggled as she tumbled head-first into the pile of black silk. I caught sight of Duncan's eye and realised he was much older than his small shape made him appear. His father's sudden death showed in his face, and my heart stilled for a moment in sympathy.

I alighted to speak a few choice words to the horse, which screeched back into its most useful shape. In the back of my head, a treacherous voice asked if I wanted to get mixed up in a murder. I told the voice it was thinking exactly like an empty-headed society girl, and I would therefore do the opposite of what it said. That gave me time to control my face, and pack away my tears.

My new bosom companion and I climbed back on board and sat beside Matilda while Patrick led us on. She needed a bath, but I breathed more delicately and tried not to change the neutrally pleasant expression on my face. I was itching to ask why her husband had been murdered, and whether the rest of us were in danger. Even inside my own head, I didn't know if I wanted to face down the potential danger or to run from it. I just didn't want to let her children believe the world was against them, as it had been against my father when he was killed.

The whole town was thick with tension, and we'd only just arrived. My heart ticked unevenly, put off by the ominous mood. I hoped no one noticed. When Patrick judged that we'd travelled far enough, he reined in the horse, unhitched it, and opened it into our suddenly-crowded quarters.

'My name is Mrs Scobie,' said the woman, flushing and ineffectually smoothing her hair. She was bereft of bonnet, gloves and shoes.

'Your husband was James, then,' said Patrick. 'My father told me about him. He was a good man.'

Tears shone in her eyes, and she turned her face away. For the first time, I saw her as a person, someone just like me, and was glad we hadn't left her in the dust.

Matilda and I introduced ourselves—I remembered to use my false name—and motioned for her to tend to her children inside while we set up a fire for breakfast. She ducked her head, cast a sharp glance my way, and bent to enter the tent. I hadn't realised she was smart. That could be a problem. Best to help her and move on before things came to a head.

Someone ahead of us shot a gun, and I jumped. Patrick explained that it indicated the diggings were open for the day. 'There's so much gold in the diggings that a thief could sneak in and find a nugget in his neighbour's patch.'

'That does sound easy,' I said doubtfully. 'Is that our plan?'

'We *are* outlaws,' said Matilda. 'At least, the two of you are outlaws. I'm just ruined for associating with Patrick.'

'Terribly sorry about that,' said Patrick, rolling his eyes for my benefit. 'Although if memory serves, you begged me to help you get away from Bearbrass, conveniently forgetting to mention Emmeline planned to find gold entirely on her own.'

'But we've made so many friends already.'

'One of our friends was just murdered,' Patrick reminded her.

I remembered being Aline's age when my own father was killed. My heart skipped a beat, and I vowed that I would risk myself for the Scobie family as if they were my own. Perhaps this was God's plan for me all along. If so, I was grateful for the chance to ease their pain.

I lugged my portmanteau inside the tent, rigged a temporary curtain for poor Mrs Scobie, and found I was suddenly exhausted. Patrick went to find water, and Matilda set up a fire for our breakfast. I wanted nothing more than tea, and the thrill of taking off my shoes. Since I was hardly in fine company—not until dinner, anyway—I did take off my shoes, and briefly considered removing my stockings and crinolines. Perhaps the colonial lack of fashion wasn't completely horrific. Or perhaps Matilda was a bad influence. She'd seemed so civilised back in Bearbrass. I lay down by the fire, and my eyes grew heavy.

'Lunch?' said Matilda.

I cracked open my eyes. 'What?'

She held a mug of tea, and I wanted it with all my heart. Luckily, it was for me. I took it in both hands and drank deeply. This time it was an odd reddish-brown, stained bloody by minerals in the water supply. It was delicious all the same, and packed with brown sugar.

'Did you say lunch?' I asked. 'And when did you change your clothes?'

'It's almost ready, but I thought you might like to dress first. We're in Ballarat, by the way. And we'll be accompanying Mrs Scobie to court today.'

'Oh!' All my clothing smelled of smoke and burnt hair, but there was little I could do about it. I dressed in wool against the heat; my silk needed to stay as clean as possible until the formal evening.

We ate damper again, but since there was no more jam Patrick laced the damper with sugar and we ate it plain, passing the lion's share into the tent where the children made appreciative noises and Mrs Scobie instinctively shushed them. I wondered how long our flour and sugar would last, and drank too much tea as I worried, knowing all the while that I should be rationing that too.

The men of Ballarat had abandoned the majority of tents around us in order to work in the diggings. Evidently they didn't come back for luncheon. Those few who remained were sick with hunger and despair.

'Uh oh,' said Patrick.

'What now?' I said.

'Soldiers. Matilda and I should hide.'

'But I shouldn't?' I asked.

He shook his head. 'You're a respectable young lady, and as British as can be. Of the three of us, you're the only one with a chance at putting them off. The longer you can put them off the better for all of us. Whatever you do, don't tell them Mrs Scobie is here—she's terrified they'll prevent her going to court today. That's why she asked us for help in the first place, to hide herself and her children until she can speak for their father.'

Matilda mimed a flirtatious wave of a fan, and disappeared into the tent. Patrick followed her with difficulty, since there were already four people inside. I passed the extra dishes to him and stood at the entrance trying to appear respectable.

The soldiers approached, looking deadly in their crimson uniforms. Their rifles were old, but no less threatening, particularly since the leading soldier had his hands wrapped around his gun as if he longed to snap into action. I'd seen his type before, but in London my name had kept them far removed from me. This was different, and I knew it. I had no social defences left, no matter what Matilda seemed to think. They kicked up dust as they came, surrounding themselves in a yellow cloud. I hoped they hadn't seen the bill advertising my status as an escaped convict.

As always, fear made me lift my chin in a futile attempt to appear taller.

'Good day, miss,' said the first, stepping sideways in an effort to see past the curtain behind me.

I smiled sweetly. 'Can I help you, sir? Are you looking for something specific, or simply fascinated by my boudoir?'

'Licence,' he said, dropping the false courtesy.

My heart ticked loudly in the silence, and I made a show of consulting the watch hanging from my bodice. Duncan sneezed, and I froze for a moment before realising the trappers hadn't heard him. 'I only arrived this morning.'

'Nevertheless. Without a licence you'll have to pay the fee—every time I see you.'

'You misunderstand me, sir,' I adjusted hastily. 'My ... er ... husband has the licence.'

'And where is he?'

'Working, of course.' I felt the rats stir, building heat uncomfortably on my legs.

The soldiers glanced at one another, and smiled as if they had known all along what I would say. 'What kind of husband would leave a pretty young wife like you all alone?'

'Indeed,' said the second, still smiling in a predatory manner. 'And in such a dangerous place, too. It breaks a man's heart.'

'I'm not alone,' I said sharply, feeling my breath catch in my throat and willing it not to give away my sudden crawling fear. 'My maidservant will be back with fresh water at any moment.'

'Then you'd best pay us before her return,' said the second. He had an extremely obnoxious waxed moustache, and it twitched in anticipation like a living thing. 'Who knows what she'll think of her mistress entertaining two military men.'

'Don't be absurd. My husband carries our money, naturally.'

'Naturally,' said the mustachioed soldier, stepping closer.

My Probability Parasol was inside the tent. I had no means of defending myself without giving away everything about my situation, and betraying the remains of the Scobie family. My heart ticked hard, but it wasn't my heart they were interested in.

The second soldier stroked his rifle fondly and stepped to my other side, trapping me neatly. My mind blanked out with terror, and I forgot to be enraged at their insolence. My sense of superiority abandoned me completely, and I was naked.

I heard a soft click from inside the tent as Patrick loaded his gun. If I didn't think of something, the leading soldier would get his excuse to use his weapon on my friends, and on the Scobie children. The mustachioed soldier took my naked hand, holding it tightly as I tried to jerk away. For a second, I was so frightened I wanted Patrick to fire his pistol and save me. But I was still British, still a Muchamore, and still myself.

'Help,' I whispered, tucking in my chin so I was facing my own feet. 'Quickly now, boys and girls.'

My rats sprang out of my pockets and leapt onto the tall black boots of the soldiers, biting and clawing with all their might. One scrambled up to the mustachioed man's face and bit him in the cheek, leaving blistered pawprints with every over-heated step.

The men yelped and hit at their faces and chests. My rats dodged them, ripping the scarlet fabric with their sharp claws.

'Call them off!' yelled the first.

'Enough,' I said, trembling. 'Get down.'

The rats obeyed and gathered at my feet, glaring at the soldiers with red eyes.

'What are they?' asked the leading soldier, raising his rifle to point it awkwardly at my feet.

'I understand your concern about my licence,' I said, smoothing down my skirts with exaggerated care so I didn't expose the frightened tears threatening to spill from my eyes. 'If you gentlemen return tomorrow morning, I'm sure you'll be perfectly satisfied with my payment of the fine, and of course by seeing my husband's licence with your own eyes. And my husband, who knows how to protect me.'

'You'll pay us,' repeated the mustachioed soldier, holding his hand to his wounded cheek.

'Naturally.'

They eyed my rats, who bounced with anticipation of another attack.

'Very well,' said the first, and walked away. After a pause, the second soldier followed him.

'Oh, excellent,' said Patrick from behind me. 'Now we need to steal someone's licence tonight. And money, too.'

'It should be easy to find Emmeline a husband, don't you think?' said Matilda, keeping her voice low. 'Let's pick someone bald and stooped and wealthy as a lord.'

My hands shook harder than before, and I sat down in the dirt to recover my composure. I still felt the mustachioed man's fingers squeezing mine, and wished I had enough water to wash away the sensation of being utterly powerless. The protection of my name was finally used up, but as long as I was free I could still save Jem and Arabella and Mrs Scobie. Now that I knew the kind of men Mrs Scobie faced, I was more determined than ever to help her.

The widow emerged and sat beside me, wrapping her arm tightly around my shoulders. 'We'll fight a pack of those limeys in court today,' she said in a voice rough with tears. 'And we'll win. Besides, that beau of yours would never have let them touch you.'

I smiled shakily at her, and didn't correct her error. 'Back in London I have a brother and sister, barely a season older than your young ones.'

She met my eye with a smile, then gasped. 'Why, you're Emmeline Muchamore!'

Chapter Twenty-Three

I stiffened. 'Whatever made you think that?' I asked.

'Your face, that's what. Excuse me, it was a surprise. Never fear, I'll not give any redcoat the satisfaction of taking you, or our bushranger friend.'

My heart was oddly calm. 'I told you, my name is Ellen Miller. The idea that I or either of my companions might be a bushranger is simply preposterous.'

'Mills,' she smiled. 'You said you were Miss Mills.'

'So I did.' For a moment there I'd remembered how to react like I was respectable. Perhaps it was the last time that would ever happen. 'How did you recognise me?'

'There's posters up all along the Eureka Flat road. I use them to help the children with their letters.'

'Has everyone seen them?'

'Some have and some haven't, but I'll wager you're not the only escapees in Ballarat. Keep your heads down and there are few here who'd say a word, or even notice who you are. These days it's those British redcoats and rich men against everyone else.'

'But I am British.'

'People already know you're with us, or they'd never have told me to look for Mr O'Connell.'

'I hope you're right.'

Little Aline stood at the tent entrance and asked to come out. Her voice cracked, and she self-consciously patted her tangled curls—a nervous habit inherited from her mother.

'Not until it's time to face the judge,' said Mrs Scobie, and sighed.

I felt awful for the girl trapped in our stifling tent, and hoped I could presume on our growing acquaintance in order to help her. Before we went to court, I needed to know the whole sad story so no surprise showed in my face. 'What happened last night? Why are you in danger from the British?'

'My Jim was celebrating with a newly-arrived friend,' she said quietly, looking at our dying fire. 'It was growing late but they were ready for a top-up. They went to the Eureka Hotel, since the lights were still on. The proprietor was there, Mr Bentley, but he wouldn't let them in. He just sat in the light sipping his own drink and laughing at them for not being English, like him and his friends. And like the trappers, which is what matters in this town. So Jim fair beat down the door, as an angry man might do when he's guilty of nothing but being a Scot.' She sighed and I bit my lip, knowing the worst of the story was yet to come. 'The men inside responded rage to rage, and before they fully knew their own minds Jim was lying dead under a tree not a mile from the hotel. His friend managed to get away. Perhaps the night would have ended differently if he'd stayed, for better or worse.

'My Jim deserves a clout on the ear for being a poor fool in his cups, but he didn't deserve that. Sam—that's the pot boy—saw Mr Bentley heading out with a shovel not long after the deed was done, and there's no doubt what that was for. So Sam excused himself from the British gent he'd been serving, and ran and told me everything. A man doesn't secretly bury another unless his conscience is black, pure black.

'If the court is forced to face an innocent man's grieving wife and children, they may find the heart to see the truth. Otherwise my Jim's just one more poor drunk, and not even an English drunk. Unfortunately, Bentley knows Jim was married. By now he'll know we're not at home, nor with our friends. He'll stop at nothing to keep the truth buried with Jim.' She bit her lip. 'So we hide, until it's over.'

'I'm sorry,' I whispered. 'I didn't know.'

'Lord bless me,' she said with a laugh. 'And what could a wee thing like you have done to stop it? It's enough that you're keeping me company, and not putting on airs.'

'How can I put on airs like this?' I gestured at my ruined clothes.

'None of us look our best,' she said, patting my hand as if I was another of her children—some part of me wished I was. Unlike my own mother, she was shouting the injustice of her husband's death for all to hear. Lower-class folk didn't have to pretend they were perfect. I envied them that. 'But it's easy to know you're Quality, all the same.' She left me to my confusion and saw to her children.

Patrick stumped back from fetching water. He took one look at my face and made more tea, which I sipped gratefully. It horrified me that 'British' had become a byword for corruption and violence, but I'd seen the soldiers for myself. I shuddered at the memory of their touch.

Patrick sat beside me in companionable silence, then suddenly said, 'My father got the idea for our tunnel from his goldfield experience, and I don't mean the mines.'

He seemed terribly pleased, and I didn't know why. I waited for him to go on.

'No one digs a tunnel system like a frustrated miner,' he explained. 'Father once told me about tunnels linking tents to the diggings, dozens of them. It's a wonder half the tents here don't simply collapse into the honeycomb of secret passageways.'

I put down the hot tin mug. 'You mean we may be able to sneak into the diggings when no one else is there?'

'Precisely. We should do it tonight, before your admirers return.'

I made a face.

'And if we don't,' he said, 'let's fly away. I should never have let you come here. Or Matilda, for that matter.'

Matilda harrumphed, but she had a wariness about her I hadn't seen before, not even when she was playing the poor savage at the Cremorne Gardens. The trappers were powerful enough and low enough to do worse than either one of her abandoned fiancés. We needed to help Mrs Scobie, find gold, and get out of town before the powder keg exploded.

'It's time,' said Mrs Scobie, straightening up as she emerged from the tent. Her two children followed her, red-faced from a doomed attempt at scrubbing. 'Thank you for your shelter, but it's time for us to face Ballarat's court—such as it is.'

'We're coming with you,' said Patrick in a flat voice.

Mrs Scobie opened her mouth to object, but closed it again without a word. I took Aline's hand, and we followed the flame-coloured crown of Mrs Scobie's head through the tents and over dirt and gravel roads to the cluster of buildings that made up the government camp. The crowd of soldiers outside the courthouse waited in orderly lines, their coats and buttons gleaming. A few ragged men waited on one side, shifting their feet. Half a dozen wealthier men stood opposite, crowned in tall black silk. I was willing to bet every single one was British born, and was surprised to find I despised them.

'You've done enough,' Mrs Scobie whispered. 'Leave, before someone recognises you.'

'They're not looking at us,' Patrick pointed out.

It was true. Every eye slid across us and fixed on Mrs Scobie. She lifted her head higher still and marched with her children to stand facing the blank bricks of the police courthouse. I wondered idly if a gaol had been built yet. Presumably in this country, a gaol would be one of the first buildings to be required—that, and a pub. The ban on alcohol didn't mean a thing, except that the trappers could 'confiscate' whatever they found. I wanted to despise those around me for drinking every night, but what else was there to do?

We waited in silence. Aline sniffed loudly but didn't break her fine posture to wipe at her nose. At last a man emerged from the courthouse. His dark clothes were slightly wrinkled in the heat, but the set of his shoulders was square. He had the look of a judge about him, and I felt myself straighten in automatic respect—and fear. I was a criminal twice over now, so the law was no longer my protector, but my accuser. His jaw was heavily outlined in thick sideburns. A British judge, for a British accused. It didn't bode well in this upside-down land.

He stopped in front of Mrs Scobie. 'Are you a witness?'

'No, sir,' she said, and her high voice carried clearly to everyone present. 'I am the widow. And these are my children, Aline and Duncan Scobie.'

There was an intake of breath, and the few ragged friends of James Scobie shifted as if they'd been tossed by a strong wind. The youngest clenched his fists, and did not unclench them. It was well known that Mrs Scobie had drawn on rare courage to appear.

'I am Police Magistrate Dewes. A grievous accusation has been made, and it will be answered.'

He signalled to someone, and they entered the courthouse and assisted in bringing out a far smaller man. His clothes were dirty and dishevelled, but he exchanged a look of understanding with Dewes that appeared to reassure him.

This, then, was the hotelier Mr Bentley. He was slender as a young girl, but his fidgeting hands were large. He cracked and popped his knuckles loudly in the quiet. I looked for evidence of murder in his eyes, as if sin was a visible thing. If it had been that simple, I realised, I'd be in the Female Factory by now.

'Mr Bentley, you are accused of the murder of the miner James Scobie,' said Magistrate Dewes. 'How do you plead?'

'Not guilty, sir,' he shouted, making Duncan jump. His eyes darted left and right, brightening with hope at the poor showing of miners—that, and the rigid lines of soldiers loyal to Britain and to wealth. He smirked, and I wanted to hurl my parasol right at him. Mrs Scobie drew herself up to her greatest height, not quite reaching the magistrate's shoulder. She was still taller than me.

Magistrate Dewes looked over her head, calling for a Mr Johnson. Johnson's red hands marked him as the pot boy who had warned the remaining members of the Scobie family to hide in case of further injustice. He shuffled forward, wide-eyed, and delivered his statement to Mrs Scobie as if she was the only person present. His story was the same tale Mrs Scobie had told me: a drunken Scobie was beaten to death and then secretly buried by Mr Bentley.

The magistrate questioned him thoroughly, making him repeat the same details over and over again. When he began to stutter, Dewes finally let him return to his equally ragged friends, and lifted his voice again. 'Is there a man here to corroborate this story?'

He waited in stony silence. 'If there is a man here who stood with Mr Johnson and can confirm this tale, let him speak.'

'There is!' Mrs Scobie shrieked, pointing at a well-dressed gentleman on the opposite side to the diggers and Mr Johnson. 'Mr Verne! He saw it all!'

I followed her gaze and immediately felt my breath catch in my throat. Mr Verne's tall silk hat gleamed as if it was newly polished. He smiled stiffly, and smoothed down his jacket with infinite care. His face flushed red, shining with sweat—but I felt my knees weaken. How could a man have such an effect before he said a word?

'Mr Verne,' said Magistrate Dewes. 'Please approach the courthouse so you may tell us what you know.'

He walked with elaborate care and stood by the magistrate. I caught a glimpse of a shining waistcoat, and realised he wore an entire vest of beaten gold. So that was why I was suddenly unable to think straight. I shook my head, clearing the magical allure as well as I could. Gold was notorious for causing all in the vicinity to find the wearer more attractive. More than one soldier shook himself roughly just as I did. I was affected by another magic too: the brass of my heart warned me that Mr Verne was quaking inwardly, facing what he believed was the most dangerous decision of his life. I willed him to tell the truth. His voice would change everything.

Mr Verne cringed away from Mrs Scobie's set face and the pale faces of her children. Taking a step backward, he collided with the brick wall and coughed to hide his embarrassment.

Magistrate Dewes asked him to say in his own words what he had witnessed, if anything.

'Nothing but a few Scottish men in their cups smashing Mr Bentley's hotel door,' he answered, and I gasped as my heart vented steam at the brazen lie, scalding my shoulders and neck despite my corset-back safety valve. I saw several soldiers smile wolfishly, and wondered how much of Mr Verne's fear of his friends was justified.

'Very well,' said Magistrate Dewes heavily. 'Since there are no other witnesses, I am left to choose between Mr Bentley's word and the word of his man, Mr Johnson. The path of justice is clear: one man's word alone is insufficient to doom another. Mr Bentley, you are free to go.'

The reaction of the crowd was instantaneous: Mr Verne's friends came forward to clap him and Mr Bentley on the back; the soldiers straightened in misplaced pride; the few who came in support of Mrs Scobie melted away as if they had never come.

Duncan clenched his small fists and stoically ignored the tears running silently down his smooth cheeks. Mrs Scobie swayed, but remained upright.

Aline chewed on something, and I realised she had torn a small piece from her dress. She turned her head and spat the miniature missile with expert aim at Mr Verne's smooth back. The tiny impact made him turn and meet her furious blue eyes. Unobserved from the back of the crowd, I saw no anger on Mr Verne's face—only shame. I wished I could aim a projectile with such subtle accuracy.

Chapter Twenty-Four

We half-carried Mrs Scobie back across the Eureka Flat toward our tent, but when we drew near she shook us off. 'I have other friends here,' she said. 'The damage is done and there's no more danger, so I can stay in my own tent safely now. I'm sorry to have brought you into our troubles.'

'Stay with us,' Patrick begged, cut to the heart that he'd found a woman he couldn't save. 'We'll think of something, I promise.'

She shook her head and smiled slightly. 'My friends will take care of us. We diggers stick together.'

'We're diggers too!' Matilda protested. 'Why else would we risk coming here?'

'Of course you are, dear,' she said gently. 'But it's early days yet. Not to put too fine a point on it, but my other friends have considerably more food.'

I blushed, but there was little more to say. We hugged and kissed the children, and let them go. The walk back to our tent and carriage was a silent one. None of us felt like either cooking or eating dinner, so we sat on the dirt and replayed the day in our minds. I wished we'd never come. So much for my newfound purpose in life. So much for freedom.

The following morning Matilda and I emerged from the tent to find Patrick pacing back and forth in front of the carriage, with his father's pistol clenched in one hand. 'We find him,' he said. 'Mr Verne. We find him, and make him tell that magistrate the truth.'

I felt the weight of despair drop from my shoulders, and agreed at once. In the back of my mind, a voice reminded me that our entire goal was to get gold and get out. I quashed it, and wholeheartedly accepted the more dangerous fate before us. Matilda's face brightened in a mirror of my own, and we set off with consciences eased to find the Eureka Hotel, stopping just once to ask directions from a bone-thin woman with a smudged face.

'What do you want the Eureka for?' she asked, and I was shocked to realise she was no older than I was, despite the squalling baby on her hip.

'We're finding a liar, and making him an honest man,' said Patrick.

'Oh, you're that lot!' she said. 'Mrs Scobie's convict friends.'

We looked at one another, and Matilda acknowledged that we were. So much for lying low. I found I liked being brave. Too much of my life had been wasted pretending to be happy and good.

'Down the track then, past the yellow pump and up the road when you find it. You can't miss the hotel, but don't expect Mr Bentley to let you in.'

Patrick jerked a thumb at me. 'She's British, technically.'

'Well, then!' said the girl. 'If you see Bentley, give him a shovel in the face for me. Oh, and by the way, Seamus Keneally has long since gone back to Clunes.'

It seemed all Ballarat knew every particular of our business. Given that most of our business was illegal, that wasn't ideal. However, it seemed the population intended to keep us safe—for now.

We walked on, interrupted more than once by an offer of tea or damper or a muttered thank you. My stomach growled, and I accepted the impromptu breakfast gratefully. People flinched when Matilda or I spoke, and I realised they were conditioned to fear a British accent. Everything in Ballarat was twisted, and I longed to make it right—for Britain.

The girl's directions were simple enough to follow despite the goat tracks in all directions. We turned a corner and saw the Eureka Hotel; a wooden structure with its name written in yellow paint above the first-floor windows.

Patrick glanced at me for a guide to the etiquette of the situation and I nodded at him to follow my lead. If it had been any use, I'd have advised him to look less Irish. Matilda's disdainful glare marked her as British despite her dark skin. We smoothed our wrinkled skirts as well as possible.

I saw a small group of diggers turned away from the hotel, and decided to rely on sheer bravado. It was just like being at home. Luckily I had years of practice faking wealth. I swanned inside the door without acknowledging the men standing guard there. Patrick and Matilda swept inside with me before the men knew what was happening.

It was dark inside, with a low bar against one wall, a desk piled with papers and pencils against the other, and rough-hewn furniture in haphazard lines between.

Mr Bentley was nowhere to be seen, which didn't surprise me. He'd looked like a man who knew when to lay low. Mr Verne, however, lay half-slumped on a table with three empty tankards at his elbow.

'Drunk,' said Patrick under his breath. 'That may help us.'

'If it gives him courage,' I said, despising all Mr Verne stood for despite the lure of his gold, 'but I suspect it'll take more than a few drinks in his case.'

Matilda and I stood opposite the drink-flushed Mr Verne and curtseyed prettily. His gold waistcoat was clearly visible, and my silly heart jumped at it again. I set my jaw and hoped I didn't disgrace us. He looked up with a fixed grin. I almost swooned at the wave of whiskey breath and shame. Funnily enough, the gold no longer affected me.

'Quick, Emmeline,' hissed Matilda. 'Show some ankle, and he'll be ours for the taking.'

Mr Verne's brow furrowed with the intense concentration of the inebriated. 'Do I know you from somewhere?'

My heart skipped a beat. 'Yes! You saw us at court. That's where you know us from. Not anywhere else.'

His eyes cleared, and my heart resumed its rhythm.

'If you're here to beg me to condemn Bentley,' he said, 'you're wasting your time. I said my piece, and that's that.'

Patrick snatched out his pistol and cocked it before I took a breath. 'I'm asking you to reconsider.'

'No,' said the man, but he froze.

'Tell the truth,' said Patrick, 'or face death this instant.'

Mr Verne grew sober abruptly. I saw a flash of real regret in his eyes, but perhaps all that gold was still creating a more likeable illusion. He held out his hands, palms upward. 'Would you kill an unarmed man?'

'An unarmed coward? Perhaps.' Patrick lowered his weapon, but his arm was stiff with tension. I glanced at Matilda, wondering if she'd realised what Patrick intended. Her eyes were bright, and I gave up on finding sanity there. I hadn't realised the practicalities of our heroic quest for justice. 'How about tomorrow?'

Mr Verne's face was stiff with tension. Fear and shame battled within him, but he looked Patrick up and down and saw no real threat—the fool. Instead he slowly pushed his drinks away. He'd found another way to make the shame stop. A better way, or so he thought. 'You're serious? You mean to duel with me?'

'That, or hunt you down and shoot you like a dog.'

'Very well.' His voice was steady, and his mouth was set. 'I'll meet you out front at noon.'

'Dawn,' said Patrick. 'We have other plans for noon.'

The man nodded. 'Dawn then. Pistols, I take it. One shot each?'

'Yes. Unless you plan to insult the truth a second time.'

'Don't do this,' I said, sick to my stomach as the situation grew even worse. We'd been brave for less than an hour and one of us was going to die for it. 'Patrick, what if you're killed?'

Mr Verne looked at me for the first time. 'I'm genuinely sorry, miss.'

'So you don't need to duel,' I said quickly, frantically trying to think of a saner plan. 'Everyone's fine. Just tell the magistrate what you saw, and we'll leave you alone.'

'No,' said Patrick, and he still trembled with anger. 'We duel.'

'I'm afraid I lack a second,' said Mr Verne, ignoring me. 'My only friends are soldiers. They'd be expelled from the service if they were involved in an illegal fight.'

'Why am I not surprised you don't have a single honourable friend?' said Patrick. 'If you have the guts to stand, you'll not need a second to stand for you.'

'And who will stand for you?' he asked.

'Other than my sister, my family is elsewhere. You and I will both have to stand alone.'

Mr Verne bowed his head. 'You're better off than I am, in that case. I have no family at all.'

'Then no one will miss you when you're dead,' said Patrick.

'True enough.' He looked blearily at his empty drinks, and waved for another. So much for British pride. Not for the first time, my stomach turned because of the actions of one of my own countrymen. 'Until tomorrow, then.'

'I look forward to it.'

Patrick and Matilda and I looked at one another, and left the hotel to walk back to our tent. Patrick walked with an easy stride, while Matilda was frowning with such concentration she barely knew where she was placing her feet.

'Wait—' I said to Patrick, catching up on his words. 'What do you mean your sister is here?'

He didn't respond. His eyes were overly bright. I stepped carefully away from him and his gun. 'Matilda? What did he mean, calling me his sister?'

'Not you!' she said, as if the fact was obvious. 'I'm his sister, truly.'

'You can't be serious!'

'Oh, but I am. Patrick and I met a year ago, in Bearbrass. I was set upon by two so-called "gentlemen" who took offence to the fact I was wearing an especially nice silk. Presumably they prefer their natives slurring and dressed in rags.'

I didn't know what to say, so I kept quiet. Having seen Matilda in rags, I knew she had a class that went beyond her dress. I remembered seeing her without a stitch on, and blushed again. Luckily she was in the middle of her tale and didn't appear to notice.

'Patrick saw what was happening and rode up on this fantastic white stallion, yelling like a madman. They fled, and Patrick escorted me home. Unfortunately, he wasn't quite quick enough to save my dress. My skirts were badly torn and my arms and face were bleeding too much to hide. That, and my fists. So my parents soon learned all that had happened, and all that could have happened, if not for Patrick's aid.

'I'm their only child, the only child they were able to have. They didn't let me out alone for weeks afterwards—their goal ever since has been to see me respectably married to whomever would take me. They each thanked Patrick in their own way. Father gave him the hot air balloon and carriage. He's infamous for them now, although fortunately Father is more than a little absent-minded, and hasn't put two and two together about the ballooning bushranger. Mother doesn't have her own things, but she has something he doesn't have: her people. She made contact for the first time since I was a child, and the elders chose to reward Patrick by making him one of us. They adopted him.

'We really are brother and sister, and Patrick has accepted his adoption as fully as he accepted the role of bushranging aeronaut. Why else would we be so casual with one another?'

'So you and Patrick aren't … oh dear.' My mind whirled, seeing every familiarity between them in an utterly different light. 'I owe you an apology.'

She waved it off, laughing at my discomfort. 'I'll not challenge you to a duel, never fear.'

So Patrick wasn't living in sin after all, and nor was Matilda, despite all I'd thought. Matilda prattled on about the continuing water shortage as if I'd never thought so ill of her. I found it terribly difficult to concentrate on her concern about the lack of rain. Knowing all three of us were unattached—Patrick, Matilda and I—made me feel very peculiar indeed.

Chapter Twenty-Five

One of our neighbours let us hide in a shallow hole beneath her tent until the soldiers had come and gone. She gave us some bread too, and we ate it gratefully. 'If you don't have a licence, that pair will come back every day until you pay the fine,' she warned us.

'Excellent,' said Matilda. 'I hope they wear out their boots.'

'They're not stupid,' said the woman. 'Sooner or later they'll find you. I hope they don't find me hiding you when that day comes.'

We took the hint and went back to our own miniscule piece of land. I tried without success to dissuade Patrick from his duel. A second death was hardly going to make up for the original murder. When I considered the possibility that he might get shot, I wanted to scream at him for being such a moron. I'd grown peculiarly fond of him—an Irish man. The blatant injustice of Ballarat was affecting my mind.

Since it was clear screaming wouldn't help, I asked to see his gun. I went inside the tent and examined each part of it carefully, paying special attention to the round lead balls that could rip through a man's chest. Long ago, I'd begun to wonder if tin was actually far from unique in its ability to understand speech. Perhaps all metals understood us perfectly, and were simply unable or unwilling to speak. One way or another, I was about to find out.

When I was sure Patrick wasn't coming in after me, I took off my corset and outer clothing. Keeping an eye on our improvised curtain, I opened the access panel in my sternum, holding Patrick's lead projectiles so they touched the ticking mechanism of my heart. I felt a fool, but if it helped save Patrick it was worth it.

'Patrick is my defender,' I told them. 'He's fighting for his life tomorrow, and he must win or Matilda and I will be alone in the world. The man fighting him wears a golden vest, and we need him to stay alive so he can testify. Please, if you are able, hit the vest. I do not want Patrick to become a killer, but if you can save both his life and his honour, I would be very—'

I heard a gasp, and grabbed a handful of my chemise to conceal my exposed front boiler. It was no use, as a violent jet of steam immediately erupted from my back. My secret was out.

'Emmeline,' said Matilda. 'What—you—your chest!'

'Come in quickly! Draw the curtain behind you.'

She did so, and knelt beside me in a meringue of skirts, round-eyed. 'Who did that to you?'

'I chose it.'

'Why?'

'For science, of course! For Britain.'

She shook her head slowly. 'How wonderful!'

'What, really?' I was more flummoxed than she was. 'You like it?'

'Does it hurt?'

'Not at all.' I took a deep breath to embrace what might be my only opportunity to show off my true heart without eliciting screams of horror. She was still smiling, so I explained the mechanism to her piece by piece—the silver valves and tubing; the segmented brass that expanded and contracted with the steam and then condensation from the twinned engines; the layers within layers of silver and brass and silver again.

'It's … brilliant,' she said at last.

I felt as if a blockage in one of the inner arteries had suddenly broken free, letting my blood flow cleanly for the first time. 'Promise me you won't tell Patrick. Or anyone else. Promise me!'

'All right,' she said doubtfully. 'I promise. Um … why did you have a handful of Patrick's shot pressed to your brass bits?'

'To help him tomorrow. Metal likes me. It might do as I ask.'

'Ah! Do you think we can win? I was hoping to drug Patrick so he missed it.'

'Much better idea!' I said delightedly. 'What will you drug him with?'

'That's the flaw in my plan. No drugs, and no money to buy some even if I knew where to go. Not even Godfrey's Cordial. And I don't know how much to use anyway.'

'Magic it is, then. But it's experimental at best. Although—'

'What?'

'I know things, sometimes. Yesterday I could sense without a doubt that Mr Verne was lying. He knows very well that Mr Bentley killed and buried Mr Scobie. I didn't speak up, which makes me just as guilty as he is.'

She snorted. 'Everyone there knew it. We didn't need magic. Now stop fussing and let's get you ready for your dinner with the Southwells.'

I made a face. 'Must I?'

'You must. If we're to buy a licence, we'll need at least thirty shillings, and so far we haven't a farthing. Patrick can keep his head in a duel, but only you can keep us from getting either ourselves or someone else arrested tomorrow.'

'Will you help me dress?'

'Of course. You'll be wearing the blue silk, I hope.'

'Naturally.'

'Must we get a licence, really?' she said dreamily as she laced me up. 'You know the money just goes to the British, supposedly to keep the law. What an insult.'

'I don't like it any more than you do. Let's deal with Mr Verne and with my so-called admirers first. Then we can try to find a way to change the entire colonial system.'

'I like the way you think!'

My own words shocked me. Everything I stood for was the same—goodness, and kindness, and fairness—but the heroic British had become the villains. It still hurt to think of it, but of course the power of Britain as a whole could never be changed by the actions of runaways and criminals like us. All I could do was stand up for the Scobie family, and pray the larger world changed on its own. In the meantime, I begged God to save Patrick's life. At least I knew He could understand human speech, whether He chose to act on our behalf or not.

Patrick spent all afternoon cleaning his gun and singing Irish songs. I marvelled that I'd ever thought he and Matilda were in love. They were far too different in every way.

He sang very well, with a haunting bass that I knew I'd never forget. The gift of song was one thing they had in common, and I hoped to hear them sing a duet one day.

Matilda fussed over me, tightening my corset and curls and brushing my crinolines and silk free of dirt. I didn't speak much, finding myself hushed by the knowledge that there was one person in the world who knew everything about me—and seemed to like it. My family had accepted me because they were my family, and Lizzie had accepted me because she knew perfectly well that I'd be done for without her aid. Matilda was different.

She spent an hour scrubbing at the stencilled numbers on the back of my dress again, and we assured each other they were as good as invisible. Together we repaired several small tears, and carefully pinned my lopsided hair up under my equally lopsided bonnet.

Without a looking glass, I relied on Matilda's approval, and the loan of her gloves. She nodded at me, looking smug, so I concluded I was as presentable as it was possible to be in this wild town.

Patrick and Matilda faced the last scraps of stale damper for dinner, and I faced an elegant repast. Too bad we couldn't trade places. I hoped I could steal both food and coins to keep us from starving—or worse. It seemed I'd become a true thief, or so I hoped. I prayed I'd get away with it this time. Patrick hadn't noticed the coal I'd pilfered from his balloon, so perhaps I had a natural talent.

The Southwells's tent was simply enormous, with dozens of lanterns shining through the canvas, making it glow like a vision of heaven. Their horses had another tent several feet away, with their carriage resting on its struts between the two. To my surprise, the main tent appeared to have a stone chimney. I walked around it slowly, and saw a dozen Georgian windows sewn into the fabric, with a roll of fabric furled above the upper sill of each one. Inside several fine ladies lined up to dance with the same number of gentlemen, carefully arranged around the steel struts holding up the roof.

It seemed forever since the ball at the governor's house and I felt suddenly shy, wishing Matilda and I could have entered together. Instead I walked in unescorted, blushing hotly with my own impropriety. Mrs Southwell greeted me without any suggestion of horror, and I was grateful for the more relaxed antipodean manners. She immediately introduced me to a Mr Gordon Verne. I barely registered the name before being rendered speechless by that hateful face.

'We've met,' he said, rubbing the red chin of a man who shaved in the afternoon.

I curtseyed desperately, hoping I wouldn't have to shake hands with the man who planned to kill my friend the following morning.

'Excellent,' said Mrs Southwell, already looking elsewhere. 'Poor Miss Mills lacks an escort.' She swanned away, leaving me with Mr Verne.

'Do you dance, Miss Mills?' he asked, holding out his arm.

I stared at the green baize wall, wishing Patrick was right about the tunnel system. If only the entire enormous tent would collapse into the ground, taking me with it.

'Please,' I said. 'Don't fight tomorrow. I beg you.'

He sniffed. 'I'd bet my vest your young broganeer won't be game enough to appear.'

I opened my mouth to assert the opposite, but I had a better idea. It seemed Mr Verne planned to reclaim his honour by showing up to the duel, and his ignorance of Patrick's convictions was propping up his sad store of courage. 'Do you really? Would you honestly bet your waistcoat—all that gold—that Mr O'Connell won't dare to face you?'

'Yes,' he said gravely. 'I will.'

'Then I'll take your hand, and gladly. Because Mr O'Connell will fight you tomorrow, and what's more, he'll live to profit from your rash promise.'

'I look forward to it.'

'For the first time, so do I—I think.'

I jumped as a gunshot marked the end of another day on the goldfields. Mr Verne's lips tightened in fear for an instant.

Before I was forced to make idle conversation, a young lady struck up a passable waltz on the grand piano standing by the stone hearth. Mr Verne bowed to me, and I felt my stomach flip over. Stupid gold and its attraction magic. I hoped it hadn't just fooled me into making a bet on Patrick's life.

Chapter Twenty-Six

Mr Verne was civil enough when he was in company. He danced with careful deliberation and passable skill. My Superior-Inferior Heels thumped softly on the dirt floor, but when we swung past the piano the sharp heels gave a hollow tap. Patrick was right after all: there was a hidden tunnel that opened beside the room's back wall. I resolved to discover, somehow, where it led.

I was unable to disentangle myself from Mr Verne's well-muscled arms until the impromptu dancing was swept aside and dinner was set out. Even then, Mrs Southwell sat me beside Mr Verne, putting a pouting Grace Southwell on my other side. I wasn't sure if I was meant to be courted by Mr Verne, or if Mrs Southwell was using me to make her daughter jealous.

Whatever she intended, that was the effect. Ignoring the simpering smiles shooting across me to Mr Verne, I helped myself to pea soup and fresh salad, roast beef and buttery sponge cake with an enthusiasm I didn't need to fake. I slipped so much into my pockets I feared I would appear excessively thick-hipped when dinner was over. Society might have been my prison in Belgravia, but I still missed the food. My newfound freedom had its downside.

Unlike most tents, this one was equipped with a retiring room for ladies to rest. When dinner was cleared away and the dancing was about to begin again, I excused myself, reasoning that I'd be alone in the next room and might be able to find a second tunnel entrance without being observed.

The retiring room was swamped in more baize and in bright yellow silk. I took the liberty of unrolling the canvas shutter above the open window—it seemed canvas curtains could be picturesque in the right circumstances after all—and had my attention caught by an elegant watercolour sewn into place on the fabric wall. It was a country scene in England's sweet hills, and I wished I could step inside. The artist used thick strokes, flawing the art and making me nostalgic for Mother's sure hands.

'Beautiful, isn't it?' said Miss Southwell.

'Oh,' I said, jerking my guilty fingers away from the golden frame. 'Very nice.'

'You're too kind.'

'It's one of yours?' I said, falling easily into the familiar conversation.

She fluttered her eyelashes at me—an effect that was entirely wasted—and held out her small hand in friendship. I paused as my inner voice called attention to her silver bracelet. My heart ticked so loudly no ordinary girl could have ignored the sound. Fortunately Miss Southwell was far more interested in herself than anyone else.

I took her hand, just touching the bracelet with one finger. The clasp opened for me as if it had never been fastened at all, and the bracelet slipped into my palm in a cool pile of links. I closed my hand and put it in my pocket as naturally as possible. The silver wanted to be stolen. Interesting.

She smiled. 'We're one lady short of a full set. Will you join us?'

'In a moment. I feel a little ill.'

She pouted at me, but when I pointed out that Mr Verne would be waiting for her she left me alone.

I tucked the silver bracelet into a cake-filled pocket of my skirt, and hoped it would be of use—and that the Southwells didn't realise they had a thief in their midst. Swallowing unexpected tears of shame, I paced up and down the small space, looking for a secret panel in the floor. The music from behind the partition was very loud.

It was no use. The only tunnel was in the main room of the tent, by the wall. It was mere inches away, and quite impossible to get to.

Or was it? I slowly, slowly pushed against the canvas, bending it outwards until it almost touched the piano. After anchoring it with handfuls of loose soil on both sides, I took off my gloves and felt around in the dirt until my fingers touched a thin rope.

Pushing the canvas a little farther into the main ballroom, I tugged up the hatch and quickly stepped inside, closing the hidden door behind me to let the canvas wall fall back into place.

The hatch muffled the music, and I was once again standing in the dark. There was nothing for it: I fumbled my way down a wooden ladder and walked slowly through the tunnel, hoping against hope that riches awaited me at the other end.

The earth smelled of Mother's greenhouse, and my eyes adjusted enough that I could walk relatively quickly. It was a far grander tunnel than the one at the O'Connells' hut—taller, and at least twice as long. I stumbled over the stub of a wax candle, and wondered how many people knew of the tunnel's location. Evidently the Southwells had pitched their tent over it on purpose—perhaps their servants had dug it out when the goldrush began. Having shaken Miss Southwell's hand, I knew she'd played no part in the labour.

I held my hands out in front of me, and came to a dead end. It was all for nothing! Unable to give up, I reached above my head and found more wooden rungs. This time, the way out was in two sections. I climbed half the ladder at my side, stepped across onto the upper section, and pushed open a heavy wooden trapdoor, which hit the dirt of the outside world and threw up a cloud of dust. My choking coughs sounded loud enough to wake the dead, but I was helpless. Even the adjusting valves on my heart couldn't clear my throat.

Peering up, I saw no one and nothing moving. There was no grass and no living thing, only string fences and an abandoned wooden frame hanging over a dark gash in the earth. I'd reached the goldfields at last, and my heart was ready to burst from my chest in excitement. If no one had heard me cough, I was most definitely alone.

Slowly, carefully, I pulled myself up, wincing as a long streak of dirt marked the front of my dress. Somehow, I didn't think the Southwells would be inviting me to dinner a second time.

I crouched on the ground, looking all around for any sign of danger. Soldiers patrolled in the distance, but they were no threat to me despite the waxing moon. I half-crawled to the broken-down wooden frame, noticing the signs of an abandoned steam pump at one end, and stood up slowly, keeping to the shadows.

This was the night I would restore the Muchamore family fortune.

Chapter Twenty-Seven

I turned in a slow circle, wondering where to start looking first. There wasn't time to wander about, not with Patrick duelling in the morning.

Tick!

There was gold directly in front of me, the sensation was as clear as if I could see it. I laughed aloud. Out of millions of people in Australia, I was the only one who could simply stand on a goldfield and know exactly where the gold was hidden.

Tick! Tick!

I walked toward it in a straight line. The ground was very rough, and my crinoline wheels bounced all over the place. One of them filled with dust and stopped turning altogether, but I didn't care. Jem and Arabella and Mother were going to be rich—richer than ever before! And so was Patrick, and so was Matilda and her friend William, and the Scobie family. And so was I. My heart beat loudly and I didn't care. In my excitement, I forgot all about the patrolling soldiers.

Tick!

'Halt!' came a shout. 'Who goes there?'

I dropped flat, pressing my favourite silk dress into the dirt.

'Identify yourself!'

Turning my head to the side, I saw two soldiers, their faces orange in the light of the lanterns they carried. Somehow I didn't think they'd believe me if I said I'd accidentally wandered onto the goldfields from the Southwells's ball.

I crawled back toward the tunnel, moving along the ground like a snake. My beautiful dress had to be sacrificed for the greater good. The tunnel wasn't far. All I had to do was get back inside and I'd be safe. I willed my heart to tick quietly for once.

'We can see you!'

I froze, hoping they were lying.

Tick, tick.

'Stand up, sir, or be shot!'

They clearly hadn't spotted the shiny mass of my skirts, so I crouched as low as I could and ran the last few steps. At the trap-door I lay flat again and slowly stuffed my legs and crinolines inside.

The soldiers didn't call out again. Their lanterns stopped moving. I lay half in and half out of the tunnel, watching them.

Tick, tick.

'Do you hear that?' said one.

'What?'

Tick, tick.

'That. A metallic noise, like a clock, or a watch.'

I mouthed every curse Lizzie had ever told me.

'He must be very close.'

They lowered their voices, stepping slowly forward. I slid backward, spitting panicked steam onto the underside of the hatch as I tried to catch hold of a rung with my foot. Instead I lost my balance and fell. The hatch shut with a clang as clear as an orchestral gong.

For a second I lay sprawled on the floor, winded, and knowing my dress was irreparably torn. Someone's fingers scrabbled at the lid above me. Of course they'd heard it slam shut; I imagined Mr Verne had heard it from town. Not to mention the hissing of my main boiler. I jumped up and ran down the tunnel, tripping over my wheels in the dark until I held my skirts up shamefully high and barged on.

'Over here!' yelled the soldier behind me. 'There's an unmarked shaft! We've got him now!'

One of my Superior-Inferior Heels malfunctioned, making the extendable heel shoot out. I stumbled on with one shoe taller than the other. The other shoe shifted sideways and I shook it off, reminded unpleasantly of Cinderella's flight from a very different ball. Hopefully I wouldn't be similarly identified. In the meantime, my remaining shoe was slowing me down. I kicked it against the wall to dislodge it, but it refused to budge. So much for that. I ran on, and dashed full-tilt into a wall. One of the wooden rungs of the exit ladder hit me right in the chin, rattling my teeth.

'Ouch!' said a voice behind me. They'd discovered my shoe.

I jumped onto the ladder and put my shoulder to the hatch, opening it with another loud bang. Two women screamed as I emerged—presumably I was a devilish vision, smeared in yellow dust and black dirt, with lopsided hair, and trailing ribbons of ruined silk.

For a brief moment I considered explaining my situation and hoping they'd understand and help a fellow traveller in distress. Then I came to my senses. I dived for the outside wall of the tent, ripping the canvas away from its weights so I could exit without gathering yet more witnesses.

They screamed again, and I didn't wait to find out if they were frightened by my merciless attack on the tent, or by two redcoats emerging from the pit at their feet. That didn't happen in London's retiring rooms.

I fled through the tent city, avoiding a crowd of revellers celebrating a lucky find. Soon I was out past the dusty edges of the makeshift town. I relied on my heart's directions to take me back to Patrick and Matilda.

Matilda found me on the town margin a half-mile from our horse tent, and she was armed with a hat and shawl to disguise my bedraggled appearance.

'How did you know to come and find me?' I asked, feeling my heart steady at the sight of her.

She shrugged. 'Educated guess. I take it the Southwells won't be inviting you again.'

'I'd imagine not. Are you hungry?'

We munched companionably on compressed sponge cake, and I chose not to mention the gritty texture was a new addition since I'd eaten it last. Matilda was too hungry to care. With Patrick's sheets of aluminium we were as rich as the Southwells, yet we were half starved.

A ragged child ran up to us and asked if we'd seen a redheaded woman in yellow with a cutlass. We answered truthfully that we hadn't, and he went on his way disappointed, having been promised a silver penny if he could find the trespassing madwoman.

I made a mental note to sew the remains of the dress into a large enough bonnet that a casual passer-by wouldn't notice the colour of my hair. Hopefully there'd be enough fabric left for that.

'We may have some issues with Patrick,' said Matilda carefully.

'Tomorrow, you mean?' I asked.

She shook her head. 'Dunne has caught up with you. I suppose the entire state saw us flying overhead, and knew we were heading this way. He found Patrick at one of the pumps and recognised him.'

'Oh no! Is Patrick all right?'

'He's fine. Dunne doesn't know which tent is ours, and he's unlikely to find us in the crowd. But there is one thing that ... well.'

'What?'

'He told Patrick about your heart.'

Chapter Twenty-Eight

I saw Patrick before he saw us. He stood outlined by the fire, with one hand on the gun at his side and the other clenched into a fist. His anger was all the more frightening because it was so unlike him.

Matilda stepped on a dry twig and he spun around to face us.

'Who's there?' he shouted. 'What do you want?'

'It's us, Patrick, calm down,' said Matilda.

He ran up to us and grabbed both of my wrists, holding them uncomfortably tight as he stared at my face. 'Who did that to you? I'll kill them myself, and have their corpses drawn and quartered!'

'He's dead,' I said.

'Good!'

I yanked my hands from his grip and slapped him hard across the cheek. 'He was my father! And he didn't do anything wrong!'

Matilda took a step back.

Patrick shook his head fiercely and reached for my hands again. I snatched them out of his way. 'You're a girl!' he said. 'You're kind and clever and peculiar—not a … a thing to be experimented on!'

'I wanted this heart, you fat-headed lout. It's brilliant, and I love it. You're just a—a—currency lad! You don't know anything.'

'I know you're no machine!'

'Yes I am! Are you going to take a sledgehammer to me, like your father?'

'No! I … can it be fixed?'

'Replaced with flesh, you mean? Of course not. Not even if I wanted to.'

He shuddered. My heart ticked in protest, and I wished it would shut up.

'I … need to think about this,' he said, and walked away. He paused and turned back. 'Your father is dead?'

'Executed, yes. Because of me.'

'Because of *that*,' he corrected, pointing at my chest.

'I asked him to give it to me—me first, before anyone else.'

'There are others?'

'No. There would have been—by now Britain would have had entire soldiers made of brass and steel. Men who felt no remorse or pain, and asked no questions. It would have been so—'

He held up a hand. His face had gone from red to white. 'Don't finish that sentence. Don't ever speak of this again.'

'—beautiful! So beautiful.'

Without a word he strode away past the glowing embers of other fires, and soon disappeared from view.

'Well!' said Matilda. 'That went better than I expected.'

I collapsed onto the ground. She sat beside me and waited until I spoke. The ground, like everything else about my new life, was hard and uncomfortable. I missed Belgravia so badly it was difficult to breathe.

'Father was … so kind to me.' Just talking about him to someone other than my siblings made me want to sob with the raw misery of his absence. 'He explained everything he did so I could understand, and I was just a girl.'

She put her arm around me and paused before she spoke. 'Do you think this is enough to make Patrick forget the duel?'

I sighed. 'Men never forget to kill each other.' I remembered my conversation with Verne and cleared my throat, forcing myself to go on. 'And I'm afraid I may have made a bet on him, too.'

'Was your father really making an army?'

'He'd have done it by now, if he was alive.'

'Well. What a … shame … he didn't succeed.'

When the black sky turned grey with morning, Patrick returned. None of us had slept. Matilda and I stayed outside so Patrick could dress.

'It's a shock,' she said, motioning toward my chest. 'He's never heard of anything like that. Nor have I.'

'You handled it rather better than he did,' I said stiffly.

'I don't have Patrick's manly urge to rescue maidens,' she said with a shrug. 'He's not disgusted by you exactly, but by the one who did that to you.'

'Then I'll thank him to keep his opinions to himself.'

'Plenty of people find me disgusting too, since I'm a mix of black and white. It's not so bad being different. Although I suppose you're the only one to be a mix of flesh and steam engine.'

'Yes,' I said. 'More's the pity.'

Patrick emerged, dressed in his best white shirt and moleskin trousers. He'd even dug up a brass vest, although he was having trouble with the laces on the sides. Matilda and I assisted him. I felt the brass sense my heart and quiver with natural affinity. My heart could be terribly undiscerning.

While Patrick was distracted, I whispered for his vest to hold onto any bullets that hit it. Patrick was a luddite and a pig, but I was still a friend to him. That was the difference between us. Hopefully, my heart could protect his.

If my theory about metal was incorrect, only luck could save him. That, or good sense, but unfortunately that quality was rarer than aluminium. Perhaps Mr Verne's cowardice would come to the fore once more, but I suspected his shame was too intense to live with now that he'd experienced its true depths. Men had died for their honour before, and would again.

Patrick didn't meet my eye, but as I knelt by his side to tighten the side laces of his waistcoat I felt him staring at my back. If only I could have emitted a jet of hot steam at will like my rats, I could have added a new burn scar to the gunpowder mark on his cheek. I sincerely hoped the sting of my slap lingered there. If he ever spoke so harshly of my father or my heart again, I'd break his nose. It might not have been ladylike, but I was well past that now. I tightened the laces a little too much, and hoped Patrick dared to offend me so I had a reason to strike. It wasn't often a lady of my birth was able to express her anger, and the power was going to my head.

Matilda and I stood back to admire our handiwork. Patrick checked his pistol for the fourteenth time that hour. He looked more respectable with a vest on and his hair properly brushed. His face was serene as usual, although his hands twitched and fidgeted.

At last he breathed deeply and turned to me. 'Please excuse my shock about your … mechanism … Miss Muchamore. You must realise it's not natural.'

'Focus on your duel,' I said, keeping myself from violence with an effort, since he was evidently trying hard to be respectful.

He took Matilda's hand. 'If this duel goes ill, I want you to have the balloon.'

'Seems fair,' she said.

'Will you use it to rescue Mother? Promise me?'

'Certainly,' said Matilda. 'But you're not going to get yourself killed today, do you hear?'

He smiled, but none of us believed it. We followed him past the tin and canvas tents to Ballarat proper and the Eureka Hotel. I felt awful for arguing with him on the last day of his life. Perhaps the Belgravia habit of blank-faced pleasantries had its merits, although I was sure the men on my street weren't inclined to duel.

'What do we do if we see Dunne?' Matilda asked me in a low voice.

'Run.'

'Why does he hate you so much?'

'Because I'm better than him.'

She paused for a second, letting Patrick get farther ahead. 'Because you think you're better than him.'

'I am better.'

'He might be low-born, but you're a science experiment.'

'A triumph of engineering,' I corrected her.

'And a thief.'

'I'm not a—oh.' The bracelet was still in my pocket. 'Yes, I suppose.'

'And have you forgotten you're travelling with a bushranger, with no decent chaperone.'

'You're with us.'

'Me? A chaperone? Hardly. You might as well use a crocodile for a guard dog.'

I hadn't thought through all the implications of my travelling companions. It seemed there was always farther to fall.

Chapter Twenty-Nine

I sensed Mr Verne's rich vest before I saw him. My stomach turned at the thought of likely bloodshed in the next short hour. The gilt paint on the Eureka Hotel glimmered in the faint light and I wondered how far away Mr Scobie's body was buried. Meanwhile, Mr Bentley slept soundly inside. I hoped he had an inkling that his supposed witness might just turn on him. It was galling to think he was at peace after shattering so many lives.

Mr Verne stood in the street, his arms tense at his sides. This time, he was completely sober. He glanced at us and I saw his shoulders droop. If he'd imagined Patrick was all bluster, he truly was an idiot. I was a little surprised he didn't run away, but I supposed he needed to stand for something after his cowardice at court. It said a great deal about British goldfield justice that he would rather face Patrick's gun than tell the truth about Mr Bentley to Magistrate Dewes. But perhaps once the duel was done Magistrate Dewes wouldn't appear so terrifying.

As we walked together up the street, Verne moved to unlace the gold vest he'd bet against Patrick's courage. I held up my hand to stop him. 'Not yet. Keep it until after the duel.'

'All right,' he said, trying not to sound excessively relieved.

'You can back out of the duel if you like,' Matilda said to him. 'None but the three of us will ever know. You don't have any family to embarrass.'

'I'll know,' he said, 'and I'll be embarrassed.'

It seemed I was right about the level of his shame. I just hoped he lived long enough to make amends—for his sake, and for Mrs Scobie. Maybe even for him.

The revolver strapped under his left arm was a pepperbox,

and I asked to inspect it. It was a beautiful piece of workmanship, with a grotesque face engraved in the pommel and a rounded wooden grip, smooth with wear. Only one of the six chambers held a bullet, so it seemed Mr Verne was more honourable than I'd originally thought. He could have prepared six bullets, and murdered Patrick with relative ease. Instead, he'd stuck to the agreed rules against a man who had to load each individual bullet between shots.

I turned away and whispered a heartfelt plea to Mr Verne's bullet to avoid hitting any of Patrick's flesh. All I could do was hope that my theories about metal were correct, or that Mr Verne was a terrible shot. Hopefully Patrick's brass waistcoat would act as armour and protect him from serious harm. Too bad he lacked the intelligence to avoid the danger himself.

Mr Verne's gold was making my heart beat rather more rapidly than I liked, so I returned his gun and let the men discuss the specific rules of their combat.

They began by introducing themselves, addressing each other with a new respect. Apparently men made friends more efficiently if guns were involved. Perhaps their idiocy gave them something in common.

'Have you ever duelled before?' asked Mr Verne.

Patrick shook his head. 'Have you?'

'Not until today. Shall we aim not to kill each other?'

Patrick looked at his gun, and for a moment a crease appeared on his forehead. 'Fifty paces?'

'Let's hope that's far enough. Do you want to shoot first, or shall I?'

'Your fine waistcoat is at stake, so I'll let you begin.'

'That's very considerate. Should I defeat you, I'll give up my waistcoat to your fine lady friend.'

'You're too kind. After all you've said and done, I find I'm pleased to have met you.'

'And I you.'

They shook hands while Matilda ground her teeth in frustration. I was beginning to think Arabella had a point when she dismissed all men as beneath her notice. They had a habit of causing unnecessary trouble. Once I had enough gold, I could hire my protectors instead of relying on the goodwill of the nearest moustache.

The two men walked slowly away from each other down the street, and I realised for the first time that a stray bullet could endanger Matilda or myself. Neither gun was known for its accuracy beyond the short range. We stood inside the doorway of the hotel and hoped for the best. I dismissed the passing thought that our actions were as foolhardy as theirs.

'Did you sabotage his gun?' she asked.

'No!'

'Really?'

'Well … I asked the bullet not to hit Patrick.'

'And it'll listen to you? Like tin listens to its owner?'

'Maybe.'

She took my hand. 'Is Patrick going to die?'

'I don't know.'

'Will you … stay with me, if he does?'

'Of course! You're all I have.'

She gave me a shaky smile and tucked a loose curl of my hair back under my bonnet. I kissed her on the cheek and we clung to one another, too frightened to close our eyes.

The men stood side-on and Mr Verne lifted his gun. His eyes widened as if he was the one preparing to receive a bullet. Patrick stood calmly, but his hands made fists.

Mr Verne shot his gun, and the bullet whammed straight into Patrick's side. Matilda screamed, and Patrick buckled and swayed. I pressed my fingernails into my palms to keep from fainting. Patrick didn't fall.

'Are you all right?' shouted Mr Verne, voicing all our concerns. 'Say something!'

Patrick lifted one hand in a wave. 'Well shot, sir!'

'Are you wounded? Shall I call a doctor?'

'Just a bruise! Shall I shoot you now?'

'Oh! Certainly. Good luck!'

Patrick straightened with evident difficulty, and sighted carefully along the barrel of his father's black Colt pistol.

I covered my eyes then, furious with frustration and just as furious at the way my heart longed to dive between Patrick and Mr Verne, saving the bearer of the gold vest. At least we'd remove it from him shortly. Hopefully I'd be able to think straight again then.

Except Patrick would wear it. I heard his voice in my head calling me kind and clever, and realised he may as well have been wearing the waistcoat already.

Tick!

Oh dear. Stupid heart. I reminded myself harshly that Patrick was nothing but an Irish lout so idiotically stubborn he'd duel a man to make himself feel better. And, thanks to Dunne, he hated me now.

BANG! He shot his pistol, and Mr Verne cried out in pain.

Patrick shoved his pistol into his belt, fumbling with the sharp edge of his waistcoat, and ran down the street to see if Mr Verne was all right.

Mr Verne stood very still, with both his hands over his chest. Suddenly I feared Patrick's bullet had hit the gap between the two front pieces of his waistcoat, and I ran to him too.

'Are you hit?' I gasped at Mr Verne, beating Patrick by a moment.

'Yes,' he said, and took his hands away.

There, embedded in the soft gold metal, was the lead bullet from Patrick's gun. It was positioned directly over his heart, squashed with its own force.

'Thank you,' Mr Verne said to me, 'for letting me wear the waistcoat a few minutes longer than I deserved.'

Patrick grabbed his hand and shook it energetically. 'Well done, sir!' His voice was far too loud, and he proudly displayed the dent on his vest where Mr Verne's shot had struck and bounced off.

Mr Verne attempted to unlace his waistcoat, but his hands were shaking. 'You earned this gold,' he said to Patrick, 'since your courage is more than a match for mine.'

'I'll never call you a coward again,' said Patrick.

'I'll never act like one. Not again.'

Just as I was beginning to be relieved enough to want to slap both men again, Matilda came up behind me. 'Emmeline! You were right about the metal. The waistcoats prove it!'

I shot her a look, but it was too late.

Patrick frowned at her. 'What precisely do you mean?'

'Er … I mean that our best wishes have been answered, and you are both safe.'

Patrick met my eye for the first time that day. 'What did you do?'

I glared at him. 'Everything in my power to keep you from getting killed.'

Mr Verne held out the left front piece of his vest to me, bullet side up.

'No,' said Patrick, pushing his hand back. 'It seems I cheated on that bet.'

'You did not!' said Matilda. 'Only Emmeline and I cheated—it had nothing to do with you. We didn't even know it would work!'

'Nonetheless,' said Patrick. 'I cannot accept any part of the spoils.'

'Then I'll accept them!' Matilda cried.

Mr Verne withdrew his hand. 'Is that true, Miss Mills? Did you alter my gun in some manner?'

I hesitated, and that was answer enough. 'Patrick didn't know.'

Mr Verne thought before he spoke again. 'In that case, our bet is void. But as an expression of my admiration of Mr O'Connell's bravery, I'll give you a consolation prize.' He pulled a slip of paper from his pocket and handed it to Patrick.

Patrick handed it to me, avoiding my eye once again.

It was a licence to search for gold, in the name of Gordon Verne.

'Well,' said Matilda with desperate cheer. 'That's better than nothing.'

'Thanks to your honesty,' said Mr Verne. 'I won't be needing it.'

My heart perked up a little. With his licence, I could walk onto the goldfields and find more gold than even Mr Verne possessed.

'I presume this will motivate you to stay in Ballarat a little longer,' said Mr Verne. 'In which case, would you care to join me for tea this evening? I may have a lack of talent for first impressions, but I'd be grateful for the opportunity to make a positive second impression. What is more, I will shortly present myself to the magistrate to make a true statement regarding Mr Bentley's actions with regards to James Scobie. I'll go at once, and tell you over dinner how I've fared. Although I should warn you, Magistrate Dewes and Mr Bentley are fast friends.'

Patrick glanced at Matilda and I, and answered on our behalf: 'We'd be honoured to eat with you.'

Chapter Thirty

Patrick emerged from our tent wearing one of Mr Verne's top hats. 'See?' he said. 'Completely disguised. The licence soldiers won't recognise me, even if they've seen the posters for our arrest.'

'Because you're wearing a different hat?' Matilda said doubtfully.

'On the contrary. Don't tell me you haven't noticed?'

'What?' she said. 'What am I supposed to see?'

He grinned at her and raised his eyebrows. 'It's gone.'

'What's gone?' she asked.

'My beard! They'll never recognise me now.'

Matilda was struck by an attack of coughing. 'Er … perhaps we should do a little more with your clothes. In addition to your … sudden … lack of a beard.'

Between the two of us, we dressed Patrick in as British a manner as possible, and unhooked the distinctive silk envelope from our carriage to hide inside the tent with Matilda. In all that time, it was clear Patrick couldn't bear to look at me. My hatred for him grew by the minute, and I wanted more than ever to just go home to Belgravia. It didn't help that he was my only hope for resisting the trappers.

After rushing about for an hour, Patrick and I sat on the ground in all our finery and waited for the soldiers to show up. I wondered what we would do if they'd seen our wanted posters.

'Do I look convincing enough to be your husband?' he asked, still facing away from me.

'You look very respectable today,' I said, but couldn't resist the opportunity to hurt him while he was vulnerable. 'No one would know you were Irish. Just try not to speak more than you absolutely must.'

'That won't be a problem,' he said stiffly, and I knew I'd scored a point.

Both of my companions were worse than vulgar. It was probably because they hadn't been brought up properly. They were nice enough in their way, but I certainly hoped their manners weren't having an effect on me. Especially Patrick. Pretending to be his wife was the greatest imposition placed on me since I'd left Britain.

A shot sounded to mark the beginning of work on the diggings. For once it didn't shock me. Apparently I was getting used to colonials using guns like clocks. The tents around us emptied. We sat in awkward silence for some hours, coughing occasionally as more dust blew across the grassless plain of tents. Clouds gathered and darkened in the sky, and Matilda and Patrick discussed them like a gambler discussed his good luck charms. Patrick never once attempted to involve me in the conversation, and Matilda's cheerfulness rang false. Noon came and went, and we ate the last scraps of food from the Southwells's ball. We fed Matilda through the closed curtain like a pet, but she didn't complain. She knew as well as we did that her face was too easily remembered.

The soldiers came at last, and I derived some satisfaction from the way their faces fell at the sight of Patrick, particularly since he was both tall and armed. He stood close to me, as if we really were husband and wife. I was torn between moving away to show I didn't need him and moving closer for safety, so I stayed still, concentrating on keeping my heart from beating too loudly. Patrick's breath stirred my hair.

I was pleased to observe that the mustachioed redcoat bore blistered pawprints on his cheek, and had been marginally less enthusiastic with his grooming wax. Our licence passed muster, and we paid them for the previous two days' lack of licence by giving them the bracelet I'd stolen from Miss Southwell. It was clear they knew it was stolen, and equally clear that they didn't care.

They left, and we all breathed a sigh of relief—Matilda

especially, since she was now able to come out of the oven-like tent. I felt oddly shamed for giving them the bracelet—not just because it was stolen, but because I knew it was reinforcing the status quo. Short of challenging each soldier and landowner to individual duels, I could think of nothing to change the corrupt system. I vowed silently that if I found a way, I would take it.

At least Mr Verne would be speaking to Magistrate Dewes about what he'd seen of Mr Scobie's murder and burial. I pictured Mrs Scobie's face when Mr Bentley was thrown into gaol and smiled.

We reattached the balloon's heavy silk envelope to its wheeled basket, and Patrick changed into his usual clothes—which I had to admit looked far more comfortable than Mr Verne's silk top hat and Patrick's brass vest. But of course it was all right for him; he was just a currency lad, while Matilda and I were ladies. As long as I remembered my place, all would be well.

I was anxious to visit our plot of land and become rich, but the time for our dinner with Mr Verne was drawing near and I longed to hear news of Mr Bentley's fate. The clouds already darkened the sky, and I began to think I'd finally see Australian rain.

Matilda dressed as if for the governor's ball. I wore my newly-fashioned blue bonnet, even though it didn't quite match the violet of my second woollen dress. There was nothing for it; I was quite possibly the only redheaded woman sighted near the Southwells's tent, and I didn't care to be recognised at the wrong moment.

Four groups of troopers asked to see our licence on the way to Ballarat proper. I was very glad we didn't have to pay the fee for being unlicenced each time, and felt sorry for those who had walked all the way to the goldfields only to end up in deeper debt before they stepped past the boundary. Worse, everyone knew that the money only funded further thuggish behaviour. I startled once again when the gunshot sounded to mark the end of work on the goldfields. For a moment, I'd thought the latest batch of soldiers had decided to fire on us.

Mr Verne waited for us in the dining room of the hotel, slightly groggified since the morning. He sipped a mug of tea, and stood when we entered. Now that he and Patrick had had their fun he was all manners, drawing back the wooden chairs for Matilda and I and inquiring about Patrick's wellbeing since the duel. Despite all that had passed between us, he seemed oddly nervous. Bad news loomed over him, and after all we'd been through I was afraid to make him tell us what it was. The hotel did not feel like a place that had just had its owner arrested. It felt like nothing had happened at all.

In the meantime, he ordered roast mutton for us, and I got a grip on my heart and attempted to enjoy a civil evening. Since he was now, apparently, our friend, I didn't need to try to find a way to steal his waistcoat from him. That was oddly reassuring. I was a thief, but at least I was bad at it.

Mr Bentley himself scuttled by and greeted us as honoured guests. We tried our best not to show revulsion at his toadying, but Mr Verne did not look up from his plate. His hands shook with ill-concealed fury. The duel really had changed him. I glared at Mr Bentley's back all the way across the room, and froze in horror.

Dunne sat facing us—facing me—with his ridiculous excuse for a top hat in his grubby hands. I'd never seen him look so happy, and his out-thrust jaw spoke of a new kind of duel. This time I couldn't cheat.

'Matilda, Patrick,' I warned, and they stiffened. 'Please excuse us Mr Verne, but I'm afraid we must leave at once.'

Mr Verne saw where I was looking. 'Ah! Your fellow escapee. I wouldn't have recognised him without your help. What a scowl! Have you had a disagreement with him since your escape?'

I clenched my hands together in my lap. 'What can you possibly mean?'

He stood up, holding out his hand for me to take. 'There's no time to explain. I know who you are—Miss Muchamore, Miss Newry, and of course the infamous aeronaut bushranger. Never fear. I have no need of reward money, and I wouldn't betray you anyway. You can hide in my room—no one will dare search through my things, not after all that's happened lately. But you must trust me.'

Patrick and Matilda stood, and Patrick gestured for me to choose our best method of escape.

I thought of the single bullet chambered in Mr Verne's pepperbox revolver, and took his proffered arm. 'Thank you, Mr Verne. We appreciate your help. Dunne was never my companion—he's my enemy.'

'I see. Shall we?'

The four of us hurried up the stairs and into Mr Verne's suite.

'Did you have enough dinner?' he asked. 'It can't be easy living on the run.'

'How long have you known?' Patrick asked, standing with his back to the door.

'I saw the paper for your arrest yesterday evening, but, if you'll excuse me saying so, Miss Newry doesn't appear to be in any distress.'

'Hardly!' said Matilda. 'I'm the only one who isn't getting hunted down at present.'

'On the contrary,' said Mr Verne. 'According to the most recent bulletin, you're the victim of a shocking abduction.'

'Who would abduct me?' she exclaimed.

'Who indeed?' Patrick agreed.

'You, apparently,' said Mr Verne to Patrick. 'Which is why the price on your head has been raised to two hundred pounds.'

'Oh dear,' said Matilda. 'I'd rather hoped Father would … do nothing.'

Patrick stared at her, incredulous.

'I left a note!' she protested. 'Aren't you glad now I didn't take any money?'

Patrick shook his head. 'What if you're caught? Your Bearbrass fiancé is waiting for you, and I doubt he'll take your reluctance as well as William.'

'I won't be caught!' she shot back. 'Not ever.'

All of a sudden I felt very exposed. My heart's brass instincts prompted me to walk to the window. I longed for a periscope to better see the scene outside, but had to settle for peeking through the white fabric.

I was just in time. Dunne dropped an oil tin, and even from the second floor I heard the hollow clatter as it hit a pile of others. He looked up at me and laughed. Judging by the joy on his face, he was finally satisfied he'd done enough to hurt me. He embodied all the small-minded criminality I'd been led to expect from his class, and had failed to find among the Irish and Scottish and Americans and Chinese at Ballarat. Then he lit a match—such a small thing!—and touched it to the oil-soaked wall of the hotel.

The wood caught. Dunne leapt on his horse and galloped away down the street, leaving Ballarat aflame behind him.

Chapter Thirty-One

Orange tongues of flame leapt up the wall, and the dry wood crackled with sudden energy.

'We're on fire,' I said.

'Excuse me?' said Mr Verne.

All the others rushed to the window and winced at the stink of burning oil.

'Capital!' said Mr Verne. 'What a brilliant idea!' He leapt at his chest of drawers and rummaged through it until he found his own pack of matches.

Patrick, Matilda and I stared as he attempted to set the chest of drawers alight.

'Are you mad?' I asked. 'We need to leave at once! I can only hope Dunne believes I've been killed.'

Mr Verne laughed. 'Don't you see? This is Bentley's hotel.'

We looked at him blankly.

'Meeting you changed my outlook, as you know,' said Mr Verne, still trying to set the furniture on fire. 'Until this morning, I was a friend to redcoats—and to murderers. That shameful life ended today, as effectively as if I was actually killed. Your Mr Dunne has just done us all a favour. If I'd thought of it, I'd have done it myself.'

'Isn't it enough to tell Magistrate Dewes the truth?' Patrick asked.

'I'm afraid I already did. He told me not to bother him now the trial was over. He had things to do, he said. Mr Bentley is an upstanding member of the community, he said.'

'How can that be right?' I said. 'Dewes is the magistrate. That's his job—catching murderers.'

'It's *not* right,' said Verne. 'I meant to tell you over dinner, but

I … well I suppose I'm still a coward, after all. Magistrate Dewes was rather unimpressed when I challenged him to a duel. He very nearly arrested me for that. I'm afraid I kicked up rather a fuss, and to no avail. But the four of us alone can still punish Bentley for what he did.'

'Are you sure?' I asked. I'd never tried committing arson before, and it deserved hesitation before I added it to my list of crimes.

'Certainly. This hotel is everything to Mr Bentley—riches, friends, protection. Without it he's nothing.'

I stepped back as the flames outside turned the window into a fireplace. Four rats climbed from my pockets and scuttled out the door.

Mr Verne chose to ignore my rodents. 'Justice is happening today, before it gets beaten down a second time by force of numbers.' He turned to Patrick, spreading his arms wide. 'Will you help me?'

Matilda produced her tin of matches. 'Sounds like fun.'

'Aye,' said Patrick slowly. 'I'll help.'

Matilda passed me several matches. 'Watch your skirts,' she said. 'It'd be a shame to ruin another of your lovely dresses.'

I lit a match, and touched it to an oil painting of a rainy hillside. The canvas caught slowly, stinking like pitch festering on a convict ship. But then the flames crept across the paint and I laughed with a strange triumph. I could make a difference after all. It was so easy.

The curtains in the window caught fire with an audible whoosh, and the four of us stared at each other. 'I believe the hotel's burning rather well,' I said. 'We should go.'

Mr Verne grabbed his few belongings and found he wasn't able to physically lift both his spare gold vests at once, not in his one free hand.

'Come on!' said Matilda. 'We'll be fried!'

Patrick hoisted one gold waistcoat onto his back, and Matilda and I took half of the other waistcoat each.

Mr Verne passed his free arm over his forehead, which was dripping wet with sweat in the increasing heat. 'My rum!'

'What?' I said.

'How else will I pay my way home?'

He abandoned his belongings and dived for the smouldering mattress, trying to pry it up with his knee. I dropped my share of the gold and helped him. The mattress hid half a dozen full bottles of rum, and three more empties.

'Really, Mr Verne!' I said.

He grinned and held out his arms. I loaded him up with all six full bottles and helped him get upright again.

'Let's away!' he shouted gleefully, and ran out the door.

The mattress banged loudly as the fire reached the remaining bottles. Matilda ran out the door after Mr Verne, and Patrick yelled for me to go ahead of him. It was hardly the eloquent conversation I was hoping for, but at least he was speaking to me with a kind of civility once more.

I ran outside, my arms aching with the weight of Mr Verne's gold. The hall was alight: a shining orange passage, hissing and popping in fury.

We weren't the only ones to follow Dunne's lead. All Ballarat was ready to blow, and we'd helped light the fuse. Too late to stop it now.

I took a breath of the relatively clear air from Mr Verne's suite and hurried down the passage, hoping my heart could handle it. The smoke made it impossible to see and I wished I'd kept a pair of brass goggles handy.

Then I remembered, I had. I draped the stupid gold segments over my right shoulder and searched my pockets. At last my finger touched metal and I drew out the goggles Matilda gave me. With them on, I saw clearly through the smoke. Brass always did work well for me. There was a single perfectly ordinary arrow on the wall pointing to the stairs, and they were headed in the opposite direction. I stumbled back the way I'd come, hoping Patrick was long gone, and almost fell over the first step.

The fire was very loud, like a hundred rifles going off in a great battle. It was so hot I couldn't think straight. My skirt was black with soot. If I'd worn cotton, I'd be on fire.

I steadied myself with one hand on the wall but it crumbled at my touch, burning my palm. Time to go—fast. My heart beat as steadily as it could, but I was breathing smoke. It was only a matter of time until I lost consciousness. How silly, to get myself killed in a fire I helped to light. Dunne would be so pleased. Even Mr Bentley might just cheer up at the news.

I ran down the stairs, staying away from the walls. The fire had completely burned through the first landing, so I clung to the picture rail above my head to creep around the ragged edges. Mr Verne's gold waistcoat clanged against my corset at the back, and I realised my bodice was badly singed and I hadn't noticed.

A single brown hand clung to the wood just where I wanted to place my foot. I stepped over Matilda's fingers carefully and reached the relatively solid stairs.

'Matilda!' I yelled.

One of the fingers lifted slightly.

I grabbed her hand with both of mine and pulled. She held my wrist like a vice, and I took it as a good sign. But we weren't strong enough to save ourselves.

'You're all I have!' I yelled. 'Pull!'

She swung up her other arm, still holding the larger back piece of Mr Verne's gold. It thwacked onto the stairs.

I grabbed her other arm, and in a few moments her face peeked out of the burning floor.

'Hello,' she gasped through clenched teeth.

'Come on!'

'Can't,' she said. 'Tell Mother I—'

'I most certainly will not!'

She blinked at me. 'Pull then!'

I braced my feet against the top step, forming a cradle of our linked arms, and pushed with my legs. Matilda popped out of the hole and landed on top of me, crushing the breath from my lungs.

'I love you,' she gasped, choking on the smoke. 'Since I first saw you.'

'It's me,' I said, looking up at her in concern. 'Emmeline.'

'Emmeline,' she slurred. And fainted in my arms.

I dragged her, step by giant step, down the stairs to the same dining room where Dunne had spotted me. If he'd meant to harm me, he'd done very well. I shook Matilda, but she didn't wake up. The ties of Mr Verne's waistcoat were caught in one of her shoes, which went some way toward explaining why she was so heavy—and so intricately, utterly, perfect in face and figure. Her lips caught my attention—full and dark and perfectly formed.

I snapped out of it. Stupid gold magic. It caused far more trouble than it was worth. Avoiding another gaping hole in the dining room floor, I jerked and hauled and dragged my lovely friend toward the nearest exit, which happened to be the gaping hole in the front wall.

A man shoved past me, knocking me over in his haste to get inside. His face was purple and twisted with rage—Mr Bentley.

'You're going the wrong way!' I said to his back as he hurled himself up the burning stairs.

Too tired to think straight, I collapsed to the floor and shuffled along half on my knees, with Matilda's head clutched to my steaming chest. I was wetting her hair with my steam, and the exposed front laces of my corset frayed alarmingly. Or was that grey cloud around her made up of smoke from my ridiculously oversized and burning skirts?

'Did you ever see anything so beautiful?' The voice was Patrick's.

I turned my head to the side, grateful again for the goggles giving me sight. It was definitely Patrick, resplendent in one of Mr Verne's golden waistcoats, and filthy with dust and ash. He climbed through a smashed front window toward me, and I was ever so pleased to see him. Even the Irish are welcome sometimes.

'Are you all right? Don't answer that.' He bent and picked us up—one in each arm—standing with a herculean effort. Step by step he bore us outside onto the cool dirt, where he laid us down as tenderly as possible under the circumstances.

'Patrick?' I whispered.

'Yes, Emmeline?'

'Please excuse the impertinence, but am I dressed?'

His eyes left my face for the first time, and widened. He took off his coat and laid it over Matilda and I where we lay, pressing it down to put out the last embers of our grand attire.

'Are you all right here for a moment? I'm going to go and fetch some tea. And a blanket.'

'Mmm,' I said, and lay down my head.

I saw two men attempt to throw water on the fire, but it was clear their pathetic buckets weren't even full. There wasn't enough water. The black clouds overhead burst and sent rain pummelling down, but they were soon spent and the fire burned on.

I glanced up at the second floor and saw Mr Verne, red-faced, at the same window from which I'd spotted Dunne's arson so recently. He waved both arms, and was shouting something I couldn't hear. His rum bottles were gone, so it was clear his life was in danger.

I tried to stand, but my legs wouldn't hold me. 'Help!' I cried, shocked at how much it hurt my throat to make a sound. 'There's a man inside! Help, somebody!'

A redcoat bent to hear me, and I pointed wordlessly at the silhouette of Mr Verne in the window, haloed in flames. He didn't waste any time, but grabbed another man by the elbow, shouting at him and gesturing at Mr Verne.

The pair of them ripped a wooden shutter from a window and beat down the flames with their bare hands. Ignoring the fact it was still smouldering, they stood perilously close to Mr Verne's window, holding the shutter above their head like a step.

Mr Verne climbed out of the window, losing his hat against

the frame, and poised himself to jump for the narrow length of life-saving shutter. I still had my goggles on, and saw him bite his lip as the embers on the shutter sent up a yellow tongue of flame.

'Jump!' I whispered, trembling for him.

Beside me, Matilda sat up and gripped my hand. 'Emmeline,' she said slowly. 'Do you see what I'm seeing? Behind him. It looks like another person.'

I turned my sharpened vision on the flames, and saw a new horror: the purpling face of Mr Bentley, murderer and ex-hotelier, and he had a flaming brand in his hand.

'Verne!' I screamed. 'Jump now! Now!'

Mr Bentley lunged for him, and Mr Verne disappeared from view. The last I saw of him was a rounded 'O' of astonishment on his face as he disappeared into the red maw of the fire. Our fire.

Moments later Mr Bentley leapt to safety, falling once more into the embracing arms of the law. He was a murderer twice over now, and the only two decent redcoats in Ballarat didn't know they'd saved the wrong man.

'Go back!' I screamed at them. 'There's someone else in there. Please!'

They didn't hear me. The hotel collapsed with a beastly scream of snapping fibres and splintering supports. Matilda sat up on her elbows, staring in stunned silence.

'He's dead, isn't he?' she said. 'Oh, Emmeline! What have we done?'

Mrs Scobie emerged from the drifting smoke of the street, a red-headed and red-cheeked vision, brimming with ill-concealed pleasure at the hotel's fall. She brought us lukewarm drinking water, murmuring reassurance and kind words. I thanked her, choking on the words.

'Don't thank me, Miss Muchamore,' she said, pushing Verne's gold beneath my skirts so it was out of sight. 'My Jim would have laughed to see this day.'

'Mr Verne's gone—killed.'

She sat back and gave a brittle smile. 'Wonders never cease.'

'No, you don't understand! He—'

Matilda squeezed my hand, and I fell silent. It was no use now. Our only respectable ally was dead by Bentley's hand, and no one witnessed it but two fainting girls.

Chapter Thirty-Two

Working together, Patrick and Mrs Scobie brought Matilda and I home, both of us half delirious still and barely able to walk. I woke at some dark hour and sat up, tapping one finger on the wall to check it was our tent and not somewhere unfamiliar. The tent binged softly to reassure me.

My rats slept in their usual compact pile. Matilda snored gently beside me, her hair caked with ash and grime and her face as sweetly innocent as a child. Two entire golden waistcoats lay neatly stacked in one corner, fitting perfectly since they were both designed for the same man. I wondered who would claim them. Presumably a large number of people would step forward shortly.

Shouts filtered through the night from outside, either a lucky miner celebrating with friends or a mob too angry to sleep. I carefully peeled off my skirts, and had to resort to cutting off the fused rags of my bodice. At least my corset was largely undamaged. My arms were decorated with black sludge and blisters. I hoped I didn't scar, and wondered if Matilda's tribe had used fire to mark the series of arcs all down her legs, visible again through the rents in her skirt. It was difficult to think of her taking part in some native ritual. There was so much I didn't understand about her.

I was reluctant to dress myself, since my blisters ached and large areas of skin on my legs and hands still felt unnaturally hot. Instead I pulled off Matilda's ruined skirts and laid the stinking pieces beside Mr Verne's waistcoat. She stirred in her sleep, moaning pathetically, and I recalled she never wore corsets to bed. I pulled at her laces, but the silk ribbons had burned into a knot, so I had to cut away the brass segments one by one.

Underneath, her chemise was still white. I saw her body through the fabric, and she looked unharmed. When I realised I was staring, I turned away. I hoped she wasn't embarrassed by her delirious comments on the stairs, and I resolved not to mention them. Had I said anything about how beautiful she looked? I hoped not.

My boilers needed refilling, and there was no water in the tent. I dressed reluctantly and went outside. It was only when I stood up straight that I realised I'd left off my crinolines. Good riddance.

The yelling in the distance definitely wasn't the sound of celebration. A pall of smoke lingered over Ballarat proper, and I felt a very improper twinge of pride. Miss Muchamore of Belgravia would never have burnt down a hotel, even one belonging to a murderer. My colonial friends were a bad influence on me after all. Or perhaps we were never very different. Either way, I liked the person I was becoming. Not only was I free, I was fierce.

I checked our fire pit and found a full pot of liquid, but it turned out to be tea. Patrick slept sitting up by the fire, with his head on his chest. Some of his hair was burnt off, and his trousers were more black than beige. He'd saved us both, then tried to stay awake and guard us. I didn't have the heart to wake him, so I drank the cold tea and decided to go and find water myself, using the spare billy to carry it back. There were plenty of people moving about the tents, so I felt relatively secure.

After fetching my Probability Parasol and donning my partially burnt bonnet, I set off for the closest water pump, easily able to see my way in the moonlight. The moon was almost full, and I wondered whether William was about to reappear and demand his share of our non-existent riches. Hopefully Matilda could put him off a second time—unlike her other fiancé.

The majority of the noise was far away, but two men sat on the ground beside the pump. They laughed together as if they'd just discovered how to purify aluminium. I froze beside a steel horsetent and listened. One man had a voice that boomed as if he'd spent all his life calling instructions down into a mine. The other man's voice was thin from prolonged illness.

'May as well burn 'em,' said the booming man. 'One last huzzah for the redcoats before I go home to my very fine wife.'

'And I to mine,' said the thin voice.

'But you'll do it?'

'With pleasure, thanks to Mr Verne's parting gift. I only wish we'd gotten the piece with the lead ball crushed into it!'

'We'll not regret it when the bank weighs our lump, my friend!'

My heart lurched, and I wasn't sure if it was a lack of water or something more. Either way, I had to take a risk. I walked out into the small space and let the men see me. They stood hastily and reached up to doff hats that they'd forgotten to wear.

'Good evening,' I said. 'How are you?'

'Rich!' said the thin man.

'Congratulations.' I winced at a shout of rage from elsewhere. 'May I ask what kind of gold you just acquired—alluvial, or quartz?'

'The kind you get from a dead man's back,' said the booming man.

I took a fast step backward, gripping my parasol.

'Not like that!' said the thin man. 'He died in the hotel, probably because he was drunk and passed out at the time. Burnt to a crisp he was. Best thing that brandy-face ever did was leave his gold behind for the likes of us.'

'Mr Verne,' I whispered. 'He's really dead?'

The booming one gripped his friend's shoulder. 'You knew him?'

'I … a little, yes.'

'Well you can't have our bit!' said the thin man. 'It's ours. We found it.'

I remembered the far greater pile of gold in our tent, and for a moment I was tempted to just walk away. 'It's all right, I won't try to claim what you've got. But … who shall I visit to give … my condolences?'

The thin man snorted. 'Mr Verne had no family, and no friends—excepting you, it seems. He spent his honour cozying up to troopers.'

'That's not true! Well … not since this morning.'

'Begging your pardon, miss,' said the bigger man, 'but it is. We don't mean to speak ill of the dead, but he stayed chummy with that murderer Mr Bentley and there's not a man here can forgive that.'

'He told the truth, in the end,' I said, since there was no one else to honour Mr Verne's memory, 'but Magistrate Dewes wouldn't listen.'

'Does it matter now?' the smaller man asked.

I bit my tongue, and remembered I needed water. Without Verne, Mr Bentley was guaranteed to stay free. But of course Mr Bentley had known that.

The men let me fill the spare billy in peace.

'Please excuse me,' I said, brimming with a curiosity that would have been unseemly anywhere else, 'but I couldn't help overhearing you as I approached. What is it that you're burning tomorrow?'

The thin man produced a slip of paper, and I recognised the curlicues of a gold licence. 'This,' he said. 'And many more besides. We've had enough of those troopers, and that's a fact. Tomorrow's the day when the licences get gone for good.'

'Oh,' I said. 'But I haven't had a chance to look at my patch yet.'

They turned to one another and laughed uproariously. 'A woman like that on the diggings, Lord bless you! You're a fine one and no mistake.'

I bit my tongue again and schooled my face into polite amusement. It was time for me to go home to London. When I was rich, I'd do as I pleased regardless of my gender. No one would be able to stop me.

I waited until I was out of sight before I let myself realise three true things: Our friend was dead, we had a new and better chance to defy the redcoats, and we were rich.

Chapter Thirty-Three

I laid back down beside Matilda, expecting to wait in the dark until she woke up. Instead, she woke me when it was already light. Patrick was heating the tea, so I dressed and told them both what I'd found out.

'Dead!' said Matilda. 'And we saw who did it, too. Poor Mr Verne … and we're rich.'

'You went to get water alone?' said Patrick. 'In the middle of the night?'

'Yes,' I said to both of them. 'As of now, the diggers are on the verge of rioting. The soldiers won't hesitate to shoot them.'

Patrick sloshed his tea in its mug. 'We're diggers too.'

'And wanted criminals,' I pointed out. 'But I want to stay. It's the right thing to do—for Aline and Duncan and Mrs Scobie, as well as all the rest. However, I promised to help rescue Mrs O'Connell once I had gold, and I'll keep my word.'

'My mother doesn't require our help at this time,' he said stiffly. 'And I don't believe any digger hereabouts will look at us for fast gold, if that's a concern.'

'Speaking of gold, wouldn't your father like to enjoy his share?'

'Not if it meant I'd turned my back from an honourable fight.'

'We're fighting the diggers' battle now, are we?' said Matilda. 'For Verne and for Mrs Scobie?'

'Do you know a better way to honour them?' he said.

'Not at all,' she grinned. 'What shall we set fire to today?'

'They—we—plan to burn the licences,' I admitted, feeling my heart quicken at the coming fight. One way or another, I was in the right place to give my all to a cause greater than myself. My life meant something, suddenly, and I could lose it as a result.

Still, I was as good as dead ever since I was transported. What did any of us have to lose—other than our lives?

'I'm in,' said Matilda.

'Aye, me too,' said Patrick.

My heart swelled with pride to be one of them. I wasn't sure when I'd finally gotten over myself, but I was glad. We buried our gold inside the tent and set my portmanteau on top of the spot to hide it. Patrick confessed that we didn't have any flour for breakfast, but we decided not to sell the vests until we were safely away. We could go hungry another day or two. Even as I agreed that it would be no great matter to skip a few more meals, my stomach clenched in hunger and I felt a wave of physical weakness sweep over me. Unfortunately, going hungry was our best course.

It was all too easy to find the protesting miners. We followed the noise of shouting and the column of smoke. The diggers had cleared a space among the tents, and a bright fire curled and danced among hundreds of licence papers.

Patrick produced our licence at once and strode forward, clutching it in one upraised fist. The crowd jostled around us, watching Patrick's strong face with admiration.

'No more licences!' he cried, and they responded with an eruption of cheering and amens.

He threw our licence into the blaze and it caught at once. I couldn't tell it from the rest, and felt a tiny moment of dread at the thought that we would no longer have the ability to prove our legal right to remain. What would the soldiers do to us?

Looking around at the thousands of men surrounding the fire, I told myself we'd draw no undue attention of our own. Besides, Matilda and I were women, and we could feign innocence far more easily than Patrick. Patrick had his gun strapped to his hip, and I was willing to bet it was loaded. More importantly than all of that, we were one of the crowd. Birth and station didn't matter anymore; we stood as one, and no one could harm us now. I saw strangers recognise our faces and simply walk on by.

Matilda fell into me as a man pushed past carelessly. I caught her and helped her stand.

'Justice,' she gasped, 'is rather less comfortable than I expected.'

'And smellier,' I agreed, glancing up by habit to the sky. There was no sign of rain. It was as if the previous night's brief storm had drained the heavens.

Across the crowd I glimpsed a flash of red hair. It was Mrs Scobie. She turned just as I spotted her and the crowd parted to let her walk up to us. 'I was hoping to find you here,' she said.

'Where else would we go?' I said, meaning every word. Belgravia wasn't my home anymore. 'Did you hear … about Mr Verne? He was with us for a single day, and now he's dead.'

'I heard.' She sighed. 'It's time now I thought of my children. I know I can trust every last man and woman here to set things right, one way or another.'

She hugged and kissed Matilda and I and walked away, leaving Ballarat and her husband's unmarked grave behind her. I swallowed tears to see her go, but there was no doubt the diggings were more dangerous than ever. Somewhere, somehow, Aline and Duncan would make a new and better life. I gasped, realising I could have given her a last wealthy gift from Mr Verne—but it was too late.

Patrick pushed and shoved his way back to us through the crowd. 'Those troopers will see reason when they see all of us! No corrupt leadership can remain unchallenged forever.'

'Not anymore,' I agreed. It was time to show Ballarat what real British honour looked like. Soon I'd be able to speak of my birth nation with pride once more.

Half a dozen soldiers stood by, watching silently as the flames shone ever more brightly. They didn't speak, and they didn't move to stop us. Instead they merely watched, measuring our resolve with cold eyes.

The soldier from our first day stood there sharpening the waxed points of his moustache. I wished I had a gun.

Chapter Thirty-Four

Several of the miners grabbed tents, carts, and carriages, and hauled them up Baker's Hill, overlooking the Eureka Flat with a clear view across at the government camp. A whisper ran around the crowd that the hilltop miners would build a fortress for anyone willing to make a stand.

'Let's get our carriage!' said Patrick. 'It's good and solid.'

'It's made mainly of painted wicker,' Matilda pointed out.

'We'll turn it on its side!' he said.

'The base is made of wood.'

Patrick didn't hear her—he was already on his way back to our tent. We trailed after him, trying and failing to remain rationally detached. A part of me said I should stop him at once. It was a very small part. I'd been itching for a fight all my life, and this was a battle worth fighting, at last. All around us the tent city swirled with defiance and hope. I wondered if Dunne had any idea what his fire had sparked, and felt perversely grateful to him.

We drank the last of our tea, packed up the horse, and hid the gold in Patrick's hollow seat. While the other two argued over how exactly we planned to get to the top of the hill, I gathered more dead wood and packed it into the carriage—just in case. In the end the horse and Patrick hauled on the carriage from the front, while Matilda and I pushed it from the back. It took most of the day to reach the crest of Baker's Hill, and the diggers' glinting stockade stood in our way. As soon as we were within sight, however, dozens of men came and helped us, laughing and clapping Patrick on the back. They dismantled part of the barrier so we could get inside. Everyone knew our names, and no one cared what we were. It was an odd sort of society, but it was one that accepted us. I slipped Father's watch into a pocket and felt myself truly relax for the first time in years.

Some of the tent-owners inside the stockade looked around in frank bewilderment, realising their plot of land had become part of an impromptu fortress. I noticed an entire shop enclosed in the metal arms, and doing a roaring trade. Starting a rebellion was a thirsty business.

Men carried pistols, rifles and even muskets. One sat on a rock sharpening the blade of his bayonet like a Frenchman battling revolutionaries. I heard Americans, Chinese, Spaniards, plenty of Irish, and many British voices raised in passionate conversation and desperate hope.

Surely we were mad to think of making a stand against the might of the military and mounted police? I checked and rechecked the balloon, and hoped we wouldn't need to fly away in a hurry.

There was no room for another tent, so we climbed into the carriage to survey the field. We had fine views across the diggings and all the way to the dust-shrouded edges of Ballarat town and the tent city.

'Do you think they'll attack?' I asked Patrick.

'Aye,' he said. 'From the hills over there, if I'm not mistaken.'

I hopped down, not waiting for his assistance. 'Time to play our part—our horse can be useful.' While Matilda set up a broad fire under my instructions, I found a decent hammer in my bag, and put my gauntlets and goggles on. It was a shame Mary hadn't packed a mesh-mask too. Just a silly wedding dress. I was surrounded by a world of optimists, and I suddenly missed Mary and Lizzie with a physical pain in my chest. Matilda grinned at me, and I was back in the moment again.

When the fire was strong enough to heat my face, I let our horse know it was about to become a wall, and tipped it over into the flames. It seemed pleased at the new development.

I hammered at the beautifully fitted curves of tin, and kept hammering until the entire horse was a flat plate, still shaped vaguely like a horse. Other miners gathered to watch, and by the time I finished there were seven more horses that binged at me to melt them down into our walls. I laid them on the fire one by one, and pounded away until I was weak with exhaustion. Someone brought me food and tea, and I ate and drank my fill, then got back to work.

More men gathered by the hour, and more horses. The wall of our stockade was two horses thick all around, and men brought more raw metal to me all the time. Patrick tried to help, but he couldn't seem to hit the most efficient points of the horses. No one could but me, although those who tried it enjoyed smashing the metal all the same. The air fairly crackled with our righteous anger—and all our stifled fears. I hoped my newfound purpose in life wouldn't get me killed before I could enjoy it properly.

Matilda went away, and came back much later looking pleased with herself. Her skirts bulged, and I wondered what she'd hidden there. My rats had burrowed down inside the carriage, showing unusual good sense.

I heard a man's voice lifted in a mighty shout and stepped away from the fire, pushing my goggles up onto my forehead. My bonnet was long gone, and it mattered not at all. No one would ever betray me to the troopers at such a time. If they did, the rest of our improvised army would kill them. Not even the gold mattered now, although I wouldn't be showing it off until we were well away.

The shouting man was making a speech. I left the last tin horse half-flattened and climbed up into our carriage to see better.

A broad-faced man knelt on the dirt with his wide-brimmed hat crumpled in his hand. He had the look of the railway about him—especially in the thick shoulders—and I guessed he'd left it to try his luck on the goldfields. It didn't look like he'd had much success.

He lifted one hand and pointed toward the sky. For the first time I saw a great flag, several feet across, bearing a representation of the Southern Cross on a shiny blue background. Whoever made it had marked the cross shape in white lines.

'We swear by the Southern Cross to stand truly by each other!' he bellowed. 'To defend our rights and liberties!'

I watched spellbound as the man raged against the redcoats, troopers, licences, judges, and Mr Bentley. He spoke with all the fire of a preacher, and I believed every word he said, even though he said it all in a thick Irish brogue. Patrick, standing beside me, looked ready to weep with pride.

'If once I pledge my hand to the diggers,' the Irishman said, 'I will neither defile it with treachery nor render it contemptible with cowardice.'

Matilda cheered with the rest, and so did Patrick and I. We were committed to the coming battle body and soul.

By the time the last horse was hammered roughly into place, it was night. The moon was full, and I remembered we'd made a promise to Matilda's native friend to give him gold by this date. I wondered where he was and how long it would take him to find us. He'd be pleased with his share, no doubt. It was more than any of us could have hoped for.

Matilda and I climbed into the carriage to make an improvised bed, while Patrick slept curled up under the back wheels. Many others, exhausted by a night and day of defiance and rhetoric, went back to their own tents outside the stockade, since the following day would be Sunday. No God-fearing trooper would attack on the Lord's day.

Chapter Thirty-Five

The ear-shattering plinking of bullets on tin woke me before dawn. I fumbled for Matilda's arm in the dark and shook her more fully awake, pulling her out of the carriage before she knew the reason for the clamour. We landed in a tangle of limbs and crinolines, and Patrick grabbed hold of both of us and pushed us beneath the coachman's step.

We poked our heads out at once, just in time to see a lone defender balance atop our tin wall and raise the bayonet he'd spent all day sharpening. He made a fine silhouette against the sudden cloud of gunsmoke lightening the predawn sky. Then he was shot, and fell to the ground without another defiant word. He was dead in a moment, and after he'd prepared so hard for this fight. I wondered if all our fates would come for us so quickly.

Patrick pushed at me, trying to get me more fully beneath the carriage.

'No!' I snapped at him, angry with myself for my sudden fear of a pointless death. 'I didn't wait around all day to lie quivering under a basket!'

He yelled back at me, but his voice was drowned out by a second barrage of gunfire.

The flattened tin horses of our fortress parped in a startled chorus. In a moment they gave up all semblance of speech. They screamed—a harsh metallic screech, like a thousand nails scraping on a thousand slates.

I clapped my hands to my ears, but it was no use. The screech of frightened tin sounded like scores of hysterical women. I heard men screaming too, and saw bright flashes of blood blossom on the shirts of men only yards away. Someone pulled on his trousers right in front of me, getting his fingers tangled in the braces.

Patrick gripped my shoulders and forced me back under the carriage, which was made of nothing but wood and wicker. I watched between the spokes of the front wheel as Patrick steadied his arm in his own personal duel, then shook his head. There were too many miners between us and the men shooting from the other side of the screaming stockade wall.

He put his foot to the step to climb up onto the carriage, and I grabbed for his boot to pull him down to dust and safety. Matilda caught my wrist and squeezed hard, holding me back. Tears streaked the dust on her face. But she was right—Patrick was no use crouched under the carriage with us.

I wished I'd thought to speak to his bullets. My heart ticked and slurred and hissed. But I wasn't afraid anymore. In the heat and smoke and darkness, I was thirsty for victory. I could be frightened later.

Patrick leapt down, landing in front of my face. For a heart-stopping moment I thought he'd been shot. But he was only loading his pistol. I waited until he climbed back up, then I crawled out and ran away across the hill where he wasn't able to stop me.

He couldn't keep me safe. We were all ringed together in our tin trap, and I might as well live up to my much-vaunted usefulness. I tripped over something warm and it yelped in pain.

When I knelt, I saw it was a wounded man. Blood shot from his leg in spurts, and I knew he was done for.

He saw my face. 'I didn't—I didn't—' he said.

'What didn't you do?' I asked, pressing down on his leg in a vain attempt to keep him alive. Warm liquid pushed back against my palm and flowed through my fingers.

'I didn't!' he said, and died.

A last gush of blood got past me, wetting the dry ground. Someone touched my shoulder and I screamed, whirling around. It was Matilda.

She smiled down at me like an angel. 'Emmeline.'

'Get back under the carriage you fool!'

She scowled. 'Hypocrite!'

Something the size of a cannonball flew up above the tin wall, and I yanked on her hand so we fell over together. She wrapped her arms around me, and I pressed her head to my chest. I didn't want my one true friend to die. If she was so much as scratched, I'd never forgive myself.

The shell exploded on the ground behind us with a boom and a gout of fire. Matilda and I let go of each other, staring face to face over the dead miner. Her mouth was moving, but all I could hear was a high-pitched ringing like a scream.

Our wall was failing. It howled to let us know we'd soon be overrun.

'What made that explosion?' Matilda yelled in my ear.

'A howitzer!' I yelled back. 'They can shoot exploding shells over the wall.'

'Very well,' she said. She hitched her skirts up to her knees and ran for the barricade.

The dead man at my feet had a gun, so I picked it up. If the soldiers broke though, I could defend myself with something better than a flick knife. And of course my Probability Parasol was carefully packed into the carriage anyway. I ran after Matilda and we crouched together against the hot tin wall.

We ducked, clinging to one another in terror as two more iron shells sailed effortlessly over the wall at the same time, spinning in an elegant dance before crashing into the earth and throwing up a barrage of fire and shrapnel.

The screaming didn't stop. It wasn't just our wall—it was our men.

'Two howitzers,' I said, and peered through a crack in the tin. I spotted both at once, one on either side of the sea of redcoats and mounted police. 'We're done for.'

Chapter Thirty-Six

Patrick materialised from a cloud of stinking gunsmoke and pulled both of us down to ground level. Muscles stood out in his neck and shoulders and arm; he'd ripped off his shirtsleeve, and I wondered if he'd attempted to help a wounded man.

'What are you two *doing*?' he hissed.

'There are two howitzers out there,' I said. 'Which means there are men trained to fire them. So we aim for them—no one else.'

'Right!' he said, sounding sure despite the wriggling fear behind his eyes. 'Can you shoot?'

'You forget, metal likes me.'

'Very well.' He crouched, ready to run to a better position. At the last moment he stopped and clasped our hands. 'Don't either of you get hurt. I couldn't bear it.'

'And you,' I said.

'I'm sorry I was such a rusty guts,' he said to me, 'about your heart.'

With that he ran along the stockade wall toward the far artillery piece, and I took a closer look at my revolver. I hadn't thought to steal ammunition from the dead man. Luckily there were six chambers, and each one was full. I pushed away the thought of having six dead men on my conscience, and begged the bullets to fire well for me and to hit the redcoats in their snarling faces.

Pressing the gun to the closest rent in the screeching tin, I pulled the trigger. Nothing happened. Matilda showed me how to prepare the hammer and I tried again. This time, I kept my eyes open. Before I pulled the trigger I glanced to my left and saw Patrick.

He perched on a carriage pushed up against the wall, and held his open hand out to the enemy ranks like a beggar asking for alms. Through the screams of tin and men and the booming of explosions, I heard his voice.

'Come on then, Barry! Toss that redcoat cully and come back to me.'

I searched the field and spotted Barry's white coat quickly among the brown horses. But that meant Officer Dry had confiscated Barry and ridden to Ballarat. Where was he now?

Barry lifted his head and whickered at Patrick. He reared, throwing a rider I didn't recognise, and trotted obediently to the wall where Patrick shoved aside part of the stockade with a delighted smile.

Barry neighed joyfully, and Patrick swung straight into his saddle and wheeled him around. Two troopers caught up with events and lifted their guns, but Patrick spurred Barry forward with a yell.

He jumped and rammed his way through the massed troops to the howitzer, and Barry kicked one man squarely in the chest with his front feet. Patrick shot another, and a third broke and fled at the sudden apparition.

Patrick leapt to the ground and wrestled something from the howitzer's back. He held it up for a split second, and my heart leapt in recognition. It was aluminium—but why would an iron howitzer have a slot for aluminium sheeting built into its barrel?

The howitzer showed me exactly why; it collapsed forward, suddenly pointing straight across instead of upward. They'd used the aluminium's magic to set the angle of attack, and now their war machine was useless. Several troopers yelped and dived out of the way before the next iron explosion divided their own ranks.

Others shouted in rage and rushed for Patrick. He threw himself across Barry's back and slapped his rear. Barry took the hint and galloped through the newly-cleared space, skewing sideways at the barrier and aiming for the opening in the wall.

He stumbled the last few paces. Blood streamed down his

hindquarters. I yelled for Patrick. Barry turned side-on and Patrick slid down his far side and tried to lead him back through the gap in the barricade. Before he took two steps, brawny arms grabbed him from inside and hauled him away from his wounded horse. I saw the wall slide back into place, and knew Patrick's heroism hadn't gone unnoticed by our companions.

All the troopers aimed for Barry at once. I heard the high screech of animal pain and watched as he fell on his knees, still trying to strike out with his hooves. The wall shook as he fell against it, still shrieking and trying to stand.

His head dropped, and he didn't make another sound. He was just an innocent beast, and now he was dead because of us. Patrick's screams for his horse broke the silence, but when realisation dawned he fell limp in his companions' arms.

The second howitzer spewed out another shell, crashing to the ground behind me. Too bad I didn't have a horse to fight with me—or did I? The wall segment immediately in front of me parped angrily. It was very poorly hammered, and its original design was clear. There were still four distinct feet planted on the ground, and a rounded back.

I tried to leap onto it like Patrick had done, but I slid off onto the hard ground. Matilda saw what I was attempting and only hesitated for a moment. She knelt and offered me her knee. I stepped up, pressed my face against the horse's shoulder joints, and wrapped my arms around its neck to help me stay on board.

'Take me to the howitzer,' I told it. 'Quickly. But—'

It was too late. The tin bunched under me and ran straight through the join where three other flattened horses touched noses.

I clung on, beaten and bruised by the unnatural movement. It skidded to a halt and I fell off, knocking over a trooper. We stared at each other in mutual surprise. It was the mustachioed trooper who'd demanded to see my licence so long ago. I hit him hard across the forehead with the iron pommel of my stolen pistol, and he slumped to the earth. It might not have been proper, but I was a colonial now. My veins ran with brass and fire, and hitting him felt just as satisfying as I'd imagined.

Someone yelled and came running across the field toward me. Someone who didn't have a uniform. Well, well. It was Mr Bentley himself. I remembered witnessing Mr Verne's murder and my fury only grew. He'd not have a third victim. I shot at him, but it went wide. There wasn't time to focus on one man.

I turned my eyes away with an effort and forged onwards. The presence of a woman on the battlefield was surprising, but the enemy had already recovered from the shock. Which meant they'd shoot me. I ducked under my horse and fetched up next to the one remaining howitzer.

An aluminium piece shone prettily at me, and I grabbed it with both hands and tugged it out of place. Its magic worked at once, and I felt light as a feather. I shot my gun wildly, hoping to keep the enemy away another few moments. If I was especially lucky, I'd hit Bentley this time. He was yelling my name—my real name—but it made no difference now.

The howitzer didn't collapse. Half a dozen redcoats lay in a living pile across the firing mechanism, keeping it from shifting. Mr Bentley climbed up them to get over the howitzer, not minding that he was kicking his supposed comrades in their legs and backs and faces.

'Stay in there!' I yelled at the iron shot, with little hope that it would listen to me. I put both my hands on the hot iron barrel, ignoring the blistering heat as it turned my soft hands to open wounds in an instant. 'Please, just blow up!'

Mr Bentley reached over and grabbed my wrist. I bashed him in that whinging face with my new sheet of aluminium, imprinting the metal with his face. He let go, but didn't fall. I hooked one foot over my horse's slippery back and wrapped my arms around its neck, holding the aluminium between the horse's tin back and my steaming chest.

'Run!' I yelled. 'Back to the other horses!'

The horse jerked and leapt and crashed back to the stockade and safety, bouncing and bashing my lower leg against the ground. I managed to look up toward our destination, and realised my horse was heading directly for the stockade wall. There was no gap.

A musketball plinged from the metal near my head, leaving a dent. I closed my eyes, focusing all my energy on holding on. Then I opened them and looked back. My howitzer was all bent out of shape, and the men trying to hold it were beginning to realise their error. They scrambled to get away, but only slipped and slid on one another, making the living mass buck and writhe.

My horse rammed into the wall with a mighty clang of metal on metal, bursting a new hole. On the other side I saw staring miners covered in dust and blood.

Matilda ran to me, holding out her arms. I heard an enormous bang, and a piece of broken howitzer the size of a dinner plate whizzed past me and thwacked into another section, sending it crashing to the ground.

I looked back and saw my howitzer blow sky-high, hurling the slender figure of Mr Bentley in a perfect parabola the height of his old hotel. The last anyone saw of him was a pale-faced figure plummeting to Earth. His despair was so palpable I reached out my hand as if to try to catch him. But his scheming, villainous life was done.

Our stockade was done, too. Miners ran to prop it back up but the troopers swarmed inside, shouting with triumphant rage and shooting their rifles as they came.

'Parp,' said my horse. 'Parp-parp-parp-parp-parp!'

I released my death grip on its neck, and Matilda caught me, stumbling only a little.

'Look,' I said, pointing at the red flank of my horse. 'My horse is bleeding.'

Chapter Thirty-Seven

Matilda half-dragged me up the hill toward our carriage. Troopers shot and stabbed and kicked their way through the far smaller crowd of miners. The walls fell silent suddenly, plunging us into a muted world of smoke and despair. It was so achingly beautiful I wept.

Miners tumbled to the ground like leaves shaken from an autumn tree. None of the redcoats faltered. The mounted police rode over our men where they lay, crushing the wounded under their hooves.

Our broad-faced railwayman stood beneath the Southern Cross flag. Tears streaked down his face into his beard. His left arm was bright red with blood and hung useless by his side as a trooper climbed the flagpole, breaking it with his weight, and took the banner away. The railwayman shivered, though his face shone with sweat. He was all out of speeches.

Matilda tried to prop me upright, but when I took a step my leg folded under me. It was wet, as if I'd stepped in a puddle. There weren't any puddles. My gun was still in my hand, so I slid it into a pocket as Patrick ran up to us, grimacing in obvious pain.

I looked him up and down, but he didn't seem to be wounded. He scowled at me. Something about me was upsetting him. I wondered if it was my heart still bothering him. Matilda seemed upset too. They slung me between them and raced on up the hill away from the scarlet wave of troops.

My feet didn't touch the ground. I twisted to look back at the railwayman. He held up a sheet of white bedlinen in his good arm.

'We lost!' I said. 'How could we lose? We were so brave, and so right!'

The troopers paused in their advance, and I wondered if there was a gaol big enough to hold the hundreds of miners still standing. Except there weren't hundreds anymore. Some were dead or wounded, moaning on the dirt. Others had long since fled.

'Run,' I said, realising all hope had bled away. 'Hide.'

'No,' said Patrick. 'We lost our fight, and we'll pay for it.'

'Really?' I said. 'Can we afford that price?'

A wounded miner reached up a bloodied hand, croaking for help at the feet of the leading troopers. He was right to beg—we were done.

A trooper looked the helpless miner in the eye and set his rifle to his shoulder. It was awkward, aiming for a man so close, but he did it. He shot him. The bloodied hand collapsed.

I saw a second trooper, mad with battle and victory, raise his gun to another wounded man. Women poured out of tents and tunnels and threw themselves over the bodies of their broken husbands and brothers and sons. They bet their lives on the hope there was some scrap of Christian charity remaining in the redcoats' hearts. Each one was radiant with love, and I wished I had Mother's talent for art.

'Stop!' I yelled.

The troopers didn't stop, but Matilda did. I fell out of Patrick's grasp and landed on one foot. Some instinct told me not to let my other foot touch the ground.

Patrick wheeled around, reaching to pick me up.

'Look!' I shouted at him. 'They're killing the wounded.'

His face drained of colour, and for some reason he glanced at my feet. I followed his gaze and saw that my left leg wasn't mine anymore. It belonged to a lead musketball, and was soaked in blood. The world wasn't beautiful at all; it was the magic of the lead playing tricks with my mind. My own blood looked picturesque to me against my pale flesh.

'Oh no!' I said, recognising the familiar sensation of shock taking over my body and mind. 'My ankle. Who'll marry me now?'

Matilda exchanged a meaningful glance with Patrick, and the pair of them ran up the hill, bouncing my good leg against the ground. I knew enough to hold up my wounded leg. It was beginning to prickle with something like pins and needles, and I suspected it was about to hurt a great deal. I braced myself for the pain to come, hoping I'd be proud enough to bear it bravely.

They threw me into the carriage and fumbled with our secret stash of aluminium, scrabbling at the silk balloon to find the necessary pockets. I noticed I still clutched the thick sheet of howitzer aluminium, and shoved it awkwardly into one of the pockets. 'Please,' I whispered to it. 'Lift us up. I don't want to be shot again.'

One side of the basket was already ablaze. While the others propped up the increasingly-weightless silk I found one gauntlet on the floor and tried to put it on. It was hard to concentrate while standing on one leg, and I wasted time trying to put the gauntlet on the wrong hand.

At last I figured it out. I put it on my left hand, ignoring the clasps, and threw pieces of wicker into the burner as tinder for the firewood. My rats parped at me, and I told them to stop whining and get to work. One stayed in the burner, and the rest jumped up onto my shoulder and then up ropes inside the silk, steaming vigorously as they did so. Our fire fizzed and sparked with exquisite elegance. The sweet smell of burning eucalyptus mixed with the coppery stink of blood, and tears sprang to my eyes at the splendour of the colours.

Our silk envelope mushroomed over us, filling faster than I dared hope thanks to the rats and the enthusiastic aluminium. I wondered how long it would take the soldiers to realise we were attempting to escape, and shoot either us or the far easier silk target. It all depended on whether they understood basic aeronautics—or just wanted us dead.

Matilda balanced on the back of the carriage, reaching up as high as she could to correctly place the last piece of aluminium. She buttoned the flap and slid down to me.

'Why is it so high so quickly?' she yelled. 'What did we do?'

'Extra aluminium,' I said. 'From the howitzer. British made, of course.'

'Of course.'

I looked across the battlefield and saw ruined tents and black craters. The sky lightened with the coming dawn, and the wounded railwayman backed away from the approaching troopers, waving his white cloth in a desperate hope that the murders taking place before his eyes were some sort of error. He fetched up against our carriage, and I reached down and gripped his good shoulder.

'I'm afraid we haven't been introduced!' I yelled at him. 'My name is Emmeline Muchamore, and I'll be saving your life today.'

He stared at me, and I held out my hand. His left arm was too weak to lift, so he tried to shake my hand with his right. Our carriage rocked precariously, and I felt good hot fire at my back. The silk filled and lifted higher, beginning to look like a proper balloon. I yanked on the railwayman's right arm, and he stumbled forward, swearing.

'Come inside, you Irish beef-head,' I yelled.

'My men!' he said.

'They'll be worse off if you're killed.'

He half-crawled up the steps, but as he joined us one man split off from the stationary troopers and galloped his horse across the debris of tents and men. His navy coat among the scarlet mass sucked away the dawn light.

It was Officer Dry—and he was coming for us.

Chapter Thirty-Eight

The carriage drifted across the ground, banging against rocks and fallen tents. I heard a scream, and knew we'd knocked over another wounded man. But it was too late, we were no longer in control. The railwayman's legs dangled half out of the carriage, and his eyes widened with shock as he realised we were flying—almost. Officer Dry reached up and caught hold of his ankle.

I held onto the charred side of the carriage, staring down at Officer Dry. He'd obviously ridden for several days before getting caught up in the battle; his beard was ragged and his grey eyes red-rimmed.

'Emmeline Muchamore, you are under arrest.'

'Officer Dry,' I spat. 'You are mistaken.'

Our balloon didn't move. Officer Dry and his horse held us like an anchor. A bald native—William—rode up beside him, but didn't move to either help or hinder him.

Matilda stood beside me. 'Come with us, William.'

'You'll fulfill your promise?' he said, and his voice was as soft as ever.

'That I will. Today.'

He tightened his knees, and the horse walked around the carriage. Matilda reached out her small hand and he took it, standing carefully on the horse's back. Officer Dry steadied his grip on the railwayman's leg. We weren't going anywhere. William didn't attempt to leap inside. He knew he was too heavy. We all stared at one another, perfectly balanced.On the other side of the hill, a man roared in sudden pain. I remembered my gun, and pulled it out. My heart's magic told me I had just one shot left. That would be plenty.

I pointed the gun at Officer Dry, feeling the balloon fret at its traces, longing to float away. 'Let go of him.'

He turned his cold eyes on me and sneered. 'What kind of lady wields a gun?'

I cocked the hammer and hoped the powder was dry. 'The kind who gets what she wants. Now let go of him.'

He grimaced with a hateful joy and drew his own pistol to brandish at me. 'Do you aim to frighten me?' I shot the ground beside him, and it exploded in a shower of dust.

He clung on to the railwayman's leg, but he hesitated.

'I fought against terrible odds today, and I fought gladly,' I said, drunk on the knowledge I'd just spent my last bullet. 'Do you doubt my will?' I levelled the gun at his heart—a pathetic flesh heart—and tightened my finger on the trigger. Knowing the gun was empty.

When he looked into my eyes he saw something there, and let go. He fell backward onto the dirt. Matilda yelped, and Patrick reached out with her and hauled William aboard as we sailed away.

I put the gun back into my pocket, careful not to let it slip from my shaking fingers, and watched the troopers pour over the crest of the hill in a final push. Patrick blew on the fire. William closed his eyes and held on. I whispered endearments to the aluminium, making friends fast.

The coming troopers shouted in rage as they spotted us. Officer Dry leapt to his feet and pointed, jumping up and down like a squalling child. Some men ran toward us, and others set their rifles to their shoulders. I crouched down, trying and failing to pull the railwayman behind the pathetic wicker. He was pale with blood loss, and too weak to haul himself to safety. Several bullets hit the burner with loud clangs, and another grazed my arm, blistering my skin like a brand. I heard tearing silk as someone shot the envelope, and yelled for my rats to clamp together the tear with their claws.

'Lose weight!' Patrick bawled in my ear.

'I beg your—' I turned and saw precisely what he meant. We

flew straight for the only remaining solid section of our tin stockade, and we were flying so low we were sure to hit it. The aluminium wanted to help us, but it needed us to do our part.

Tick, tick.

Matilda dived for Patrick's locked chair and I knew at once what she was thinking. Our heavy gold was about to get us killed, tipped ignominiously back into the trooper's range. Officer Dry would have us arrested the instant we hit the ground—if we lived that long. So she was going to throw it away.

'No!' I yelled, and grabbed my portmanteau, doing my best to haul it over the side in a leathery pile of scrap metal, spare shoes and steel parasol.

I wasn't strong enough to lift it—not anymore. The railwayman's eyes widened with understanding, and he made a supreme effort to get inside the basket, ending up prone but safe. He gripped the bag with his one good hand. Between us we pushed and pulled it across the floor and up and over the broken wicker side. It fell to the ground and our carriage lifted higher at once.

Tick, tick.

Matilda closed the lid of the gold-filled compartment with a hollow clap, and she came back to me. Together we stared at the spilled contents of my old life. My parasol had sprung open like a pale flower; my left gauntlet lay palm-upward with the fingers splayed; and my wedding dress spilled from the open top of the portmanteau in a white froth.

'Oh,' I said as the sight grew rapidly smaller. 'I never got to wear it.'

'Hmm,' said Matilda. She pushed me down to the wooden floor and shoved my skirts up to my knees without so much as a by-your-leave. My heart beat louder, but I didn't care.

Tick!

'What have you done this time?' she asked me.

I looked at my left ankle, and it suddenly hurt very much. Instead of swooning, I gritted my teeth and pressed my lips together to mute my moans. Swooning would have been better.

On the opposite side of the carriage, Patrick tore off his one remaining sleeve to tie around the railwayman's bleeding shoulder. Only Matilda would notice if I wept a little, but I was the only truly British person on board, so I called on my Muchamore pride and managed not to cry out at the blistering pain.

'I lost more blood than this when I was just a girl,' I said stoutly, 'and I was hardly hurt at all.'

Tick, tick.

'Good to know,' said Matilda, humouring me, and she pressed at my leg with her fingers, searching for the bullet.

'Leave it,' I told her. 'The metal's holding in the blood. It can't do me any harm now. Besides, it's making you look prettier than ever.'

'Very well,' she said doubtfully, and pressed her skirt against the wound to staunch the bleeding.

Tick, tick.

'Oops,' she said. 'The shot came out the other side. Is that bad?'

She showed me a hand covered in blood, with a comically squashed lead ball.

'Do you think a harder metal would be more or less effective as a projectile?' I asked.

'I think you're hysterical.'

'Shouldn't I be ... oh, I don't know, louder? If I was hysterical?'

'Excellent point.' She dropped the lead over the side of the carriage as if it was nothing.

Patrick finished tending to our friend and crouched beside me. 'It will be all right. We're safe now.'

I didn't answer, thinking instead of the wounded men we'd left behind. For the first time, I was viciously glad to be an outlaw. If those redcoats represented the law, I wanted no part of it. We might have lost, but we still won. Matilda wrapped my leg in uncharacteristic silence, and I knew she was remembering the fallen as well.

'My name is Lalor,' said our companion.

We introduced ourselves, and for a moment I thought Patrick would offer us some tea.

'I'm sorry to have failed you,' he said to Mr Lalor.

'Failed?' Matilda interrupted. 'Someone had to make a stand against those rat-hearted tyrants.' My rats stared at her. 'Er … no offence meant to present company.'

Patrick collapsed against the far wall. 'Barry,' he whispered. 'What have I done?'

'We lost good men,' said Mr Lalor stoutly, 'but we didn't lose.'

Even Matilda paused at that. 'We surrendered. You waved the white flag yourself.'

'And you all saw the murders that followed, I presume? On the Lord's day, too. Every newspaper in the country will tell Australia and the world what happened today, and our courage will weigh heavier in men's minds than any victory.'

I wondered what I would have thought, reading about such a battle way back in London. He was right: even my old self would question everything the redcoats stood for.

'We lost, but we lost to a pack of cowards, and everyone will know it. Those poor dead men have proved the justice of our cause. From today, everything has changed. You'll see.'

'Mr Bentley's dead too,' I said, too tired to be either pleased or sorry about one more soul gone to Judgement. 'I saw him.'

Tick, tick.

Patrick lifted his head. 'I bet Mother draws a picture of us, and what happened here. Someone will see it and make hundreds of copies.'

'Thousands,' I said, remembering the achingly beautiful blood and the courage of our dead friends.

We flew on in silence, not knowing where the wind would take us. All that mattered was that we left Ballarat behind. We'd lost and won the greatest battle of our lives.

Tick.

Hisssssssssss.

Oh no. Not now.

Chapter Thirty-Nine

'What was that?' said Matilda.

Tiiiiiick.

'What was that?' said Mr Lalor.

Tiiiiiick.

'What was that?' said William.

'Oh!' said Matilda, understanding what was happening. 'Look away, gentlemen, if you please.'

She produced a bottle of clear water from her skirt, spilling several lumps of high-quality coal as she did so. 'Sorry dear,' she said to me, and ripped away the front of my dress. 'While you lot prepared for battle I decided your heart might need taking care of too.'

'Mmph,' I said, trying not to move as she tugged at my corset laces, pulling them out and throwing them aside with the steel segments. I noticed two more lead bullets embedded in the metal, and that her hands were very beautiful. Also, I was naked from the waist up. Matilda had a tiny smirk at the corner of her mouth, but she didn't say anything untoward. My heart told me she wanted to—and she wasn't delirious, either.

'I'm not particularly good with engines,' she said instead. 'You'll have to tell me what to do.'

'Front and back,' I whispered, finding myself out of breath. 'Half-fill the boilers. Should be all right …' The noise of my ticking heart was silent for the first time since I was a child. My foot no longer hurt. Matilda bit her lip in concentration, and the movement looked so magnificent all kinds of peculiar thoughts paraded through my head. 'Hurry …'

She hooked open my sternum access panel and her shoulders

relaxed as if she knew exactly what she was doing. I wondered if my lead bullet was powerful enough to make me look beautiful to her, like she looked to me. Later we'd have to compare notes—for science. Suddenly I remembered the lead shot was already out of my leg and tossed away. Which meant Matilda really was that beautiful. Oh dear.

'The boiler is … ?' she asked.

'Not the bit with coal in it, or the pipes. The bit in the middle.'

'Ah!'

A moment later she shut my sternum and squinched around to my other side. Her warm hands felt around on my skin for the clasp of the main access panel in my back. I felt perfectly serene even as my vision blurred and my heart refused to switch over to its backup engine. The water hissed as Matilda poured it into the over-heated brass of the primary boiler. She slotted it back into place with a neat click, and we both waited, kneeling, to see if she'd saved my life.

'Oh!' she said in delight. 'I can see it beating! Is that how it's meant to go?' she asked.

I laughed helplessly, and turned to embrace her. 'Yes! Yes that's right.'

She clung on to me, dripping tears down my naked back. 'I was so scared!'

'Me too.'

'It's so … elegant! All the little joins and compartments. I've never seen something so perfectly made.'

'I'll have to teach you to maintain it.'

'Please!'

We sat back on our heels and grinned at one another.

'Emmeline?'

'Yes?'

'Do you think you should put some clothes on?'

I looked down at my naked breasts, and was startled to remember Matilda had just destroyed my very last dress. 'Oh.'

My corset lay in segments around us. I reattached the laces and Matilda helped me put it back on. We asked the men to pass us Mrs O'Connell's dress, and Matilda tugged it on over what I was already wearing.

'What are you smiling at?' she asked.

'When we first met, I thought it was my duty to civilise you.'

'Oh?' she raised an eyebrow, and her fingers stilled on my laces. 'How's your progress so far?'

'Not good.' I wondered if I was delirious, and decided it didn't matter. 'Fortunately.'

'Can we turn around yet?' asked Patrick. 'We can't hear a word you're saying over the crackle of the burner.'

'No!' I said loudly. 'Not yet.'

'All right,' Matilda said, tying one last bow. 'That will have to do.'

She lifted her head to address the men but I reached out and hushed her, placing my finger on her lips. 'Not yet,' I whispered.

For once she looked uncertain. I didn't take my hand from her lips. Something was happening—something important—and I couldn't figure out what it was.

Her eyes brightened with suppressed laughter. She knew something I didn't.

'What's happening to me?' I whispered.

Matilda pressed her lips against my hand in a swift kiss. It startled me, making my skin shiver. I snatched my hand away. We stared at each other, kneeling face to face.

She breathed deeply, keeping her eyes fixed on mine. I wanted more than anything to share her breath and life. One shimmering curl of her hair strayed across her cheek. She smelled of eucalyptus and coal and silk.

I had no secrets from her—none at all—except the fact that if I didn't kiss her my heart would break. Again.

So I kissed her, and she kissed me.

'We're all right,' said Matilda loudly, sitting back comfortably.

'You gentlemen can turn around, if you like. Emmeline will be just fine, I'm sure of it now.'

'Glad to hear it!' said Patrick, smiling at both of us. 'Would anyone like some tea?'

'Mmm, yes,' I said, choosing to ignore the break in my voice.

Matilda and I knelt close together. She sang an ancient song I loved but didn't understand. The five of us flew on over coppery grassfields and silver forests, with our box full of gold.

Tick, tick.

THE END

I made certain choices in portraying an Aboriginal woman of the time, consulting with Dr Anita Heiss and others in order to try to make ethical writing choices. Some of the terms used for Aboriginals in the book are offensive ('native', 'Aborigine', and 'tribe', for example), as I compromised between a tragic history and a light-hearted story. The most glaring fiction is the pattern of scars on Matilda's body. Because many Aboriginal religious rituals are kept deliberately secret, I chose to fictionalise her past rather than inadvertently reveal something sacred (or pretend her childhood contained nothing of note). I also used British names in order to avoid using the Aboriginal names of the dead. Matilda and William would have had other names as well, but they have not been spoken or written here.

Some of the characters, locations, and events are real (such as the Eureka Hotel and James Scobie), and others are entirely fictional (including Scobie's family, Verne, Patrick, Emmeline and Matilda) and I left out Mrs Bentley. The latter was a truly fascinating woman, who was pregnant at the time of these events, yet lent her husband a dress on the night of the fire (presumably to help him get away unnoticed, despite the fact he was on a police horse at the time), and who may in fact have killed James Scobie herself (eyewitness accounts place her at the scene expressing delight at the instant of Scobie's death).

Many of the least plausible aspects of the story were taken from history. Some transported convicts were recorded as 'deceased' by British courts; horses handle balloon flight quite well; the goldfields really were laced with secret tunnels; the Southwells's tent was based on a real Ballarat tent used for holding balls; at least one shop was enclosed within the Eureka stockade; the lost battle at Eureka prompted real change. Many of the inventions, including the cogged railways, were real inventions that simply didn't catch on.

After the Flag Fell

A Choose Your Own Adventure-style bonus to *Heart of Brass*

This is the page where you keep records of your item/s, personality, and skills. You can grab pen and paper, or follow tradition and cheat.

You begin this story with a single magical item made from one of the following metals (choose one and mark it)—listed in order from least to most precious in 1854 Australia.

*This is the only thing you need to choose before beginning the story on **Page 1**.*

- _ **Tin Spoon:** has rudimentary communication ability.
- _ **Iron Tea Caddy:** makes you physically stronger.
- _ **Brass Goggles:** fine-tunes the senses in useful ways.
- _ **Lead Ball:** increases your emotions, for better or worse.
- _ **Silver Pocketwatch:** can connect with organic life, which is medically useful.
- _ **Gold Nugget:** makes you more charming.
- _ **Aluminium Locket:** neutralises your weight, making you unusually graceful.

During the tale you'll need to keep track of the following by marking them with an X.

Trust: _ _ _ _ _
Caution: _ _ _ _ _
Sharpshooting: _ _ _ _ _
Mechanical Skill: _ _ _ _ _
Poor Health: _ _ _ _ _

*If you have marked off all five of your poor health lines, go to **Page 18** regardless of other instructions.*

Possible Goals:

It is possible to achieve all of the following in a single play-through, but it's far from easy. You might prefer a different path, a different story or a different life. The real-life equivalent of the protagonist achieved three of these goals.

1. Your arm is better (either healed or improved).
2. You are married.
3. You have helped Australia become independent of Great Britain.
4. You have gained the right for all Australians to vote.
5. You have remained committed to your ideals of democracy and justice.
6. You are rich.
7. You are in possession of magical items made from seven different metals.
8. You live happily ever after.

There are three 'good' endings, two of which can be achieved in various ways.

Or you can collect all of the six gruesome ways to die.

I saw the flag fall. That glorious Southern Cross, shining with hope for every man who'd been grubbing in the gold-studded dirt for so long … gone. One of the soldiers—one of those blasted redcoats that attacked us diggers on the Lord's day—climbed our flagpole and tore down our stars.

The battle was lost by then, and our stockade was broken in a dozen places. Our rebellion was finished, though I couldn't bear to admit it yet. We had our guns and a little magic here and there, but they had more. I felt my eyes burn with anger, and was unashamed to let my tears fall.

We were just diggers looking for gold and hope and a new life in Australia. By 1854 the only ones getting rich on the goldfields were the redcoated soldiers taking the little we had with their overpriced licence fees. In the end we'd burned our licences and built a rough boundary fence: the Eureka Stockade, a gathering-place on Bakery Hill where Irish and Scottish and English and Chinese and all the rest joined together as one. It wasn't a fort, it was a symbol: we deserved better.

We were willing to fight for our lives, but we weren't ready. So when the redcoats marched to crush us our stockade was quickly breached, our numbers decimated, and our flag torn down.

I didn't even hear the gunshot that sent a musket-ball my way. It hit the metal of my waistcoat and slid upwards, lodging in my shoulder and shattering the bone. I tried to move my fingers, but I couldn't. Nor could I lift my arm. My part in the fight was done, and I knew it. If I was lucky, I'd lose my arm rather than my life. I looked around for our flag, hoping for one last glimpse before we were overrun, but it was gone.

The dead lay in slag-heap piles. More than a dozen men I'd encouraged to make a stand would never stand again. Others lay moaning, and I decided that since I could still walk I'd best make myself useful. I headed towards the closest wounded man, wondering what I'd do for bandages when my own shoulder was dripping blood down to my fingertips. Two redcoats reached him first—and killed him.

In another life I'd have been too shocked to move, but this was Eureka, and I understood instantly that the redcoats would kill anyone who wasn't quick enough to flee. I still had my gun, but it was no use against the crushing tide of history.

I spotted a pile of slabs nearby—big enough and untidy enough to keep me hidden.
If you choose to hide under the timber, add a mark to Caution and go to Page 4.

A hot air balloon drifted across the battlefield, and a wealthy-looking woman reached out her hand to invite me aboard.
If you choose to trust her, add a mark to Trust and go to Page 5.

A Scottish acquaintance of my friend Duncan Gillies saw me and yelled, 'Peter! Mr Lalor! I have a horse for you.'
If you choose to trust him, add a mark to Trust and go to Page 7.

There were tunnels beneath the hill. I knew I could escape and hide in the bushland and no one would ever find me.
If you choose to hide in the bushland, add a mark to Caution and go to Page 9.

If this is your second visit to Page 1 within one play-through, go to Page 61.

Easter Egg #1

If you'd like to make the same choices as the historical Peter Lalor, the sequence is as follows (except, sadly, with no magic or mechanical limbs): 1, 4, 7, 12, 9, 13, 10, 20, 24, 21, 22, 26, 37, 70, 38, 43, 67, 68, 47, 45.

I happen to know one of Peter Lalor's descendants. If Lalor had made different choices, she might not exist. Of course, if he'd truly believed in democracy (as people assumed he did until he emphatically proved otherwise), Australia might be a better nation today.

Someone had discarded a sword nearby and I used it to lever up a crucial slab that shifted another, and another—allowing me to crawl inside the pile of timber before releasing the sword so the slabs fell back into place.

Redcoats called out, 'Where is Peter Lalor? Tell us!'

No one told them where I was. Staying perfectly still, I watched in horror as the blood from my shoulder pooled beneath me, leaking out from beneath the slabs to where it could easily be seen. Outside, I heard women screaming at the soldiers to spare their husbands and sons. Close by, I heard laboured breath. I wasn't the only wounded man hiding as the soldiers butchered our companions. My heart stuttered in my chest, shaming me twice—once for the terror stealing my breath, and once for my uselessness when good men most needed my help.

At last the soldiers were all gone, and brave women searched the battlefield for survivors. I crawled out from my shelter and pulled the shirt off a dead man to staunch my bleeding shoulder. He was one of mine: a common man trying to scrape a living from the goldfields only to lose it to the greed of the wealthy. Now he'd lost his life as well. I didn't even know his name.

My vision blurred from pain and loss of blood, but my legs held me up well enough.

Add a mark to Poor Health.

Add a mark to Mechanical Skill.

My acquaintance with the horse was calling for me. I went with him. **Add a mark to Trust and go to Page 7.**

I headed for the bush to keep out of the way of the redcoats. They were bound to continue looking for me. **Add a mark to Caution and go to Page 9.**

The rich woman assisted my awkward scramble into the hot air balloon just as the soldiers spotted me and immediately fired several shots, careless of who or what they hit. I saw blood staining the wooden floor of the basket, and it wasn't mine.

Getting in the balloon wasn't enough. It floated far too close to the ground, and made all of us a target. The woman hurled her portmanteau over the wicker edge of the basket in order to save me instead of her belongings, and I realised it was her blood on the floor. I was too dazed to thank her, or to protest that I'd caused such trouble. The balloon was packed with people, and they'd all risked themselves to save me.

Together we drifted away from Ballarat, flying at the mercy of the wind. The pilot was Irish, like me, although the woman who had hauled me aboard was British. An Aboriginal woman tended to her wound as the pilot bound my shoulder. I still couldn't move my fingers, and my whole arm was a dead weight.

To distract me from the pain, the pilot showed me the mechanism of the enormous balloon—using a controlled fire to lift or lower the varnished black silk. Strange to think that we were flying like birds based on nothing but the power of warm air. I had expected to feel afraid to be in the sky, but instead it was strangely calming.

The British woman's friend gave me an aluminium locket. She said she hoped the unnatural grace it provided might help me in future battles. So she was wealthy too—or had been until the battle. I felt a surge of pride that our Southern Cross had brought together such an array of good people.

'Where to?' said the pilot. 'It's looks like we're heading for Geelong.'

Add a mark to Mechanical Skill.

Add Aluminium Locket to your items.

'I have friends in Geelong,' I said.
Go to Page 24.

'The sooner we separate the safer we'll all be,' I said. 'This area looks familiar. If you're able to let me down I'll go to my friend Mr Mason for shelter.'
Go to Page 12.

'Is it possible for you to let me down a little farther in this direction?' I asked. 'My friend Stephen Cummins is definitely loyal to me.'
Go to Page 13.

I couldn't remember the Scottish man's name, but I remembered he was a single man, like myself. That was a relief, when I could hear women sobbing over their dead all around us. I couldn't bear to look at them, but as I stared at the ground I caught a glimpse of a calico skirt soaked with blood. One pale hand still curled around a fold of cloth. I wrenched my gaze away before I saw her face. One of her shoes had been cast off as she attempted to flee, and it lay a stone's throw away, still as clean as when she put it on. The other shoe was torn, broken, and soaked with her blood.

'This way, Mr Lalor,' said my redheaded friend, and ducked into a low tin structure that had been somebody's makeshift home before Bakery Hill was chosen as the location for our gathering. I couldn't help noticing it was smoking gently, like many other rude hovels and tents unfortunate enough to be blasted by howitzers that morning.

To my surprise, most of the inside floor was taken up with a gaping hole, and the little ground that remained barely fit a rather clunky stove and boiler attached to a winch. My companion stepped down into the hole, landing on a wooden platform within. With few options for escape, I stepped down with him and watched as he flipped a switch on the engine and waited expectantly.

The stove and boiler was in fact a steam-powered winch for our platform, but the release valve was blocked by a piece of shrapnel. Reaching up, I pulled it out and our platform immediately moved down into the dark, creaking in time with puffs of steam above.

Once we reached the base of the shaft, Mr Gregor—that was his name—led me through a dark tunnel on foot until we finally emerged into bushland, where the promised horse was waiting.

'Thank you, Mr Gregor,' I said, desperate to prove I remembered his name after all.

'You should ride,' he said, directing a sympathetic grimace at my shoulder. 'The horse is yours, if you want her. She'll find her way home again once you dismount. Are you sure you're all right on your own?'

Add a mark to Mechanical Skill.

'This area looks familiar. Thank you for the horse.' I went to my friend Mr Mason for shelter.
Go to Page 12.

'I know my way from here. The horse will be very helpful, thank you.' My friend Stephen Cummins was definitely loyal to me. I went to him.
Go to Page 13.

I wandered in the nearby bushland for a full day and night, so thirsty I didn't feel hungry. My shoulder turned red and swollen, stretching the skin painfully. I still couldn't move my left arm, and I was convinced I'd never be able to use it again.

The trees around me whispered and cackled, and I heard creatures scuttling all around. Half-metallic abominations chittered and clanked in the branches above. In the darkness, I sometimes saw glowing eyes—or perhaps they were stars glimmering through the trees. A pack of dingoes found me just as the sun greyed the Eastern sky. I shot and wounded one of them before they dispersed.

It grew harder to remember what was real. I didn't have any more bullets, and I needed a doctor. And water.

Add a mark to Poor Health.

Add a mark to Sharpshooting.

I made my way to the Mason family's house.
Go to Page 14.

I made my way to the Cummins's house—it was farther, but he was a better friend.
Add another mark to Poor Health, and go to Page 13.

I stayed in the bush.
If your Trust is higher than your Caution, go to Page 15.
If your Caution is higher than your Trust, go to Page 17.
(If your Trust and Caution are equal, choose either Page 15 or 17.)

Stephen Cummins rapidly found a surgeon who could be trusted. At that point, I'd have accepted a passing redcoat if he'd said he could make the pain stop.

The surgeon was a tall man, grey-haired, with a stoop that made him look like a mountain with legs. After cutting away the bloodied rags of my shirt, he swore in a leisurely fashion before directing me to lie down on a wooden pew.

'I have good news and bad news,' he told me, sharpening a long knife with a whetstone.

'Oh?' I said.

'I don't have any chloroform,' he said cheerfully. 'Or ether, for that matter. And I'll have to use salt to clean the wound, too. That won't be pretty. Not even a drop of whiskey, which is sad indeed. If you didn't want any, I'd have drunk it myself. Oh, and I doubt you'll see that arm again in this life. That's the other bad news.'

I smiled weakly, wondering if he was entirely sane. 'You mentioned good news?'

He grinned, setting the knife down beside a hacksaw that I wished I hadn't seen. 'I'm very fast.'

My friends distributed themselves all around me, pinning me to the pew with all their strength. It didn't seem quite right having surgery on a wooden bench above a dirt floor, but what else could I do?

'Ready?' said the doctor.

'Ready,' said Stephen.

I closed my eyes and willed myself to remain still. It was no use. When the knife sliced through my skin and muscle I convulsed wildly despite the best efforts of everyone present. The doctor switched to the saw and cut through the bones of my arm near the shoulder, hissing through his teeth as he did so, then happily announcing, 'Almost done!'

When he'd tied off my arteries so I didn't bleed to death, he pronounced himself to be finished. I took a ragged breath, only to scream it out as the salt he poured on my bloody stump sucked away all the moisture in the area. He signalled for a bucket of water, and slopped it over me, leaving me soaked from beard to britches—but at least it washed away the salt.

'Now I'm really finished,' he said. 'You look great!'

I was too shaky to sit up, and it took all my self-control not to hurl myself at him in a blind fury. It helped to remind myself that all I'd have done was fall on the floor.

The entire operation took less than a minute, but that fifty-three seconds left me more shaken than the entire battle, including the moment when the bullet first hit me.

If your Poor Health is zero, go to Page 64.

If your Poor Health is one or two, go to Page 20.

If your Poor Health is three, go to Page 25.

If your Poor Health is four, go to Page 52.

If your Poor Health is five, go to Page 18.

I soon wished I'd stayed hidden on Bakery Hill. The distance to the Masons's house had grown five times longer overnight. My shoulder throbbed, and my arm was a dead weight.

There weren't many houses outside of the gold-rush town of Ballarat, and those that existed stood empty as their owners sought their fortunes elsewhere. I wondered if they'd all return to their original homes now we'd lost our battle for a fair go. The weight of our failure pressed down on me.

When I arrived at the Masons's mud-and-timber house, only Mrs Mason was there. She blanched at my bloodied appearance and immediately pressed a cup of lukewarm tea and a fresh bandage into my good hand. I felt greatly restored at once.

'Thank you for your kindness,' I told her. 'You're a true—'

'I'll go and get my husband at once,' she said, and left before I could say another word.

Add a mark to Poor Health.

I waited for their return.
Add a mark to Trust and go to Page 59.

I fled to the bush instead—she could have been fetching anyone, even soldiers.
Add a mark to Caution and go to Page 9.

Mrs Cummins recognised me as I staggered from the trees near their house. She called Stephen at once and together they helped me through their wilted vegetable patch and into their slab hut, applying a fresh bandage and giving me plenty of much-needed water. It was tinged red from the iron in the soil, and reminded me uncomfortably of the battle, but I drank it gratefully.

Stephen cooked fresh damper for me, lacing the dough with sugar and telling me to eat as much as I wanted and then to sleep in their bed.

When I awoke some time later, Stephen and Mrs Cummins redressed my shoulder, glancing at one another with silent horror as they bared my wound to the full light of day.

Stephen was concerned that our friendship was too well known, so he'd crossed the gully while I slept to ask Father Smythe's permission to shelter me at the Presbytery. There was already a two-hundred-pound bounty on my head.

'What do you say, Peter?' he asked.

I went along with his suggestion and moved to the church under cover of darkness.
Mark Trust and Caution and go to Page 10.

I went and hid in the bush instead.
Mark Caution and go to Page 9.

I went to the Masons's instead.
Mark Trust and go to Page 14.

If you have a Tin Spoon, go to Page 32.

Otherwise, go to Page 33.

I wandered through the bush until an Aboriginal family found me. By then I was barely rational, and slipping in and out of consciousness. In a delirious waking dream, I imagined universal suffrage—not just landowners, but all colonial and British men. Not just men, but all colonial adults. Maybe even, someday, all Australians—landowners, ordinary men, women, and Aboriginal people.

I woke up screaming as the natives sliced through my upper arm with a machete, switching to a hacksaw when they reached the bone. They'd tied me securely while I slept, and I was unable to move. Women stood by with burning pieces of wood, and they burned what was left of my arm until I passed out. When I woke up a second time, they gave me water and sweet fruits and nuts, and I realised they'd saved my life. With my one arm, I untied the remaining laces of my metal waistcoat, and offered it to them.

Using fire-warmed rocks and pieces of wire, they flattened the moulded metal and, after a great deal of discussion, carved a hunting scene into the back piece. A herd of kangaroos sprang for the upper corners of the vest as stylised hunters ambushed them. It was complicated, delicate work and I revised my opinion of their metalworking skills.

As night fell, they held the picture before their cooking fire and it danced with light through miniscule holes. Then they gave it back to me, keeping the front pieces of my waistcoat for themselves.

A few already spoke a little English, and they laughed without malice at my first attempts to communicate. They washed and redressed my wound every few hours, and it soon became clear that they possessed their own brand of medical knowledge.

I realised I was waiting for the noise of gunshots, and made an effort to calm myself. This world had its dangers, but I was far safer than I'd been in some time. I curled up and slept peacefully under the starry sky.

I chose to stay with the natives for as long as they'd let me.
Go to Page 19.

I went to my acquaintance, Mr Mason.
Go to Page 14.

I went to my friends at Geelong.
Go to Page 26.

I stood at the lip of a deep gorge that still had a few muddy patches indicating that it only carried water after heavy rain. It hadn't rained in days. Christmas was yet to arrive, and the weather was already stifling. I wondered how long the mud far below could sustain my life.

As I considered my situation, the shadows under the trees opposite me shifted, and I realised there were people on other side of the gorge. They were natives, so they could have been locals or trackers. If they were trackers, I was done for.

I shrank back into the spiky underbrush and fled. They didn't pursue me, as far as I could tell. Unfortunately, I couldn't stay awake forever.

Add a mark to Poor Health.

If you have an Iron Tea Caddy, go to Page 15.

Otherwise, go to Page 18.

My wound stank with putrescence. In my delirium I fought redcoats, but no matter how many I fought there were always more. I struggled mightily, and fell facedown on the dirt. My lifeblood softened the hard ground, and I died there in the mud.

Over time, the Lalor legend grew. People said my ghost still walked the bush and wailed from abandoned mines all over Victoria. They said I was angry that Britain still ruled the land where my soul was doomed to wander.

Ten years later, Australia became an independent nation, and my ghost was finally laid to rest … or was it?

THE END

You have achieved Goal 3 and Goal 5.

Instead of urging me to leave, the natives adopted me. It was a strange new life without electricity or books, and I often wondered what my ten brothers and sisters would think of me— but I eventually settled down. I learned to hunt and fish (very poorly), and made friends. On clear nights, I slept under the stars. I married and had children, and as the years passed without major interruptions from the outside world, I grew less and less concerned with laws, gold and political systems. My children grew up, and I even learned to speak the language of my adopted people … more or less.

I lived happily ever after.

THE END

You have achieved Goal 2 and Goal 8.

I woke up slowly from a dead faint, confused to find myself in a church, and missing an arm. 'Hello?' I croaked.

Stephen burst into congratulations and questions about how I felt. The Eureka Stockade battle came back to me—as did the memory of the musketball in my shoulder.

'Are you all right?' Stephen asked again. 'How do you feel?'

'I feel … actually, I feel quite well, under the circumstances.'

'That surgeon saved your life! Unfortunately, you have several bits of lead still lodged into what remains of that left shoulder.' He lifted his hand to squeeze my shoulder for comfort, then thought better of the action and let his hand drop back to his side. 'Normally he'd advise leaving them there, but he noticed redness and swelling in the area, and didn't have the right implements to dig any deeper. You're still infected, and I doubt your body has the strength to overcome it without another surgery.'

I tried to smile, but my muscles were spasming with shock all over my body. All the same, I was alive and still at liberty, so I was grateful for that.

He smiled. 'Once we're done taking measurements for your new arm, shall we arrange a second operation to remove that lead for you?'

'New arm?' I echoed.

'Oh yes,' he said with alarming enthusiasm. 'A better one.'

'But the lead should be removed first?' I asked.

He nodded, abruptly solemn.

'No thanks,' I said. 'I can't go through that again.'
If you have a Silver Pocketwatch, go to Page 21.
Otherwise, go to Page 18.

'All right,' I said, working hard to keep the tremor from my voice. Better to face another operation than a painful death.
Go to Page 24.

My Geelong friends fitted me with a new mechanical arm, controlled by a number of cogs and levers that enabled me to operate it quite skilfully with my right hand. Alternatively, I could set it into a fixed position, or do certain basic actions by steering it with my chin.

The craftsman they'd hired in preparation was talented enough to have built several hidden compartments into the metal 'bones' of the frame, and my friends gave me a little money and some bandages to keep inside my arm at all times, as well as a small bag of top quality tea leaves.

My arm creaked somewhat and was uncomfortable to sleep on, but it smelled wonderfully of Chinese tea. It overheated in the sun, but it could stop a bullet—and each metal finger could take considerable weight on its own. All things considered, it was better than ever.

You have achieved Goal 1.

Add a mark to Mechanical Skill.

Go to Page 22.

Some instinct made me keep the fragments of the musketball that almost killed me.

The trauma of the battle had already activated the metal's innate magic. I felt the heightened awareness most acutely when the sun rose. Each day at first light I remembered the shock of that Sunday battle at the Eureka Stockade, and wept.

Lead was most popular with artists because of the way it increased emotion. It hurt sometimes, but I embraced the pain. Other times I was filled with an overwhelming joy and pride.

In time, my body healed completely. I knew I was lucky to be alive.

Add a Lead Ball to your items.

Go to Page 26.

Easter Egg #2

The Eureka Stockade happened in 1854.

Peter Lalor's arm was amputated due to the musketball wound in his shoulder. He married Alicia Dunne—the woman who secretly nursed him at Geelong—just seven months after the Eureka Stockade battle. The following year he was elected to politics and promptly fell out of popularity when he voted in favour of a repressive land bill that was detrimental to the poor. 17,745 Ballarat people signed a petition against the bill. He ignored them.

The Welcome Nugget was found in a tunnel under Bakery Hill in 1858. At the time it was the largest gold nugget ever found, weighing almost seventy kilograms. The first two men who saw it immediately fainted in shock and delight.

Australia achieved Federation in 1901 (twelve years after Lalor's death), although the queen is still technically our head of state. Australia had an unusually peaceful path to independence.

Universal suffrage, while also a largely peaceful process, was a long time coming.

Non-landowning men began to acquire the ability to vote soon after the Eureka Stockade battle—probably as a direct result of that conflict.

Landowning South Australian women were given state voting rights as early as 1861 (six years after the Eureka Stockade battle).

Some Aboriginal people had the right to vote relatively early. Others only achieved full voting rights in 1965.

In Geelong, my friends quickly found me a surgeon. He was Chinese, shorter than me but with an imperious manner, like a well-fed cat. If my friends trusted him, so did I. After all, I had no better options. I noticed he'd taken off his shoes and his bare feet were soiled from the dirt floor, but I didn't say a word.

He soaked a cloth in chloroform and held it to my face. In his bag I saw several large knives and saws along with pliers and syringes. He saw me looking and quickly shut the bag. I couldn't help noticing a second, larger bag beside it that clinked as he knocked it with his foot, but I didn't say anything.

After just a few breaths of the sickly-sweet rag I felt consciousness slipping away. The doctor was still talking, but I couldn't hear what he was saying. Within seconds, I was asleep.

When I woke up, all the infected tissue had been sliced away from my body and some silver pieces had already been affixed to my exposed bone in preparation for fitting a mechanical limb.

I was terribly grateful for modern medicine, knowing that a similar operation would have killed me if it had been attempted just twenty years earlier.

Go to Page 21.

I glanced down at the bloodied stump where my left arm had been and promptly passed out. When I woke up two days later, my arm had been thrown down an abandoned mine shaft.

The operation was declared a great success. I was terribly grateful for modern medicine, knowing that a similar operation would have killed me if it had been attempted just twenty years earlier.

Go to Page 21.

My friends moved me to Young Queen Hotel in South Geelong, where they kept me hidden until my health was fully restored.

Miss Alicia Dunne nursed me in secret there, and talked to me when the view of the four walls and single narrow window felt like a cell. She was extraordinarily patient with me as I slowly regained my health, all the while risking her own reputation to tend to an outlaw. I soon realised she was also growing prettier every time I saw her.

Just as I most longed for eloquence, I became a stammering fool.

Set Poor Health back to 0.

I decided she probably didn't want a man like me, and it was best not to say anything at all.
Go to Page 38.

I was sure she was in love with me too, so I kissed her.
Go to Page 27.

I suspected she might harbour some feelings for me too. Perhaps. I gave her my original metal item to show how grateful I was for all her selflessness.
Unmark your original metal item and go to Page 37.

If you have a Gold Nugget or Brass Goggles, go to Page 35.

Otherwise, go to Page 28.

I moved to kiss her and she jerked away in shock, trailing loose bandages across the floor.

My heart sank as I realised what a blockhead I'd been. 'Please forgive me, Miss Dunne. That was presumptuous.'

'Yes,' she said, and approached warily to continue her work. Clearing her throat, she said, 'Is your family well?'

'They are,' I said, keeping my voice steady with an effort. 'Thank you. And how is your mother?'

'Much better, Mr Lalor.'

'I'm pleased to hear it, Miss Dunne.'

She pushed back a golden strand of hair that had escaped her bonnet, and gave me a wan smile as she packed up her bag ready to leave. 'You're healing nicely. I'm not sure you have any further need of my help.'

I talked to her about my feelings.
Go to Page 29.

I gave her my original metal item as an apology, and a sign of my sincerity.
Remove your original metal item, and go to Page 37.

'I will not bother you again after this conversation,' I said, and heard the note of begging in my voice as she paused in the doorway, 'but my foolish actions have given you the wrong impression. If you would ever consider having a man such as myself, I would marry you.'

She stared at me, unconsciously pulling out a long curl of yellow hair. It was some time before she spoke. 'If you are a lothario, you're certainly not good at it.

'Not at all,' I assured her.

If your Trust is higher than your Caution, go to Page 37.

If your Caution is higher than or equal to your Trust, go to Page 69.

Sometimes, my thoughts turned to my many brothers and sisters scattered throughout the British Isles, America and Australia. Sometimes, a longing for the grey sky and green grasses of my Irish homeland made my heart ache. But then I'd look around me at grey-green trees, red earth, and a blazing blue sky, and the burning kiss of the Australian sun on my skin would comfort me.

At night the rain on the roof sang me the same old Irish lullabies Mam used to sing to me, long ago. It wasn't so different after all.

My heart was at peace and my conscience clear, and I lived long enough to appreciate how special that was.

THE END

You have achieved Goal 5 and Goal 8.

My friends gave me a new gun, and arranged for me to practise my shooting in the hotel's deserted stable while my left side continued to heal.

The quiet made me think often of the family I left behind in Ireland. Three of my ten siblings lived in America, fighting on opposed sides of the civil war. I prayed they never met in battle.

Add a mark to Sharpshooting.

Fighting to change a nation was pointless. I decided I'd fight only for myself.
Add a mark to Caution, and go to Page 40.

We lost at Eureka, and still won hearts. I decided to gather men around me and fight for independence for Australia.
Add a mark to Trust, and go to Page 41.

'Parp-parp-parp!'

It was my tin spoon. Something was badly wrong. I shushed it and listened. There were voices outside, and far too many footsteps. Soldiers!

I peeked out through gaps in the wooden door to make sure they didn't have the house surrounded—yet—then I slipped quietly out the back door and away into the bushland.

My heart was pounding but I forced myself to tread slowly and carefully until I was out of hearing distance. Then I ran until my chest burned and I no longer knew where I was.

I pressed on through the trees, determined not to be caught.

Go to Page 9.

I heard a branch snap, and the careful crunch of human footsteps attempting to make as little noise as possible. The footsteps stopped and someone spoke in a low voice, giving orders.

Soldiers!

Holding my breath, I attempted to creep away through the bushland.

'Lalor!' one of them yelled. 'There! By that rock!'

I gave up on hiding and crashed away into the trees. Branches stretched across my path and long silver leaves whipped at my face. The world filled up with the smell of eucalyptus and sweat, with the noise of my own harsh breath and the yells of the men pursuing me. Before I could get out of sight one of the younger soldiers cannoned into my legs, sending both of us sprawling onto a carpet of dead leaves. I reached for a weapon but he stomped on my wrist, breaking it. The leaves were sharp against my skin, like ants already crawling on my broken body.

I howled in pain and fury, though I knew better than to expect kindness. There were grey clouds gathering in the sky above, and I had a terrible premonition that I'd never see blue sky again.

The rest of the soldiers caught up and congratulated one another for my arrest. They forced me to walk back into town where I spent the next two days in an oven of a cell, utterly helpless and low on water. A doctor did what he could for me, but he avoided my eyes. He didn't expect me to live long.

My fame was my greatest enemy. The trial was a sham, and I was rapidly sentenced to death. I spent my last night standing at the high window of my cell, my eyes lifted to a clear and shimmering sky. When the stars faded with the coming dawn I turned away, unable to bear the sight of my last sunrise.

Within the hour, I was hung from the neck until dead. So much for justice.

My friends requested my body, and buried me in a ceremony that soon turned into a bloody riot. I had become a martyr for the cause of suffrage: a symbol greater than any one man could be.

Many more ordinary, desperate people were arrested, and dozens sentenced to death after trials as hasty and unjust as my own. The excessive punishments only added fuel to the fire. Not even death, it seemed, could stop the rising tide of justice. The fight for universal rights grew stronger than I could have imagined. Even the scattered and diverse Aboriginal nations united together, joining their voices with miners, ex-convicts, and women to demand universal adult suffrage.

Five years later, all Australians were given the right to vote. The nation was changed forever.

THE END

You have achieved Goal 4.

I saw a travelling show once, as a boy. The showman demonstrated the power of electricity to make my hair stand on end. It prickled all over my skin, and felt more magic than magic itself.

Kissing Miss Dunne was a little like that, and a little like finding gold, and a little like wearing a suit that had been tailored to fit me exactly.

She kissed me back.

If you have a Gold Nugget, go to Page 36.

If you have Brass Goggles, go to Page 37.

'Oh!' She pulled away, her eyes wide. 'I shouldn't have done that. I know you have gold magic so it doesn't mean a thing. My apologies! It won't happen again.'

'No, I— Alicia!'

She fled, trailing bandages, with her bonnet clasped in one hand.

'Miss Dunne!' I cried, attempting to follow her despite my weakened state.

The last I saw of her was a flash of silk skirts as she hurried around a corner. I never set eyes on her again.

Go to Page 38.

Miss Dunne understood me perfectly, despite my lack of eloquence. 'Oh!' she said, with a blush that made her more beautiful than ever. 'I'm so glad you feel the same way I do.'

She took my hand in hers, turning it palm-upwards and thoughtfully tracing the fine lines with her finger. 'I had an idea the other day … do you trust me?'

'With my life,' I answered honestly.

'Perfect,' she said. 'In that case, I have a lot of work to do tonight.'

She packed her things and left before I had time to ask what she was going home to do.

Go to Page 70.

I disliked idleness, especially when it was mixed with real danger to anyone who remained my friend. The two-hundred-pound bounty on my head rarely left my mind as I wondered if a cell might be preferable to a hotel room I was unable to leave.

Time passed, eventually, and Stephen Cummins burst into my room one afternoon so excited he was barely able to draw breath.

'Calm down man!' I said. 'What is it? Is your wife safe?'

He took several deep breaths. 'Your arm looks good.'

'That's not why you came all this way.'

'No,' he said. 'It isn't. You've been exonerated—you, and all the rest.'

'Do you mean to say I'm not an outlaw anymore?' I asked.

He shook his head happily. 'No more running or hiding. You're a free man!'

I dived for my clothes and made myself respectable as hastily as possible.

'There's more,' said Stephen. 'The mining tax is virtually abolished.'

'Oh!'

'And you and I just became eligible to vote—along with every other miner in Victoria.'

My head was already spinning. It was so much good news all at once.

Together Stephen and I ran outside, as energetic as children, and danced on the dirt road in front of the hotel. The clear sunlight warmed me from the outside in.

I was no longer an outlaw, and my whole life stretched out ahead of me. Stephen stopped suddenly as the same thought occurred to him.

'What will you do now?' he asked.

I was no stranger to guns and bloodshed. If I'd helped achieve so much, I could achieve more if I continued to fight.
Go to Page 31.

I was famous, and no longer in danger of arrest. I decided to become a politician, and make a difference that way.
Go to Page 43.

I went back to my previous job as a railway worker.
Go to Page 44.

Now that mining was viable, I returned to the goldfields to try once more to make my fortune.
Go to Page 57.

I'd never stolen from anyone before, so even after making the decision to become a bushranger I hesitated. There was a particular stallion I had my eye on; a good racer with steady nerves and a dark coat speckled with white. I watched over that horse for weeks before I could bear to actually steal him. By the time I crept into his stable and led Blacky away, I knew that he liked a treat more than he liked his master, so I fed him a series of apples as we walked through the gate, over the field, and away into a new life. He kept quiet for me all that way, crunching happily, and by the time I ran out of apples he was used to me.

'Be fast and quiet, and I'll have more apples for you soon enough,' I whispered.

He blew out a breath, which I took as agreement. I swung up onto his back and we headed into the bush together.

From that time on he was my companion. We stole other horses, money, pocketwatches and nuggets, but we were true to each other. I lost some friends, and gained others. When Blacky and I had done well, everyone was my friend. But it was Blacky who slept beside me in the rain when there were no other true friends close by.

The companions who had sheltered me after the Eureka Stockade battle still cared for me, and when my crimes didn't keep me fed my friends looked after me, hiding Blacky and me from the authorities and giving us any food and supplies they could spare. I'd abandoned my morals, but they never did.

If you have an Aluminium Locket/Iron Tea Caddy/both AND at least two Sharpshooting marks, go to Page 45.

If you have an Aluminium Locket/Iron Tea Caddy/both OR at least two Sharpshooting marks, go to Page 62.

Otherwise, go to Page 63.

We made a new flag and took over the same section of Bakery Hill where we lost our first battle. It was never an ideal place to fight, but the ground there was already baptised with my blood, and it reminded everyone of the cost we'd soon have to pay. It also reminded us of the chance we had to truly make a difference. We were a contradiction: sombre as dusk, bright as stars. This time, we were ready.

One of my men gave me a tin spoon for luck. It was the only magical metal he owned.

The soldiery attacked before dawn on the Lord's day, but this time we were expecting it. I'd set men on sentry duty all around our new, stronger stockade, and had hidden more than half of our men in an extensive network of tunnels and compartments below the hill.

It wasn't the shouts that woke me—it was the tremendous crash of our primary trap collapsing under the weight of some hundred redcoats, who fell screaming into the hole we'd made for them. The men I'd chosen for that part of the battle set to, shooting and stabbing any who tried to attack. Most of the trapped men didn't fight back—they were wounded, or dead, or too afraid.

I heard the horrible squelching and choking of battlefield deaths as I ran to my own station near the flag. My breath came in gasps, and I realised belatedly how utterly terrified I was. But it was far too late to remedy that. My life was no longer my own: it was an idea. The idea of a new nation of free democratic Australians. So, silently cursing my own hubris, I followed the plan I'd outlined two days earlier, and climbed on top of the wall.

There, silhouetted neatly against the dawn sky, I stood tall and tried not to think about what a perfect target I made as I shouted at both sides, 'Leave behind your old ideas of home and hearth. This red land is ours now, and we can shape it to our will— together! We will lay down our arms and stand together under this Southern Cross—forever!'

There was a hush as I stopped speaking. All I heard was a single man quietly moaning, down in the trap. I didn't know whose man he was, but the main force of redcoats was already close enough that I could see their faces. For a moment, I thought they'd really lay down their arms and the entire battle would turn to friendship.

Then I saw the rifle lifted to point right at me, and the *crack* as it fired split the silence.

Add a Tin Spoon to your items.

If you have an Iron Tea Caddy/Aluminium Locket AND two or more Sharpshooting marks, go to Page 46.

If you have an Iron Tea Caddy/Aluminium Locket OR two or more Sharpshooting marks, go to Page 65.

Otherwise, go to Page 63.

I was elected easily—almost too easily. Eureka had made me a hero, and no one even asked what I intended to do with my newfound power. My brother Richard had long since gone back to Ireland and became a member of the House of Commons. I told myself that if he could be a politician, I could at least try.

Soon I forgot all about my initial doubts. I owned land and had a steady and decent income for the first time. I was given a brand new silver pocketwatch so I'd never be late. Strange, to think that such a small thing would once have been my greatest treasure.

Add a Trust mark.

Add a Silver Pocketwatch to your items.

If you are in a relationship, go to Page 67.

Otherwise, go to Page 68.

I returned to the goldfields and took my time reconnecting with old friends and deciding where to stake my claim.

Ballarat was different. There were fewer people searching for gold as the rush began to fade, but those who remained walked taller. No one hid from the remaining redcoats, and there were fewer tents and more huts and houses. Children played and laughed among the pit heads, and women gathered under the gum trees to have tea together.

Other women staked their own claims, and carried their own pistols and papers. The sprawling settlement remained a rough and ready place, but it was a true town now rather than a camp.

If you have Brass Goggles AND at least two Mechanical Skill marks, go to Page 50.

If you have Brass Goggles OR at least two Mechanical Skill marks, go to Page 30.

Otherwise, go to Page 56.

My wealth only grew as I carefully invested in other men's sheep farms.

I retired well before accident or old age brought me low. As a result, I lived in peace and comfort until the end of my days.

THE END

You have achieved Goal 6 and Goal 8.

I leapt back inside the stockade just a moment too late. The shot struck a glancing blow to my left shoulder. There was a roaring in my ears and it wasn't until one of my own men gently took my pistol from my hand that I realised the redcoats themselves were yelling, 'Southern Cross! Southern Cross!'

I'd expected to become a martyr—yet I lived. We'd won.

The story of that day spread from coast to coast at lightning speed. Men and women from all over Australia travelled to join us. Many redcoats abandoned their positions to support our cause. Even the wealthy and powerful came to Ballarat, including the aeronaut Emmeline Muchamore, who had flown in a balloon above the first Eureka battle. She noticed the logistical difficulties of feeding such a large company, and offered to host our growing army at her own estate. The vast majority accepted her offer, and we moved en masse into the mansion and valley that soon became the final battleground for our struggle.

Australia became an independent nation exactly two years after the first Eureka Stockade.

You have achieved Goal 3.

Add a mark to Trust.

After that I turned to politics. It was time for me to get real power.
Go to Page 43.

I returned to my previous work as a railwayman.
Go to Page 54.

I went back to the goldfields.
Go to Page 57.

One of my assistants had the gall to present me with a petition signed by 17,745 Ballarat citizens asking me to reconsider the bill.

'Forgive my impudence, sir,' he said, 'but are you sure you want to prevent women from voting? Your people elected you because they believed you would uphold democratic values.'

'Democracy means good government,' I told him, putting the petition in a drawer. 'Not total chaos where everyone with an opinion gets the power to make their voice heard.'

He hesitated. 'Your definition differs from the common one.'

'That will be all, thank you,' I said sharply.

'Yes, sir,' he said, and wisely left the room.

I refused to risk the good life I had. Letting women vote was too much.

Go to Page 45.

Under the circumstances, I signed the bill to let women have the vote.

Go to Page 30.

Faced with losing my reputation and displeasing the people who elected me, I supported the bill to let women vote. It passed by a narrow margin.

My investments plummeted in value, but it was worth it. This was what democracy looked like in Australia.

Go to Page 30.

If you have a Lead Ball and/or a Gold Nugget, go to Page 58.

Otherwise, go to Page 48.

The magic I carried drew me right back to Bakery Hill, where I bought up most of the old claims there and spent my days wandering the tunnels remembering all the time I'd spent digging them out such a long time ago. I worked with other engineers to build steam-powered pitheads over the shafts. Soon the shafts were so deep they blocked the sunlight completely. I didn't mind. It meant I could look up and see the stars throughout both day and night.

One afternoon my torch caught a glint of light in the soil, and when I took a closer look I discovered what appeared to be an enormous gold reef. I chipped at the rock around it until my fingers bled, although I didn't feel the pain.

It was no ordinary reef. I'd uncovered the largest gold nugget anyone had ever seen, so large that I fainted from the shock. When I came to and knew it was no dream I looked up and fainted a second time. After I awoke, I sat on the dirt floor and breathed steadily for a long moment, glancing at my prize only briefly until I felt sure I could trust myself not to swoon a third time.

It was the Welcome Nugget, and it weighed almost as much as I did.

Add a Gold Nugget to your list of items.

You have achieved Goal 6.

If you have all seven metal items, you have achieved Goal 7.

Go to Page 45.

Easter Egg #3

Peter Lalor's Bakery Hill Speech:

Fellow diggers, outraged at the unaccountable conduct of the camp officials, in such a wicked licence hunt at the point of the bayonet as the one this morning, we take it as an insult to our manhood and a challenge to the determination come from the monster meeting yesterday. Now I call on you to fall into divisions of eighty men, according to your weapons, and to choose your captains from the best men among you. It is my duty now to swear you in, and to take with you the oath to be faithful to the Southern Cross. Hear me with attention. The man who, after this solemn oath, does not stand by our standard is a coward at heart. I order all persons who do not intend to take the oath to leave the meeting at once.

Let all divisions under arms fall in, in their order round the flagstaff.

We swear by the Southern Cross to stand truly by each other, and fight to defend our rights and liberties!

When I saw so much of my blood and flesh and bone scattered across the dirt floor I lost consciousness. It was too much for a mere man to survive.

I never woke up.

THE END

You have achieved Goal 5.

Easter Egg #4

For the version of this story that is 'true' within the *Antipodean Queen* series, the correct sequence is: 1, 5, 12, 9, 13, 10, 25, 21, 22, 26, 37, 70, 38, 31, 41, 46, 43, 67, 68, 49, 58, 30.

Page 46 happens at the same time as the events of another interactive story, *Attack of the Clockwork Army*, which is available for purchase as an app via https://www.choiceofgames.com/category/user-made-games/

You can play *Attack of the Clockwork Army* as one of Emmeline Muchamore's siblings, or as your own character in a slightly different reality.

If your Trust is higher than your Caution, go to Page 55.

If your Caution is higher than your Trust, go to Page 30.

(If Trust and Caution are equal, choose which you prefer.)

I enjoyed the straightforward work of the railway after all I'd been through. It was hot work, and hard, but I enjoyed the daily test of strength in my arms and back. Piece by piece, the railway reached out across the landscape. The steam train was coming to Australia, and I laid the welcome mat with my own hands.

It was a sunny day like any other when my friend Tommy hammered an iron spike off-kilter. Instead of fastening the rail before him it shot up and out from his hand and pierced my left eye. At that speed, the spike was as damaging as a bullet, and it went straight into my brain.

I was dead before the apology formed on Tommy's lips.

THE END

Bakery Hill inevitably drew me in, and I worked with other engineers building steam engines to hoist and lower men and soil from the shafts. The shafts grew so deep they blocked the sunlight completely. I didn't mind—it meant I could look up and see the stars throughout both day and night.

Our work improved mightily and our spirits were high until one day I was drenched in boiling water as the engine above me blew its boiler. My skin crackled and blistered, and I was blinded by the pain.

I groped for the wall, knowing that if the winch failed I was done for—but I wasn't fast enough. The entire shaft collapsed, trapping me deep underground.

So I was killed and buried on Bakery Hill after all.

THE END

If your Trust is higher than your Caution, go to Page 56.

If your Caution is higher than your Trust, go to Page 44.

(If Trust and Caution are equal, choose which you prefer.)

My passionate speeches were made all the more powerful because of the magic I carried with me. The more speeches I gave, the greater the crowds grew. Women turned out in droves, cheering and waving placards. Several Aboriginal elders met with me personally. They wanted to learn how to regain a little of what they'd lost since the arrival of the First Fleet, and I wanted to teach them. It was a heady time, fuelled by newfound optimism and the momentum of my fame. In the end, the bill was amended to include all adult residents. It passed by a single vote.

The realities of the change in the voting structure came as a shock to many. I lost my seat in the backlash at the next election. Democracy hurt me personally, but I had suspected it would. I remained convinced I'd changed Australia for the better.

After such a contentious achievement I lost my home and my land, but I gained friends. On my fiftieth birthday, those friends gave me a beautiful pair of brass goggles that I wore constantly around my neck. They reminded me that I'd kept to my ideals of democracy and justice, and when I looked at them I was grateful for all I still had.

Add Brass Goggles to your items.

You have achieved Goal 4 and Goal 5.

After that, I lived moderately for the rest of my life.
Go to Page 30.

After that, I tried the goldfields one last time.
Go to Page 44.

If you have a Gold Nugget, go to Page 60.

Otherwise, go to Page 14.

Mrs Mason returned, flustered, and showed me into her wardrobe. 'There's a reward for your capture of two hundred pounds. Use my husband's razor to shave your beard, and get dressed in my clothes. It could save your life. I'll be back as soon as I can.'

I dressed with difficulty, and was scowling at my bonneted face in the mirror when I heard a knock at the door. When I opened it a crack, praying the dim light within would shield me, I saw an entire troop of soldiers.

'Is Peter Lalor here, ma'am?' Their leader was already looking at the next house. I gathered he didn't have a high opinion of women's good sense. My own opinion of Mrs Mason was rapidly rising.

'Certainly not,' I said, trying desperately to sound feminine. 'Miss Wiggins said he was an outlaw now, and I mustn't speak to him. Would you like to come in and check?'

'Thank you, ma'am, we'll be on our way.'

They left in good order, and I sagged in relief. My arm was bleeding again, ruining Mrs Mason's dress.

When the Masons returned, they were both terribly apologetic that they didn't know anyone who could operate on my shoulder. 'We have a horse. Is there someone else who might be able to help you?'

'Yes,' I said. 'My friend Stephen Cummins. He'll know what to do.'

Mr Mason walked beside me all the way, talking quietly to help me stay conscious.

Add a mark to Poor Health.

Go to Page 13.

That was the second time I'd been shot in the same shoulder. I tried to crawl to safety, but I passed out. Much later, I discovered that one of the soldiers recognised me, and told his fellows I was dead. For the moment, no one was looking for me.

I woke up several days later with a brand new metal arm. It was obvious from the light weight and the indented shape along the inner arm that it contained someone's melted-down aluminium locket. I was impressed.

Desperate to be useful once again, I practised sharpshooting with my good arm while I recovered.

Add a mark to Mechanical Skill.

Add a mark to Sharpshooting.

Add an Aluminium Locket to your list of items.

I was no stranger to guns and bloodshed. It was time to fight for more.
Go to Page 31.

I'd had enough fighting for a lifetime. I went back to my previous job as a railway worker.
Go to Page 30.

I deserved a better life. I returned to the goldfields to try once more to make my fortune.
Go to Page 57.

You are rich.

You have achieved Goal 6.

If your Trust is higher than your Caution, go to Page 63.

If your Caution is higher than your Trust, go to Page 45.

If your Trust and Caution are equal, you can choose either page.

I was awoken from a dead sleep by the clatter and shouting of soldiers on horseback closing in on me. Leaving all my possessions behind I fled through the dark bushland, knowing that it was hopeless. I was on foot, and alone. My luck had finally run dry.

'Lalor!' someone yelled. 'Stop or I'll shoot!'

But I couldn't stop. It wasn't in my nature, and we both knew it. When I heard the *crack-crack-crack* of rifle fire, I thought he'd missed—but then my legs folded under me, and I fell to the ground. I struggled to crawl away, but none of my limbs worked properly.

Instead of struggling, I rolled over and breathed my last lying flat on my back, watching the stars through the leaves. My vision turned slowly to darkness as my lifeblood drained into the soil. The stars faded one by one until there was nothing left.

THE END

My arm remained attached thanks to the speed of treatment. Eventually it recovered completely.

You have achieved Goal 1.

Go to Page 22.

The bullet struck me a glancing blow, knocking me from the stockade wall as the soldiers remembered themselves and our battle began in earnest.

It all felt strangely familiar …

Go to Page 1.

Easter Egg #5

There's only one way to get every achievement in a single play-through. Here are some clues to help you:

First, choose your original item wisely. Timing is everything.

Second, remember the lesson of Eureka: Sometimes, you have to be willing to bleed to ultimately win.

Rich friends are useful, but even bad friends can teach good lessons.

Thirdly, when it comes to love, don't be presumptuous. Or cowardly.

Fourthly, peaceful negotiation takes time. And you ain't got enough of that.

And finally, power corrupts—but I hope it won't corrupt you.

Good luck, and welcome to your own version of history!

I enjoyed the prestige and safety of being a landowner, and my darling Alicia bore two children—Annie and Joseph. I'd never been happier.

For our tenth wedding anniversary in 1865, Alicia commissioned a painting of our whole family. It was worth more to me than any treasure or magic.

Go to Page 68.

In a flush of democratic enthusiasm, one of my fellow politicians wrote a bill proposing to give women the vote. I was never quite sure if he was serious, but female suffragettes embraced the concept with marches and pamphlets distributed throughout the land. It was time to make a decision—for better or worse.

My political position would become vulnerable if women could vote. It was better to shut them down.
Go to Page 47.

That bill put my whole lifestyle at risk, and had the potential to ruin my family, but voting rights was what I got into politics for. I supported the bill.
Go to Page 48.

It put my whole lifestyle at risk, and had the potential to ruin my family, but voting rights was what I got into politics for. I went a step further and wrote an amendment to the bill that gave the vote to all adults—landowners, ordinary men, women, and natives.
Go to Page 49.

'I've lingered too long,' she said to me, backing away as if I was a savage dog. 'Shall we part as friends?'

'Thank you,' I said, with just enough honour left to keep my voice from betraying the depth of my dismay.

Go to Page 38.

The following day she returned with a leather bag almost as large as she was tall. Judging by the way she dragged it along on an array of tiny wheels, it was as heavy as her too.

She unlatched the bag and produced a piece of metal with a flourish. It was a little larger than her hand, and inexpertly beaten into an incomplete cylinder.

'Is that—' I asked.

'A tea caddy?' she smiled. 'Yes. It was my grandmother's, and it's magical. I thought your arm could use the extra strength.'

'That's … thank you,' I said.

'Thank me if I can fit it properly,' she said, bending over her bag to draw forth a travelling stove, flint, brass goggles, and an array of tools. She packed the linens from my bed around the door and opened the window to vent the smoke, then removed my shirt and took some measurements of my arm before heating the iron caddy over the stove and improving the shape to fit me.

I watched her, rapt, for some hours, making myself useful by fanning the smoke outside. At last she declared herself satisfied and slid the flattened and rounded tea caddy onto my upper left arm, making a few minor adjustments while it was still warm.

'Is it fitted correctly now?' she asked, frowning in concentration as she checked for rough points.

I was somewhat distracted by the sensation of her breath against my bare chest. 'Will you marry me?'

She looked up. 'Is that a yes?'

'Is that?' I asked, feeling lost but determined to have an answer to my proposal. I'd spent enough of my life waiting for good things, and from now on I'd seek them out and catch them when I could.

'I asked you about the caddy first,' she said with a cheeky smile.

'It's wonderful,' I said. 'Yes.'

'I thought so,' she said, comfortably aware of her skill.

'And …?'
'Yes,' she said. 'Yes, I will marry you.'

Add an Iron Tea Caddy to your items.

You have achieved Goal 2.

Go to Page 38.

Acknowledgements

Writing a novel takes a certain madness, and my enablers include my parents Phil and Wendy, the PWDDA—especially Tabby, Will (you know what you did), Ben, Fish, Emma, many others over the five years between concept and publication, and of course my partner Chris and my children.

An interactive story is a special creature. Thank you to the beta readers/reviewers Sam Kabo Ashwell, Chris Banks, Dominia Bloodrose, Ben Crispin, Julian Fleetwood, Ann Jensen, Selina, Chris Northey, Helen Northey, Brian Rushton, Emily Short, James Walker.

www.ingramcontent.com/pod-product-compliance
Lightning Source LLC
Chambersburg PA
CBHW032105180726
48284CB00002B/465